D1051210

TABOO

Also by Kim Scott

TRUE COUNTRY
BENANG: FROM THE HEART
KAYANG AND ME (with Hazel Brown)
THAT DEADMAN DANCE

TABOO

KIM SCOTT

Small Beer Press
Easthampton, MA

Taboo copyright © 2017 by Kim Scott. All rights reserved. The moral right of the author to be identified as the author of this work has been asserted. First published 2017 in Picador by Pan Macmillan Australia Pty Ltd., 1 Market Street, Sydney, NSW, Australia, 2000. First Small Beer Press edition 2019.

The author would like to acknowledge that early draft extracts from this work were first published as 'Collision', *Kenyon Review*, March/April 2017. Gambier, Ohio: Finn House, Kenyon College; and 'Departure', *Review of Australian Fiction*, Zutiste, Inc., 2015.

Small Beer Press
150 Pleasant Street #306
Easthampton, MA 01027
smallbeerpress.com
weightlessbooks.com
info@smallbeerpress.com

Distributed to the trade by Consortium.

Names: Scott, Kim, 1957- author.
Title: Taboo / Kim Scott.
Description: First American edition. | Easthampton, MA : Small Beer Press, 2019.
Identifiers: LCCN 2019016455 (print) | LCCN 2019017048 (ebook) | ISBN 9781618731708 | ISBN 9781618731692 (alk. paper)
Classification: LCC PR9619.3.S373 (ebook) | LCC PR9619.3.S373 T33 2019 (print) | DDC 823/.914--dc23
LC record available at https://lccn.loc.gov/2019016455

First edition 1 2 3 4 5 6 7 8 9 0

Set in Sabon LT Pro. Original typesetting by Post Pre-press Group.

Printed on 30% PCR recycled paper by the Versa Press in East Peoria, IL.
Cover design: Sandy Cull, gogoGingko. All rights reserved.
Cover image: Sandy Cull. Skull from Shutterstock.

To Ryan Brown, *ngan ngoon*

OLD HAUNTS

Our hometown was a massacre place. People called it taboo. They said it is haunted and you will get sick if you go there. Others just bragged: we shot you and poisoned the waterholes so you never come back.

We had heard all this, and we heard it again as we lifted ourselves from the riverbed and went back up the hill into town. Some of you may wish to imagine our decaying flesh, our shuffling tread and a collective moan emanating from our slack jaws – as if we were the undead, indeed. It was never like that, and we are hardly alone in having been clumsy, in having stumbled and struggled to properly speak and breathe and find our place again. But we were never hungry for human flesh or revenge of any kind.

Our people gave up on that Payback stuff a long time ago, because we always knew death is only one part of a story that is forever beginning . . .

*

And so this story will start here, where the wind has suddenly dropped and the sun glowers in the eerie red light of a dying sandstorm. The many falling sand grains whisper, thunder crashes and rumbles down the rocky river valley and lightning glitters on the chrome of a semitrailer cresting where the highway chokes to become the plummeting main street of this little town in Western Australia's Great Southern: Kepalup.

The old name means 'place of water' or, perhaps, 'welling', but the signpost points to a cluster of buildings either side of a dry, old creek emerging from a low, near-barren range on Western Australia's southern coastal plain.

The truck driver, surprised by the sudden descent, touches the brake. His foot goes flat to the floor. Tries to change gear; cogs clash and grate.

The truck's chrome glints, tarpaulins tremble, wheels roll faster and faster.

Propelled by tons of wheat, freewheeling down the street, the driver's bowels loosen, his gear stick flops about. The poor man leans on the horn and he, passenger and truck make a wailing chorus.

In the pub, frothy heads of beer shiver with the truck's passing.

The numbers on the speedometer continue to rise.

A little group of people have gathered on a patch of grass beside the Local History Museum. They are here for the opening of a Peace Park.

A large, bald and well-dressed man leaving the edge of the group suddenly sees the charging truck and scurries from its path, arms flailing and little feet a blur. An older man, refusing to be distracted by the tons of glass and metal rushing between them, stares after the bald one but all the other faces, like flowers following the sun, track the vehicle as it thunders by:

Museum

Town Hall

Café

Supermarket

School . . .

No child is harmed. Also unharmed, drunks fall out of the top pub, their gaze (along with that of the Peace Park attendees) trained upon the truck's dusty, wagging tailgate. It seems the runaway vehicle has created a void that vision is obliged to fill.

The driver's eyes, by contrast, dart here and there seeking an exit, an escape clause, some soft shoulder to roll on.

As if tempted by the scent of fuel, the truck veers briefly toward the roadhouse, then weaves back and, departing the other side of the bitumen, snaps a railing and takes down a succession of small trees and shrubs as it bucks and bounces across the flood plain. Slowed at last by deep, coarse sand, it makes one last, dramatic gesture (reminding one observer of a feebly breeching whale) and rises into the air a little, before falling on its side.

Birds flap into the sky, screeching indignation.

The motor hiccups; stops.

Wheels spin on, as good wheels do.

From a distance – the aloof view, say, of those birds – a pattern is dissolving and reforming again: bunches of people at the museum, pub, café, roadhouse, the little park; then all moving together and flowing down the street. A car stutters ahead, pulls up at the road edge of the river crossing.

A bystander – perhaps even you, dear reader – might anticipate an explosion, a great ball of flame. But there is no explosion. Already, the so-recently startled birds are beginning to resettle among the slow and incrementally turning leaves of the patient trees.

A human figure emerges from the window of the truck's cab door. A girl, a young woman perhaps. Standing easily on the side of the cab, she bends to help someone exit. A strong young thing, then; athletic. The other person seems much older, or injured. Having been helped (hauled) from the cab, he immediately sits down on its still-closed door. Hurt? Tired?

He looks around, back into the cab, and then tentatively makes his way down after the young woman, though less nimbly.

The two of them stamp their feet on solid ground as if reassuring themselves. They listen to the wheels spinning and a luxurious, whispering sound: wheat, slowly spilling from the vehicle.

Come close. Closer.

A small pile of wheat is growing beside the trailer, fed by a thin, grainy spout from the upper corner of the tarpaulin. Golden, it has both the look and sound of great wealth. The tarp slips a little so that the thin stream becomes a golden chute, and then the tarpaulin pulls away like an upside-down stage curtain and a wide, low wave of wheat makes the girl step back once, twice, three times. She stops, transfixed by something in the trailer as the wheat continues to flow around and behind her.

Imagine a figure sitting in a deep and rapidly draining bath: head and shoulders appear, then the upper torso, knees . . . In the trailer, beginning with the dome of a dark skull, a figure is being revealed.

This figure slides a little, shifts.

The tarpaulin slips again.

The golden grain continues to flow across the ground.

The figure begins to rise. It must be the moving grain, but it seems as if the legs lever it upright and it steps from the upturned trailer and stands, swaying with the high weight of its skull. The girl, the figure, they stand facing one another, feet invisible beneath the grain.

The wheat dust, the light of the sandstorm, the after-effects of the accident . . . What is it the girl sees? Something like a skeleton, but not of bone. At least, not only bone. The limbs are timber. The skull is timber too, dark and burnished, and ivory dentures – stained as if by chomping, inhaling, gustatory human life – grin exultation.

A gauze of gold dust and light motes swirls from its broad shoulders and around the rippling cage of its ribs.

Long shanks lever the pelvis, itself a solid thing of smooth river stone and timber glowing at its centre of gravity.

Kneecaps too are smooth stone, but the rest is bone and polished timber and woven grass, seeds and brightly coloured feathers and even fencing wire. Cords of sinew, of neatly knotted fishing line and – is it human hair? – meet moistly at each mobile joint.

The figure sways toward the girl, led by the heavy skull, and then glides to her, arms low and open, each beautifully defined and delicate hand held palm up. Its whole being is a smile.

Hands clasp; firm, warm, uncalloused.

And now the wind gathers strength; a melody plays across the visual rhythm of those ribs; hollowed, meticulously carved spaces begin to whistle and timber limbs begin an accompaniment. Thunder cracks and booms, it rumbles in the riverbed.

The figure teeters, begins to move, to slowly fall apart and maybe tumble . . .

*

We thought to tell a story with such momentum; a truck careering down a hillside, thunder in a rocky riverbed, a skeleton tumbling to the ground. There must be at least one brave and resilient character at its centre (one of us), and the story will speak of magic in an empirical age; of how our dead will return, transformed, to support us again and from within.

One may as well begin, 'Once upon a time' . . . Except this is no fairy tale, it is drawn from real life. We remember Dan Horton. He will seem a stereotype, even a caricature, this stooped and elderly man in faded towelling hat, sensible clothes and lace-less boots. Real life has its stereotypes and caricatures. Dan Horton was one of those rural men who, in the middle of conversation, will suddenly crouch and, clearing a little plot of dirt with the heel of his hand, draw diagrams with a stick or calloused finger.

So.

So.

Once upon a time, Dan Horton squinted through his kitchen window into the heart of light. Out there, beyond his sight, the earth – having been stripped and raked and poked – was desiccating in the wind. Sand rose from the razed ground and was swept away in clouds, persisting only in fine ridges beneath the fencing wires and heaped against posts, trees, dead sheep or indeed any lifeless body. This wind gives the coastal dunes their sharp edges, and stings the flesh of anyone caught in the paddocks.

Sunlight streamed through the streaked window and glinted on the stainless steel sink.

Dan's wife Janet had died two months ago, yet her clothes were still in the wardrobe, her slippers under the bed. She'd left him. Passed, people say today, not 'passed away'. She is past. Dan had only just changed the bedsheets; it was the first time he'd attempted this particular household task. He supposed that men today helped their wives change the sheets, helped with the cooking and the dishes and all of that. Breastfed too, probably; Dan had seen there were these lady-milking machines.

His adult son had not been at Janet's funeral. Overseas perhaps? Married even? He had little idea where or how that young man lived, not since he had responded to Dan's ulti-matum – my way or the highway – by walking away from God, the farm and the family. Of course Dan regretted his words.

The bedsheets had helped Dan dream of Janet, and each morning she faded away and he had to once again reckon the absence in his world.

The phone rang, startling him; hot tea slopped down his shirtfront. One hand holding the shirt away from his skin, he put down the cup, plucked the telephone from its cradle and pressed it to his ear, grimacing as the wet shirt fell against his skin. He began untangling the telephone cord, an action repeated so many times it had become in itself a comfort.

'Dan? Dan!' It was his brother, Malcolm.

'I'm sorry. Thinking.'

'You know her voice is still on your answering machine?'

He did. He did indeed. He pressed on; there was something he must tell his brother.

'You remember Tilly? One of those babies we fostered for a time? She was walking and talking and . . . her mother took her back.'

'Well,' said Malcolm. 'I remember how Janet was when she left. The father was a rapist or something, wasn't he? That was a terrible year. Wheat wasn't much more than $70 a ton.'

'Tilly, she's coming to Kepalup. There's a group of Aborigines coming for the Peace Park opening.'

'She's with them?'

'It's her family.'

'Her mother was white.'

'Distant relations, perhaps, the way we think of things. But they have a strong sense of family, Malcolm, you know that, and . . .'

9

'Well, I wish they'd look after their families, that's all. Think about the children you and Janet fostered. There should've been no need, and who of them ever contacts you, eh?'

'Well, this one has. Someone on her behalf, anyway.'

'Where they staying?'

'Caravan park, Hopetown. Be here some days, apparently.'

'Why?'

'Told you, the Peace Park. Something about some stories. Dreamtime. Language or something. You know, culture stuff. Malcolm, I think they want to visit Kokanarup. They want to come onto the farm. "The massacre", he said.'

'I wish they wouldn't use that word. Massacre.'

Dan continued; they wanted to reconcile themselves to what happened here, to have their Elders come back particularly. Of course it was a long time ago and – here Dan and Malcolm agreed – there was no real evidence of any more than a few Aborigines being killed. Undoubtedly, some were; they both remembered finding a skull wedged by the rock waterhole when they were still children . . .

On their own property.

You could see what people meant about skulls grinning. All those teeth. In Dan's memory the skull was sunlit bright.

Janet's body would be rotting by now. Putrefying. The coffin would keep the insects, the worms and maggots away for a while.

Her car was still in the shed. He would have to get rid of that too.

'Taboo, isn't it?' His brother's voice in his ear. 'For them to come here, I mean.'

Dan said nothing. He waited, impatient for Malcolm to go on, but – as was the way between them, each imbued in the same family tradition – he remained silent.

There were often these long silences in their conversation.

Tethered, Dan stretched the telephone cord as far as possible, moving to where he could avoid looking directly into the heart of light. He was thinking of how the dead might yet return. Hoping and wishing he said, 'I prophesied as I was commanded: and as I prophesied, there was a noise, and behold a shaking, and the bones came together, bone to his bone . . .'

Malcolm responded automatically.

'Ezekiel 37.'

It was a game they'd played since childhood; one brother would quote a bible passage, the other give the reference.

'Resurrection. Oh, Dan.'

There was another of those protracted silences.

'Remember those two old Aboriginal woman? I've been thinking about them, Malcolm. Gins, we used to say. Married Irish twins. How we used to treat that family. They must all be related to them, the people coming. Tilly must've been too. Must be. She was long gone, course, the old girl, and Tilly a baby, almost a toddler when she left and never a hair on her head hurt. She thrived with us.'

'Janet was distraught.'

'Beside herself.'

She was beside him, back then. The boy had been upset by Tilly's absence too, Dan remembered, even though a child himself and still at primary school, he had gone very quiet for weeks afterwards and kept to himself.

'Malcolm, I'd like to invite them to the farmhouse. Kill a lamb, chill it. We can have a barbeque, a chat.'

'Think they will? Taboo and that?'

'They *want* to visit. They'll be at the opening of the Peace Park.'

There was another long silence.

Janet leaned in the bedroom doorway, studying him. Their

two little dogs lay at her feet. Dan blinked. She was gone. The dogs remained, whining and anxious.

'Malcolm, will you come pray with me? I'd like us to pray together.'

'Yes, this evening. I'll bring some chops.'

Dan put the phone away. He picked up a rock from the sun-drenched counter, held it in his hand. It was wonderfully smooth and warm.

Dan looked through the window. Malcolm's house was just down the track, across the highway, another gravel turn-off. Not so far, half a day of walking perhaps. Not that they'd ever done that. It would be a long walk. Snakes. And between the two houses, closer to the river was the old farmhouse. The massacre farmhouse, he'd heard people say. Blocks of stone and corrugated iron in a yellow paddock.

Now his own house was haunted, and he was glad.

*

Gerald Coolman stepped from the little bus near the top of the main street of King George Town and stood alone to watch it drive away. *Now* he was out of jail. His lips moved and he spoke to himself, mouthing words of an ancient language few would recognise.

He took several long and deep breaths, calming himself. Feel your skeleton moving inside the flesh, feel the spaces within. Turning his back on the view of the harbour, he began the walk to the outskirts of town. He did not take the main highway, but one parallel. Nearly an hour later he came to an intersection near the Aboriginal Centre; how neglected and run-down it looked. The first place he went was Aunty Margie's. He didn't knock at the door but went down the driveway to an open shed, something he'd done many, many times. The young men sitting in the sun at the shed's doorway looked up and smiled. They shook his hand and hugged him. They offered him a dirty plastic bottle with a short piece of plastic inserted in it, and a bucket of water.

Smoke wreathed the grins and teeth of these brothers, rose from their whiskers and through their hair. Gerry said he was not going to start those old habits again.

'Found the Lord?'

'Nah. Better than that.'

They turned away. Lowered their heads over the bottle and bucket.

'Only a bit of weed. A bit of green. Not the other stuff.'

*

Gerald sat in the doorway of the shed as the others walked away. He breathed lightly, his anxious heart pattered. Their feet crunched gravel spread so thinly between asbestos fence and asbestos house that weeds had punched through. Fibro, people said now, not asbestos. Fibro and weatherboard.

Bougainvillea erupted on the fence, lunged at the house and, falling, made an archway. Beyond, at the bright end of the driveway, a car grumbled left to right. Gerry heard the sound of the small stones flicked by its tyres and saw the two pedestrians turn, and also exit stage right.

This little house, this shabby backyard of weeds; a child's bicycle, a rotary clothes hoist. It felt an enormous space. The big old sky above.

Gerry sat in an old school chair. Metal frame, wooden seat. The sun warmed him. He realised he was smiling.

Get some work. Or an education. Find a way to stay off the stuff. After all, he'd managed that inside, more than twelve months now.

Natural, wanting to celebrate at such a time.

He scratched himself.

*

He'd only been inside a few weeks this time. A parole issue, that's all. It had been a disappointment in a way, because on his previous stint his cousin had been running 'culture classes', 'workshops'; whatever you wanted to call them. A long timer, Uncle Jim. Wirlomin boys had looked up to him, and those attending the classes had been mostly his own nephews and cousins and grannies. Another member of the extended family sent Jim wordlists, genealogies, language and songs and stories and photos and stuff he was putting together with old boy, Jim's dad. One of the screws was helping, even. Jim had had that knack of enlisting people, women particularly.

They were teaching themselves, in prison of all places. They'd memorised vocabulary, and listened to recordings of family, most no longer alive. Had sat around a whiteboard in their baggy greens while Jim played recordings and – there was no getting around it – lectured them. A pyjama party for grown men, but no party food, no women, no grog. Not so many laughs. A barren room.

Jim's father died. It was best he never saw his boys turn up at the funeral in chains and prison greens. Would've hurt him. His voice was on lots of the recordings.

Then Jim himself was gone. Had they only played at respect, in that prison cell, listening to Jim? Jim did go on and on.

It was true what people said: every old one left a hole in the world when they died, when they took language with them. That old language was a world itself, and one by one the words let you in. But individuals who could connect you to it, re-introduce you, they were necessary too. Someone needed to step into Jim's shoes.

Gerald used to lie flat on his back on his cell bed, and let what they called a dead, extinct language roll through his skull. Move his lips and tongue, say the words out loud. Let them reshape him from the inside out. That was under a low ceiling, a prison cell. Now he had this big sky, this fresh breeze.

A woman appeared. Nita. Aunty Nita. Nan. Old Girl. A childhood memory: her cold hands and the first time – a boy looking into her upturned eyeballs – he knew himself a lone consciousness, a single self.

The bougainvillea spilling over the doorway had concealed her so she first appeared as a bloom among the thorns and clinging vine, and then the blank gaze of her sunglasses turned to him, her long grey hair lifted in the breeze, and her attention reached out to him.

The face was expressionless, open to the world, her chin lifted. She held her arms slightly raised, a little in front and out to each side and the hands palms down. Her tread was very light, and – no doubt her blindness was part of it – there was something tentative about it; a distinct moment when the foot remained poised in the air, not yet committed to that necessary next step.

Gerald walked toward her, his footsteps softly crunching, stopped a few metres away and bid her good day in the old language.

'How are you, Gerry?'

In the old language, he told her he was well.

She tilted her head to one side. 'You talking language, now. Proper blackfella, unna.'

He agreed with her, again using the old people's tongue.

'You reckon that's our lingo?'

He said he did, and went to her. They embraced, lightly. She accepted his peck on the cheek.

'You happy, Gerry?'

'That old me's not who I am now, Aunty. Language, the old culture, that's what Jim showed me.'

'If it helps, my boy. Good. But those young girls, Gerald?'

'They're safe, Aunty. Don't start that. I never did nothing; that was Gerry, you know that.'

'You working?'

'Will be, but gotta camp coming up. Workshop. Back to country.'

'Getting paid?'

'Not about the money, my aunty.'

'In prison, you one of the dancers there last NAIDOC, unna?'

'Singer, Aunty.'

'What's it stand for anyway, that NAIDOC?'

'National Aboriginal and Islander Day of . . . committee of . . .'

'You go? NAIDOC Ball?'

'No.'

'You ever been to a ball, Gerald?'

'No.' Gerry spoke again in what he believed was the old people's tongue, then: 'That's the real me.'

Nita raised an eyebrow; a surprising gesture for a blind person, at least for those that did not know her.

'Yeah. Giving up all the other shit . . .'

What did the old girl mean by her little smile? Holding her face up all the time like she thinks she is a holy person.

'I know my problem.' Gerry kept speaking. 'Drugs. Violence. That's not who I really am.'

'You gunna get in touch with her, Gerry?'

'I am. That's what Jim wanted.'

Nita stood there, head nodding.

'You always been good with words and promises, Gerry.'

'More than just words, Aunty. You never knowed the real me. Nobody knows.'

She just kept nodding her head.

'Was my brother, that last time.'

Her blind eyes stared.

Gerry gestured goodbye, mouthed the words at her, went away like she wanted him to. Started the long walk down the driveway. He remained proud of himself.

There might be a bus. He could maybe cadge a lift. No. He was gunna walk. There was no need to rush. Old people, they used to walk. Eat only good food. Be together around a fire under the same old sky he was under now and he could be right in their world – be right inside and among and part of, like breathing the air or a fish swimming in water or a child beginning to dream in their mother's tongue and the world springing more to life each day . . . He could live and find himself in the language, in the stories, the songs and all that. Not in books. His land was his book. These were the very thoughts he'd entertained and cultivated in his prison cell.

Gerald sighed. Looked along the road. A car went by.

He walked on the edge of the road, where the bitumen crumbled a bit, along a strip of gravel and weeds. Bottle tops, cigarette butts and wrappers of various kinds. Throwaway bits of people's lives.

Houses and cars, the weed-tufted gardens, the snaking hoses and kids' toys.

Gerald walked between houses he'd known forever, and some that were new to him, fresh brick and tile with carports and two or three crammed where there'd been just one.

People had good houses now. All sorts of help to get ahead, to get to where you could scratch and struggle with the white people. Join the assimilationists.

A footpath. A weedy gap between it and the road on his right. Footpath the other side too. Someone walking there, staring straight ahead. Houses either side, blankly staring at one another.

The shabby shopping centre. The laundromat, once its social centre, was closed. It must've been a phantom dryer he heard, spinning.

*

Once he'd followed a schoolmate along here. Pioneering family, he told them all, though both his mum and dad worked at the TAB. Kid stole money from his mum's purse. Bought a big bag of lollies, a plastic shopping bag meant for groceries but filled with jelly snakes and chocolate buttons, with coloured sugar in all the shapes of domesticity: teeth, babies, cigarettes, bottles, cars, pets . . .

Primary school years. Gerald the youngest in the group trailing behind the TAB kid, scrambling for the sweet things he threw over his shoulder. The kid threw lollies onto the roofs of shops, a bus stop. Sugar collected in gutters. He kept walking. Some of the others were jumping to try to see what was on the roofs; one began shinning up a drainpipe.

The TAB kid was pleased and so very full of his power, scattering sweet and desirable things, controlling the little crowd.

One of Gerald's older cousins went up to him. Grabbed his bag. Hit him a few times, laughed at his tears and jeered his stumbling departure. Then passed handfuls of lollies around the triumphant circle that remained.

Gerald was halfway into town already.

Traffic came past as if set in motion by a distant machine at small and irregular intervals. Whoosh. Whoosh. Like explosive exhalations. The sound got on his nerves. Kept him edgy.

He walked past buildings – big boxes – all along the highway, bright red yellow blue beige boxes too, with large letters screaming at him. A hill of shabby houses rose on his right, granite rocks and tufts of grey trees here and there among them. To his left, the land continued to slope, flattening to become sports fields. When he was a child it was a Native Reserve here. Before that, a camping ground.

Pa Harry Hopetown in a shabby greatcoat, sitting beside a smoking fire, slipping among paperbarks and mosquitoes. A big drum of methylated spirits, the shaking cup and pale cordial within.

The summer easterly blew in Gerald's face. Blew, he reminded himself, from ancestral country, from where the sun forever rises. Even today, even with lowering clouds like this.

Gerald's lips moved. He mouthed some of the words he'd got from his dead family and his brothers in prison.

His feet took him across the slope a little away from the top of town, paths only used by poor pedestrians, by single mothers and little children. Ex-crims too, obviously. He went by the back of supermarkets and trucks shovelling merchandise into shopping malls. A community radio station. A panelbeater. The drab rear of a video store, no longer in business. Skirted around the old cemetery. Lots of white people, but no Noongar ever buried there. Remembered that girl grinding her pelvis against his, fucking among the bones. Dead people never scared him. No old massacre was gunna keep him from his real home.

He was tiring already. Didn't walk much lately. He cut across a deserted stand of petrol bowsers, a school further up the hill, an empty squash court on his left. Buildings from his childhood, from before he was born.

Walking toward the beach, he detoured into another huddle of small brick bungalows. Knocked on a door.

Last night, his last inside, Gerald dreamed of Kokanarup.

The door opened, and his mirror image greeted him. No, not quite his mirror image. This version had particularly glossy, bloodshot eyes, the teeth were not so strong, the lips looser. This doppelganger's skin was mottled and greasy. His twin smiled silently, stepped back to let him enter the room.

'Only weed,' he said. 'Bit of weed's alright. Bit of green never hurt no one.'

'Yeah, well, I need somewhere to stay and you owe me,' said Gerald. 'Again.' And he stepped across the threshold.

DEPARTURE

The city's Central Bus Station was built upon the principle of a large shed and, except for the enormous windows on one wall, barely disguised as such. Inside, a vast grey plain of concrete was enlivened not only by the dancing dust motes and large, sparkling rectangles of sunlight on the floor, but also by firmly anchored patterns of bright plastic chairs. A schoolgirl entered the building and, veering widely around the chairs, paused at a vending machine. The machine accepted her money, gave nothing in return.

The woman behind a pane of glass marked *Enquiries* looked away. She touched her stiff hair, pursed her bright lips and tapped the keyboard before her. Small particles of what seemed to be skin flaked from her cheekbones.

A would-be passenger, clutching at baggage and clothing, stumbled into the building as if pushed. Hissing, the doors closed. Outside, a hot wind continued to moan and twist in the angles of the building. The schoolgirl, Tilly, perched at the very corner of one platoon of chairs, and bent her head to her electronic device. Voices in her skull competed for her attention; she did not hear the wind, the doors; had not even heard her own footsteps.

Again the doors parted and an old woman stood between them, holding herself against the buffeting wind and beckoning two small children to join her.

The woman was perhaps seventy years old, the children of primary school age. Each child – a boy and a girl – had a bright backpack. The woman wore loose, colourful layers of clothing and her abundant hair was tied back, silver curls spilling against her skin. She looked around the sunlit departure room and saw Tilly, in pleated private school uniform and hat. Tilly pulled her sleeves down past her wrists, and wrapped her legs around one another so tightly that they might have been woven together and the one loose shoelace the only thing awry. Her eyes were fixed to her phone, and tiny speakers pressed into her ears. Her fingers danced and her lips moved as she breathed some internal voice.

The Enquiries woman shuffled toward the glass doors, a hand flicking at the wrist to gesture that the old woman and children must move away from the doorway. A bus pulled up and, as it lowered itself with a subdued hiss, its door sighed open. Elderly passengers stepped cautiously onto the kerb and, seasoned campaigners, looked around for alternatives to the glossy woman and sliding glass doors that confronted them.

A little group of bodies had attached itself to the belly of the bus, and watched the beast being gutted. Another group began to gather to see it stuffed again.

Tilly turned at a touch and, skilled by habit, unstoppered her ears. Dangling the tiny speakers in one hand, she put her head to one side, and politely performed: Yes, what do you want?

'Where you from, bub?' asked the silver-haired woman, keeping an eye on the children's ascension into the bus.

'Here,' said Tilly. 'From my mother's belly.' Faltered. 'Well, I used to live in . . . I'm at boarding school.'

The school's name was emblazoned across her small frame: on the round straw hat, the tie, at one breast. Her shoes were sensible shoes, neatly polished; her socks smooth, and folded at the ankle.

'I'm Gloria,' the woman said. 'Gloria Winnery.' Her eyes moved to the windows of the bus. Tilly wanted to step around her but could not.

'Who's your family then?'

'Oh, my mum is white.' It was dismissive. 'She passed away.' Tilly glared at the older woman, and continued on to prevent any more questions and to get it over with. 'My dad was Jim Coolman.'

'Oh, I'm sorry. You're that Wirlomin mob.'

'Yeah.' Surprised.

'You poor thing, losing both your parents.'

Tilly gave a little snort. 'I only met my dad this year.' She looked past the woman to the bus. The silver-haired woman's attention moved to the children, who had claimed their seats and were now pressing against the glass. Tilly danced around the coloured shawls, the silver hair and waving arm. 'See ya,' she said, glancing back from the steps of the bus.

'Where you headed, bub?' Gloria called after her.

From beside the driver, Tilly called, 'Kepalup,' and kept moving.

Seated near the back, unpacking phone and earbuds, Tilly allowed Gloria a little wave. The old woman was clutching her hands to her chest, as if distressed. Tilly wasn't feeling so wonderful herself.

She put her bag on the seat between herself and the aisle and leaned against her reflection; beyond that was the rush and flow, the spiky, shape-shifting world of traffic lights, of shouting signs, of corners of glass and brick and steel, of vehicles merging and separating; people were fragments and shadows in tilted panes of glass and scattered shards of sunlight. Tilly's fingers gripped each shirt cuff; her fingernails were gnawed to the quick. Smoothly, with the practised ease of a nervous reflex, those raw fingertips found the text from her Uncle Gerry:

Hi Tilly get Esperance bus to lake grace 2moro. Someone will pick you up there for the camp. Gerry.

She'd replied, *Ok,* and a phone call from Nan Kathy had sorted it. Gerry was her dad's cousin, Noongar-way; connected by generation from an apical ancestor, as the legislation speaks it. Before he passed away her dad had as good as asked her to make this trip, go to this camp. 'For me,' he might as well have said. 'For all of us.'

Tilly told herself it was nice of the old woman (Gloria?) to be concerned about her, but she'd rather she wasn't. One of the children at the front of the bus turned, waved to Tilly. Did they know about the taboo, too?

She caught the driver's glance in his rear-view mirror. Closed her eyes.

*

Already, several of the passengers had turned to look at her, some more than once. In some cases, they had gone to some trouble to do so, and smiled reassuringly. Tilly did not feel comforted. People had told her not to see hurt where there was none, not to be paranoid. Trust yourself. Even Gerry had said it. Love yourself. Be grateful.

She administered to her telephone.

Her reflection there, too.

Outside the bus, unnoticed by Tilly, was clear evidence

they'd left the city. White lines stuttered along the bitumen and Christmas trees trumpeted orange blossoms from fence corners and road edges. The many masts of a forest of some other tree, tall and straight, sailed by. For a time, the bus sliced through undulating, bright yellow rectangles that were irregularly hemmed by fences, only otherwise interrupted by a thin line or threatened stand of shabby trees crowning a slope. Vast expanses of bright yellow flowers rippled when the wind rolled across them.

Tilly was so attentive to her screen you would not think she realised two old women were talking about her. Each turned their head to look, turned away again. Their skulls leaned to one another. Tilly pulled her wrists deep into her shirtsleeves. Sipped at a water bottle.

'Pulling over for a toilet break.' The driver's amplified voice startled her. 'Back on the bus in fifteen.' He made a performance of looking at his watch and named a time. 'Grab a snack if need be. We'll pull up again around lunchtime.' He rose to his feet, singing, and the passengers, save those few laughing and singing with him, went among the billboards and bowsers, headed for bright shelves and cellophane.

It wasn't one of those new roadhouses, in which everything is integrated. Vehicles, except those refuelling, parked haphazardly at a distance from the bowsers. There was a little copse of peppermint trees; green, mowed grass; and a path to the toilet block. From behind a tall fence, two llamas stared at Tilly with impertinent expressions. A sign:

You can feed the llamas!!
Feed $1 per bag in shop.

Another on the toilet wall:

These ARE NOT public toilets.
They are privately run.
Please do the Right Thing!
If you need to use our toilets please use the shop also.
Thank you.

Inside the door, large above the basin, in strong red letters:

NOT DRINKING WATER.

Tilly went into the shop. With a twinge of anxiety, she passed her fellow passengers going the other way, back to the bus. She grabbed a bottle, handed the man some money. Checking the change as she left and realising she'd been short-changed, Tilly turned around within the doorway. The shopkeeper was smirking; it seemed the skin of his face might split. He teetered toward her with a curling index finger.

Tilly turned her back on him.

Back on the bus, Tilly pulled a bright plastic lunchbox from her backpack. Gave it prime place among her luggage.

Trees closed in on each side of the road, then were flung back again and reduced to scattered clumps, or a thin fringe running beside road or fence and the expanses of bright yellow. 'Canola,' she heard someone say, though not addressing her; people looked away at her glance. The undulating yellow was a backdrop, a blanket, something you might fall back upon. Be helpless and pinned down, held there and hurt by some greedy twisted fucker.

Smothered under this sky.

Tilly pressed her knees tightly together, folded her arms very tight.

One of the women across from her held out a plastic

container of sandwiches. 'We've made ourselves too much, love. Help yourself.'

'Oh no. Thank you very much, but I'm full, really.'

The old woman smiled, but seemed disappointed. Before she could withdraw Tilly seized and displayed her own open lunchbox. 'Something sweet to finish off?' The plastic box was brimming with brightly iced cupcakes. 'I baked them for the trip.'

The women's faces creased and folded, crumpled with pleasure. They struggled to rise from their seats. Two pair of little old hands reached toward Tilly, fingers trembling.

'Baked them yourself you say?'

'Yep, got up early especially. Ate too many already, myself.' Though in fact, she had eaten one.

'Mmm, taste even better than they look.'

'Aren't you the clever girl then?'

Tilly closed the lunchbox when they'd had their fill, and clamped herself back into the music.

*

Road signs held up words and made them strange. She realised they were not from any song or film or book she knew: Wagin, Narrogin, Kojonup, Katanning . . . Wangelanginy Creek: a place, it might be said in the old language, where all the voices are together speaking and where, perhaps, beyond the roaring tunnel of glass and metal that held our Tilly, some innocently babbling brook remained, some safe and sheltered course with its own momentum continuing.

Tilly removed her tie and curled it in the hollow of her upturned hat.

At the next stop, the driver – stretching and scratching himself as Tilly stepped from the bus – asked, 'Where you getting off again, love?'

'Lake Grace.'

'Staying there?'

'No. Kepalup, or Hopetown.'

A passenger glanced quickly at her, then away again. A woman on her way to her car turned her head at the name and two women leaning against a car watched the bus leave.

Tilly was wrapping herself in her playlist, her photos, all her friends and the world she wanted kept close:

You lubbly sing
Watta dog
Yey party bitches
Thas rite niggas u 2 blue.

Tilly took the lunchbox from her bag, looked at the cakes for a while. She snapped the lid shut, put the box properly away. Sipped water.

Attending to her homework, Tilly made her way into some old novel: *Dracula.*

On the long scar of bitumen ahead, a minor murder of crows prepared to have their feathers ruffled. A couple took reluctantly to their wings, a few hopped away from the furred carcass as the bus buffeted them. Further ahead, a bloated kangaroo thrust its limbs skyward.

Tilly, bent to the old English words on her small screen, may not have noted the shadows lengthening, or the vegetation changing. Outside, mallee bristled at the bus's approach, then writhed and thrashed and shivering leaves applauded the blustering vehicle's departure.

Despite the fine soil lifting in the wind, shadows remained etched in earth: trees and fence posts, clods of ploughed soil, even a bull ant defiantly gripping the road's bitumen edge.

A thin stand of towering trees closed above the speeding bus, and in that brief tunnel of filtered light the trunks and limbs referenced the barely sun-kissed flesh of most of those in the bus; might have reminded them of their own sheltered, intimate parts; Tilly's secret skin too.

Deep red gum oozed from old wounds on the scarred trees; dark fluids seeped and coagulated.

The bus shot between two paired trees as if through a gate.

Sinking into some old story, Tilly was slipping away from her new friends, their fashion and idols, their boyfriends and bands, their films and photos and gathering energy. Even so, she did not see the clefts and limbs, the gateway of trees, the eagle hovering far above. She heard no rattling leaves, no shivering applause.

One side of the road was forest reserve, mostly what's called jam tree. Small, erect trees standing shoulder to shoulder like a sullen crowd, dull with dust. The other side of the road was bare earth, a haze of soil hanging just above the surface and sand heaped at the base of fence posts. Clouds moved across the bare sky, slowly shape-shifting.

Tilly raised her head. Saw the glass screen beside her. A dead snake on the bitumen. More crows. A shallow pool by the road held a patch of blue sky that rippled. The bus swerved a little.

'Lake Grace coming up. One passenger getting off here, cup of tea and toilet in another hour if everyone can hold until then please.' It wasn't a question.

Tilly read the speed signs. Saw a jeep, recently polished and ostentatiously parked across the entrance of a driveway. Three metal cut-outs of a poppy flower leaned in its open cab. The town labelled with a metal sign. The same colourful metal poppies again, each the height of a person, standing around the fence of the preschool.

Lest we forget.

The Great War.

Farm equipment: For Sale. A pub. Supermarket. Curly Wigs Hair Salon. Eatitup Café. Guns Safes Steel.

The bus pulled over at a roadhouse the other edge of town.

'Got someone to meet you, love?'

'Yes thanks.'

But there was no car waiting at the roadhouse.

Faces in the windows of the bus turned to her, for a moment like a school of fish. All eyes on Tilly, on her backpack and the Aboriginal flag imprinted upon it.

'Tell you what, love, have a word with the roadhouse. You got money? You can wait in there, at a table. He won't mind if you just sit.'

Not fifty metres away, the proprietor held open the door. He was a big man; Tilly would need to press against him to get through the door. His shirt tight against his bulging belly; skin like damp beach sand; strands of dark hair pressed against his skull.

Then there was the sound of another engine, of tyres flicking small stones. The school of faces in the bus windows turned again, lured by glass and sunlight-edged chrome. A dented and dusty four-wheel drive utility pulled up parallel to the bus, facing the other direction. The utility's tray cover was torn, and a thin cord dangled by a broken taillight. Its motor coughed and grumbled. The girl stood in the space between the two vehicles. The bus driver looked down the tunnel of his open doorway. The faces in the bus floated this way, that, like coy goldfish not wanting to stare.

The ute's tinted passenger window opened slowly, teasing the curiosity of the passengers. The onlookers saw two men inside. Twins? Of Aboriginal appearance. Approximately thirty to forty years old. Unshaven. Passenger appeared to be drinking, your grace.

'Tilly?' said the man in the ute. He gave a small belch.

'Gerry?' Tilly said, looking from one to the other.

'G'day, Tilly,' said the driver.

'Gerry,' she repeated, relieved.

'Hop in.'

The bus throbbed, waiting.

That girl in school uniform, no tie or hat; socks down, her skirt surely too short for school rules. She had flounced from the bus, now leapt into the back seat of the dual-cab. Kept her backpack with her, not in the tray.

'Yeah, plen'y room in the cab, Tilly. You don't want your bag in the back. Blood and all sorts of shit there.'

They accelerated away before the bus door had closed.

The roadhouse manager, still with one hand on the open door, raised the other in a wave of departure and the car horn squawked a reply. He looked at the bus, and gave a gap-toothed leer.

Eyeballs rolled away with the bus. The roadhouse door closed.

THE KILLERS WE GIVE HER TO

Tilly sank a little into the seat as the car accelerated noisily. Felt a little thrill. Music on, the volume very low.

'Hi Tilly, long time no see,' said the driver.

'Hi Gerry,' she said. 'Or . . .' Looking from one to the other.

The passenger said, 'He never tell you 'bout his twin? We're both Gerry. I'm Gerrard, he's Gerald.'

'Oh, I see,' said Tilly, laughing in what seemed relief. 'Must've seemed a good idea at the time.'

'Mum and Dad drunks, true. They couldn't tell us apart most of the time either.'

It was disconcerting for Tilly, seeing the twins. Like a mirror, almost; a split-screen. One wore a collared shirt.

'Jerries!' said the passenger. '*Schnell, schnell! Achtung*, English dog. You ever read war comics, Tilly? Ever watch *Hogan's Heroes*? Not the WWF, not that Hogan. Hulk Hogan? Nah, you too young to know that stuff.'

The passenger – Gerrard? – transferred his beer bottle from one hand to the other hand and held up his arm. A number one was tattooed there. 'Gerry One, me. That's number two there.' The driver, Gerald, tilted his head in acknowledgement. His long sleeves hid any tattoos he might have.

Tilly nodded. She offered them the remainder of her cakes. The driver took one, and she waved them before the passenger.

'Don't like sweet things, *those* sweet things. Beer man, me,' he said, and held up his near-empty beer bottle. 'Finish these off before the camp. Dry camp. No grog or gear of any kind.' There were several full bottles at his feet. 'Gerry'll drive all the way. Skipper.'

He held up the bottle in a salute to the driver, then tilted it to his mouth.

Tilly settled the container of cakes on the console between the twins.

'Your dad, Jim, he's first cousin to us, Tilly. You call us uncle, know that? Our way.'

'Yeah, I know that.' She looked to Gerry, the driver.

'Jim's girl, Tilly. It's too good you're with us, Tilly.' He said a word she did not know. 'That means very good,' he explained. Tilly's lips moved, trying the new word.

'Alright then.' The passenger scoffed a cake. Had a second.

'Too deadly. You ever been down this way, Tilly? Ancestral country, our country.'

'Dad said I was fostered here, but I don't remember.'

'That's right. Only for a bit. Your mum took you back.'

'Dad,' she hesitated for a moment, then rushed on. 'Mum never said I was fostered, not who or where or maybe I don't remember.'

The driver spoke. 'You was fostered with Hortons, who got Kokanarup. You know about Kokanarup?'

'I don't remember much. Nothing really.'

'Know about the massacre?'

'Yeah, Dad told me a bit about it.'

'This farm is where the old wadjela was killed 'cause he was messing with our women, wrong way.'

'Assassination,' said Gerald. 'Not an uprising.'

'He broke the law. He could've been with another woman. Law. Then his brother and the police got a permit and they killed every blackfella they could find, chased them away, poisoned the waterholes . . . Winchester rifle invented about then, see.'

'Well, some stayed, bro.'

'Our old granny and her sister.'

'Great-great-granny.'

'How come they survived? Stayed?' Tilly could not help herself asking.

'With white men, I guess. Twins.' The two men glanced at one another. 'Married and all.'

'They needed the women, but a proud black man is no use to them.'

'Maybe they were in love,' said Tilly.

'Yeah.'

'Your dad did all the research, even though he was inside. He reckons can't blame 'em for what their old people did. He reckons they're alright. Told us to get in touch. The old girl, Mrs Horton, even went to see him. Last thing your dad said to me: "When you get out, take my Tilly down there."'

'Yes, I know. Lovely. Take her to massacre country. Back to the white people, the killers' family we gave her to when she was little.'

'Not like that, Tilly.'

Sand pelted the windscreen. Twisted cords and eddies of brown and red in the air.

'Sandstorm again. They ripped all the trees out, didn't they? All the soil just blowing away, years and years now.'

The few trees fringing the road tossed their noisy leaves as the car shot by.

'Thunderstorm coming maybe.'

The passenger Gerry regained hold of the conversation. 'You know most blackfellas never even stop near Kepalup 'cause of what happened. That murderer. 'Cept the grannies. And you.'

Tilly saw the bird as they hit it. The bright flurry of feathers. 'Fuck.' The car slowed.

'Need a piss-break anyway, brother. S'cuse me, Tilly. There's a park just up here.'

The bird was caught in the bumper. Surprisingly intact, it was nevertheless dead. Feathers moved, but it was only the wind. Still warm, and light too; not much more than the weight of its feathers. Tilly wondered if angels were like this: hollow-boned, needing to preen themselves. Its eyes like glass, its claws folded, its feathers bright green and red and so very, very soft.

Tilly heard the stream of urine hitting the ground, and was again on the enclosed back veranda. Snotty-nosed, weeping, dishevelled and sore. Having given in. Knowing the chain, the smell of dogs. Light in the dimpled glass louvres. The smell of a freshly lit cigarette. A streetlight, pale stars.

She got back into the car. Closed the door.

The driver joined her.

'He's a drunk, but harmless if you can put up with his prattle. Couple of hours to go, which with his already-old-man's bladder will probably mean a few more stops.'

They sat in silence for a moment. He yawned. 'Dunno what he's up to. See if I can hurry him up.'

Tilly waited in the car with the window down to feel the wind on her cheeks. The bush rattled in the wind like small bones; an irregular, building rhythm. A flower like a paw waved from beside a rusty and tilted yellow bin; hands clutched, arms swung and reached.

A kookaburra laughed like a maniac.

Something howled.

Tilly felt someone beside her; looked, but there was no one. She tried to fall into her phone. No reception.

When they resumed it seemed the driver's turn to do all the talking, to tell her the story of their life and their own family's connection to the area, despite the massacre, and in contrast to other Noongars who were all shitty-arses and too scared to even visit. It began to rain, a fine, misty drizzle.

The wind had dropped.

The windscreen wipers squealed softly on each return stroke, as if pleading.

'Piss-stop, bro?' said the driver.

Tilly realised she had been asleep.

They pulled onto an arc of gravel beside the road, up close to another yellow bin into which the passenger tossed the empty bottles that had been rolling around on the car's floor.

The light was coloured with smoke. Or was it sand? Tilly could smell smoke.

'Musta been bushfire not far.'

'No more, not with this rain.'

The driver must have exhausted himself with talking. He fell back into silence, and now the passenger had regained his voice.

'Wanna cone, Tilly? You smoke? Don't mind if I do?'

She did not answer immediately; he turned back to her.

'No, I don't mind. No, I don't want any.'

Because then she might be shivering with fear again. The feel of the dog collar, the dry dog food in her mouth. Doug yanking the leash.

The car was slowing. Passenger Gerry wound down his window, and exhaled smoke. It was shredded in the roaring wind.

'Cut through on the gravel?'

'Yeah, roadworks ahead anyway.'

Dust churned behind them.

'Save us twenty minutes, half-hour maybe.'

The car skated sideways, maintaining momentum but heading for the ditch. Then straightened suddenly. Inside the car their heads moved from side to side like loose puppets.

'That's clay. Musta had more rain here.'

The driver nodded grimly, slowed. Tilly had begun taking driving lessons. She kept an eye on him. He was the sensible one, she thought. He'd rolled his sleeves. She saw the number 1 on his forearm. And also on the arm of the drunken passenger, who wore his shirt inside out. For all she knew they could be swapping their shirts every time they stopped.

Just a stupid schoolgirl, that's all she was. Trusting herself to drunken twins. She had reason to trust one of them, but probably not the other.

She said nothing.

Her cakes had been eaten. She stuffed the empty container into her school bag.

*

Yet another dead kangaroo lay stiff on the edge of the bitumen road, its forelimbs pointing straight at the sky, head to one side as if coy about death. Tilly did not smell its scent. Had never known that smell, nor seen a kangaroo as big or as dead as this one. Even now saw it only through a screen, like in a movie. A boring movie.

'Old fella said drop in today, unna?'

'I'll ring him.'

'Thought you said it was our country?' said Tilly.

A grimace the only reply.

They came onto the bitumen again while he was on the phone. An intersection. The passenger pointed – unnecessarily – to the right. 'Away from town,' he said softly to himself.

'Right then, Mr Horton. We'll see you about twenty minutes, just past the crossing.'

He hung up, turned to his twin. 'You know the turn-off?'

'About seven k's this side of Kepalup,' Tilly said. 'I googled it before,' she said in response to their look. 'I didn't remember it. Don't remember nothing of being here.'

Sand lifted from the paddocks and rolled in billowing waves across the road and into the dense scrub on the other side. Rose again like smoke. The many stiff and leathery leaves coated in dust. More and more of a certain small tree, crowding.

Rain came in a fine mist. Bathing the plants, thought Tilly. Refreshing them.

One of the twins spoke. 'This is your country, Tilly. Our old people lived here.'

'So I've heard.'

'Coming into it now. More of this.' He pointed to an untidy, blue-grey and large-leafed plant. 'Tallerack. See 'em best at night.'

Gerry belched and, leaning toward his brother, turned to Tilly in the back seat. 'Not many blackfellas been here for a long time, since nearly everybody was wiped out . . .'

Tilly said nothing. She was here when she was a baby.

'Taboo,' said the other twin. 'But you been here and nothing happened.'

Tilly's brow wrinkled. She was, it seemed, returning with one, perhaps two, drunk, stoned and distant relations.

They slowed, turned left into a narrow gravel and sand track. Immediately the trees closed around them so that only now and then was there a glimpse of sky.

'Ok,' she said aloud.

*

In years to come Tilly will dream this entrance again and again, blending details as her experience and imagining increase, building on details that, recalled and examined, wither to something threadbare when she wakes, an irritant scratching the inside of skin.

The little track slipped aside at the point the bitumen road, rushing elsewhere, begins to curve. There is an older bitumen road that cuts across this curve and, although overgrown with tough and cheeky plants that have reasserted themselves there, you can still pick out the hard smooth surface, and follow it on foot. Between the two strips of bitumen there are three water-holes set in granite. Thin slabs of stone still cover each of them. And the water, dark and cool, gathers there from rain running down the rock. One of the waterholes is never dry, not in the longest of summers. Fed by a small spring, the dark, cool water brims, cusping at the stone edge.

It is easy to become lost in such reverie. To immerse oneself, to drown. Tilly had been rushing behind two who were drunk, were tripping or otherwise shifted in their selves, and then everything tilted, was sliding away. The very quality of sound changed. The tyres settled in the dirt, broke a thin crust of damp sand. Sand clung to the tyres, was flung away, dispersed. Grey sand, grey mist, drizzle, a grey forest of small trees that, standing close to one another and with their limbs folded compactly at the same angle, might have been a company of soldiers, a silent crowd breasting a fence line, spilling over it and shuffling closer and closer, halting in the instant before a glance found them. Jam trees.

Passenger Gerry, very serious, gave the old word for the tree. Another belch.

A sweetly scented timber, jam tree. There are many kilo-metres of fence posts made of this tree. Grey posts in straight lines, rammed in the earth, strands of wire linking them, the top one barbed. A hard, dense timber. Strip away the bark, and see colours swirl cream and dark chocolate on every limb.

Tilly: 'What?'

'I said very important tree for us, Tilly. Rub the ash on the babies, put it in graves. Tapping sticks too.'

'Seeds, and gum to chew on,' his twin continued. 'At the workshops, you'll see . . .' He said the words for the old instruments fashioned from local trees.

Gerrard looked at his brother. Tyres whispered on the sand and gravel.

Tilly mouthed one of the old words he'd used.

Tilly felt herself lighten as they crested a rise and the forest opened up. The trees were taller and more widely spaced, their warm and light-coloured trunks reaching to an expanse of sky. Then they dropped from the crest into the shadows again.

'Meet him at the grave.'

'Horton?' asked the other twin.

'Same family, eh?'

'Yeah, must be the grandson or great-grandson or something. Ancestor the killer cunt, s'cuse me, Tilly.'

'You been here before?' said Tilly.

'Nah, not us.'

'The man we're meeting, what's his name again?'

'Dan. Dan Horton.'

'That's who I was fostered with?'

'Yeah, your dad said.'

'Was it here, this place, or one of their other farms?'

'Dunno.'

'The old house, I think.'

A house squatted on the other side of the creek they were approaching. Made of stone blocks and mortar, and so white it might have been bone, its two dark, blank windows looked across a sloping expanse of brittle, yellow grass to the creek. The new iron roof was a dazzling contrast to the messy clutter of old corrugated iron sheets, rusting machinery and tangled wire that surrounded it.

A four-wheel drive utility was parked beside the house. Its taillight brightened, and it moved away, distorted reflection trembling in the window glass. A loose sheet of corrugated iron banged in the wind. A door knocked again and again in its frame. Nearby, a nest of dugites coiled and twisted together, moving slowly in a shaft of sunlight that sliced the gloomy cold of the stone well around them.

The car turned just before the creek crossing, and disappeared among the trees.

TWO BIRDS NOW

Tilly's car came down the last slope; tyres splashed in the shallow river and left brief, damp prints at the edge of the creek bed before being immediately coated with sand. Tiny rivulets caused by the disruption disappeared almost immediately.

Tilly saw the white utility parked just off the track. An old man stood beside it. Pale as a ghost and with two tiny dogs at his feet, he held out one arm to indicate an even smaller track. His clothes were faded and worn, a pale blue towelling hat pulled low on his head.

They parked.

The dogs strutted, bristling, toward the twins and Tilly. Gerald (so far as Tilly could guess) stepped toward the man with his hand held out. 'Mr Horton.' The dogs shied away from him, took shelter behind their owner.

'I'm Gerry Coolman; rang you earlier.'

'Yes of course. Pleased to meet you.'

'My brother, Gerrard. People call us both Gerry – makes it easier.'

They looked to Tilly. She was by the car, looking away from the little dogs that pranced around her, yapping. Dan Horton called, 'Blacky. Whitey.' The dogs ran to him and one, two, leapt into his waiting arms.

He bent, and they jumped to the ground again.

'Tilly? I don't suppose you remember, from when you were a baby? My wife and I, you were our foster-child.'

Tilly shook her head, no.

''Course your mum took you back soon as she could, soon as she was well again.'

He moved to embrace her, but Tilly held out a hand, and so they shook hands rather formally, with the careful courtesy of diplomats. Dan tilted his head, moved his eyes. 'The grave is this way.'

A small clearing. Paint flaking, a picket fence more grey than white. The concrete block above the grave plot had broken midways as earth subsided. Butterflies of light on the ground. Carved into a timber cross:

William Horton. 1848–1881. Killed by natives.

'That's what this place is known for these days, I'm afraid. And what happened afterwards, as you know. My wife, rest in peace, always wanted to work with you people to do something about that.'

Jam trees swayed and brushed against one another. The sheoak whispered. A bird made a harsh and sceptical noise. Wispy clouds rushed across the little patch of blue above them.

'Nothing about all the Noongars killed then.'

One of the twins lifted a hand, almost reached for Tilly as she moved away; the other touched Dan Horton's arm. The three men stood for a moment, then followed the girl down a thin path.

Pools of water were scattered like islands in the dry, coarse sand of the creek bed, with rocks and tussocks of reeds at their edges. Between them were banks of sand, deep and soft and difficult to walk in. Their feet fell easily, sank, were difficult to lift again. Dan led them to a firmer way that wended between the pools, and mostly they kept to that.

Occasionally, between trees, they saw the old white stone farmhouse further up the slope of the dry paddock.

'There are so many different stories about what happened here,' said Dan.

'Took turns going out with a Winchester,' said one of the twins.

'Some say scores killed, but the paperwork . . .' Dan hesitated.

'Poisoning the waterholes,' said the other twin.

They walked as a group, one or the other stumbling when they strayed into deeper sand. Trees lined either side of the creek bed.

Then they came to a place where the creek bed was a little wider and, on a flat sheet of rock near its centre a circular stone wall, not much more than knee-high and about two metres across, brimmed with algae-thick water.

'Needs cleaning out,' said Dan. He lifted long strands of green muck with a stick, flicking it onto the ground around them. 'My grandfather built the walls around it.'

Tiny rivulets of water ran across the rock, pushed aside grains of sand, disappeared.

Dan cupped his hands and drank from the well.

'You can drink it. Hard water, but perfectly ok. Stock thrives on it.'

The sand around them was dimpled with many more prints than their own.

Gerry, turning, taking a step here and there, pointed to the prints in the sand. 'Look at this.' He breathed with the old people, let their sound move in him. Looked at Tilly. 'That's our language. Kangaroo. Racehorse goanna. Porcupine, you say echidna. Look.' He pointed to the footprint of a bird, and named it in the old language. 'Crow,' he translated. 'He must've took off.' The single footprint, then nothing.

Gerald placed the heel of his hand on a patch of clear sand, touched his finger to the soil a few times and made a tiny, perfectly formed footprint. Then he named a specific spirit creature, basically human but miniature in form.

'That's clever, that is,' said Dan.

Tilly saw that some of the plants had also left prints in the sand, patterns where the wind had bent their tips to the soil, and repeatedly moved them to and fro.

'Can we sleep over some time?'

The men looked at Tilly, surprised.

'Someone has to, sometime. I lived here when I was a baby and nothing happened. No evil thing. No devils, no taboo thing, I mean. My father wanted me to come back here, meet you.'

Dan looked at the twins; who looked at one another, then to Tilly.

'But Tilly we never lived here then, with you,' said Dan. 'Not this place.'

They kept walking. We are all descended from Adam and Eve, Dan was saying. He seemed to insist.

They followed a line of old posts that led from the creek, past the house and continued over the crest. Wire dangled from some of them, and porcelain conductors were displayed like small trophies well above the heads of this little bunch of ambulating onlookers.

'The old telegraph line,' said Dan. 'Put that through in the 1870s. About the same time the Hortons, about the same time our family,' he glanced at Tilly, 'settled here.'

'Noongars used to climb up and grab them conductors, chip them away for spearheads,' said Gerald. 'Before . . . When there was still a few here, living their own way.'

'Maybe they wanted to listen to what people were saying,' said Tilly.

A couple of corrugated iron sheds stood away from the house. Dan led them to one that, leaning against a solid stone wall, gave the impression that it was part of a much more soundly built structure. They walked among the gloomy iron, through the stone wall.

'Old shearing shed,' said Dan, proudly. Light flooded in a great wash through a large opening in the other wall, but did not dispel the gloom and shadows in corners, and behind drums and tarpaulin and a heap of tyres. There was a timber floor, a timber railing coated with dust. On the wall a saddle, a yoke. Beneath the dust, the rotting timber and rust, they could smell the years, the sweat and lanolin. Strong roof timbers spanned the space so high above their heads.

'A convict built this. A stonemason.'

They walked to the house.

'Maybe you're not so interested in the buildings, white man's heritage and that?'

'No problem, Mr Horton. We appreciate your trouble.' Gerry winked at Tilly behind Dan's back.

Dan paused; he placed his finger into one of a series of holes in the mortar. 'This must've been made by a spear. See, several of them. Aborigines attacked the house.'

'You reckon? Like an attack, an uprising?'

'But, another time, I'll show you waterholes on the property.'

Gerald gave him the old word for such rock waterholes. Tilly understood this was for her benefit.

'Yes. Well. And there's a soak, that's all walled in with

stone. They must've done that. I never thought before, but the Aborigines must've helped build that, don't you think?'

His listeners murmured agreement.

'We used to find stones, grinding stones at our property a little downriver. They'd stand out, because different rock. Must've come from a little spot down near the river mouth, we reckon.'

'The reef there?'

'Yeah.'

'I know that spot.'

The windows reflected figures circling the house. Poking it. Turning their backs. The glass was old and flawed and the people it showed were also distorted, and there were many more than four. Again, a sheet of corrugated iron clanged in the wind. A door knocked in its frame. A window rattled. The wind dropped for a moment, and then dust rose and the dry yellow grass hissed as another gust came rushing up from the creek bed.

'There was a bit of a cellar, but they filled it in in my grandfather's time. Snakes kept getting in there, apparently.'

About fifty metres away, a broken wall of stone, a dip in the earth, a vexed tangle of blackberry bush.

'An old well there. Dry now. There were always snakes there; couldn't get rid of them. Keeps us all happy this way, know where they are.'

They gazed at the small ruin. No one moved toward it.

'But, like I say,' continued Dan, 'come to tea with me some time. Tonight? You'll need to go back on the bitumen, head back to Kepalup just a few kilometres. You'll see the road – Horton – named for us. You'll see the letterbox. Stay and have a look around meantime. If you like.'

*

The white utility disappeared into the trees of the creek crossing, and they saw it emerge again, following the track up the opposite slope. Again it disappeared, and soon they did not even hear it.

A cockatoo jeered.

'Go back to that spring, walk along the creek?' suggested Tilly.

'Sure thing, boss,' said Gerry. 'You go all shy there for a bit?'

Again the house windows showed a girl and two men walking away, then more figures, trembling and shifting shape in the flawed glass. Unseen by the walkers, a snake crossed the space between them and the building, its rippling undulations as uncanny as some old and forgotten magic.

Back at the creek bed they saw how an old flood had here and there woven what almost looked like screens between the trunks and limbs of trees either side of the sand; screens of sticks and twigs, leaves and feathers – it was unclear where the edges were, where they began and ceased.

Tilly stopped and turned in a circle on her heels. In an open space, she saw the house on the bleached and prickly slope. Trees crowding the edge of the creek bed bent toward her, ushering her away from its gaze.

'I don't remember a thing. Jeez. I was just a baby.'

'Yeah, but you helped make sure family always been here.' Gerald thought himself the serious one. 'Our old granny married a white man, maybe she wanted to forget, and then you come lived here, too little to know and . . . Old man Horton trusts us 'cause he remembers the old women, he remembers our family.'

Again he pointed to prints in the sand, naming in the old language the animals and birds that had made them.

'I dunno them words,' said Tilly.

'Learned them in prison. Your dad was teaching us younger fellas . . . Well, not all so young.'

'Pity he was never around to teach me.'

'That's why we're all down here, Til. In our old country.'

'Your dad never really been here either. He only knowed to wind up the windows and keep driving. 'Cause of the massacre, see,' the other twin said.

Tilly pointed along the creek bed, to a single tall tree in the distance and an eagle perched on one of its lower branches.

Gerald spoke its name in the old language.

'Don't see 'em low down like that much,' said Gerrard.

The eagle and the three people studied one another.

'Eagle, he don't sing. Not like us curlew – us Wirlomin. That's our totem, Tilly.' Gerald said the old word for curlew. 'Scary when you hear them, boy. Lots of people reckon, "death bird", 'cause of the sound.'

'Not many around now,' said his brother.

'Bit like us then,' replied Gerald.

'Maybe none,' said Tilly.

'Maybe they just keeping quiet. Camouflaged. You might never see one, think it's just a stick of wood.'

The brothers began to sing. They were transformed by the song, the singing of it. Then it faded. Surprised at themselves, they listened to the sound of the wind, of insects and birds.

The eagle opened its wings. It seemed for a moment it might even fall but, wings straining, it rose into the sky.

'That song,' Tilly began.

'Not an old one. Your dad made that one up. First couple of words are from an old song, but no one really remembered how it went.'

'It's beautiful.'

The eagle spiralled higher and higher as they watched. Became a small thing, easily lost in the sky.

No storm, but still those heavy clouds gathering on one side of the sky. Darkness was coming upon them.

Gerald checked his phone. 'Pay the old fella a visit, unna?'

Tilly shrugged.

'Sure,' said Gerrard. 'He asked us.'

'Rest of them won't be there for hours yet. Got held up somewhere.'

The car drove away, and the trees leaned back from the water and sand, reached for the sky again. Light thickened, became something almost palpable.

*

It was only a short distance, but already the trees sprang from the darkness ahead of them and bent over the headlight beams. The car slowed. Through a filigree of leaves: a globe shining down upon a front door; a window outlined in yellow light.

Footsteps crunched on gravel. Tiny, dancing tongues of flame: a small barbeque arrangement close to the house, glistening iron plate dripping grease on the fire. A low wall in the fire glow, two hunched cats. Globes smouldering beneath slow eyelids.

The three at the front door listened to one muffled singing voice, the piano's simple accompaniment. Tilly slipped around the corner of the house, waved them to the window. They looked upon Dan at the piano, singing. The dogs content at his feet.

They knocked again at the front, more loudly. Heard the small dogs barking, claws scrabbling the other side of the door which now swung open. Little dogs swirled around them, growling, and then were gone. Dan shook hands with one of the twins, put a hand on the shoulder of the other and with this firm grip, pulled them into the house. Tilly remained just outside the door, her back to them and her arms wrapped around herself. The little yapping dogs bouncing around her.

'Git.' She waved her arms and stamped a foot. The dogs retreated to Dan, who gestured at Tilly. 'Come in,' he said.

The walls of the small entrance hall displayed framed paintings of horses drinking from a stream, and photographs: farm animals and machinery, stiff portraits of ancestors and family.

'My brother did the paintings,' Dan said, but he pointed to a small photograph of a woman with a toddler on her lap. 'Recognise this photo, Tilly? The little girl, perhaps?'

Tilly peered closer.

'It's you, Tilly, and my wife. Bless her.'

The woman was smiling. The child looked suspicious. Tilly recognised neither of them.

'That's your frown alright, bub,' said Gerald.

A large table sat just off centre of the expansive room. The upright piano pushed back against the wall. A guitar and mandolin were propped beside it, and the walls were covered with large sheets of hymn lyrics, handwritten in thick pen:

Though I walk in the valley of death . . .
Just a closer walk with thee . . .
Lead me Jesus lead me . . .

The light from a single, suspended globe did not quite reach the cobwebby corners of the room.

Six places were set on a tablecloth of checked plastic. The cutlery and crockery did not match. Dan lifted a metal cover. Steak, sausages, chops, evidently cooked on the outside barbeque.

'Can you grab the salad from the kitchen, Tilly love?'

Dan opened the plastic bag of sliced bread, and invited the men to sit. He folded his hands ready for prayer as a disgruntled Tilly returned, then closed his eyes and began to speak.

Tilly glanced quickly at the twins; one twin raised his eyebrows, the other had his eyes closed and his palms together. Tilly's hands were under the table. She dug her nails into her palms, very hard.

'. . . the certainty of your holy word, oh Lord. Our conviction and faith is in your word. Amen.'

'Amen,' said Gerald.

Dan looked around at his guests. 'Our meal is waiting for us. I think we should help ourselves, don't you?'

The little dogs, stiff and trembling, investigated the shadows by the fireplace. A spider moved to the centre of its web in a high corner of the room.

Dan indicated the vacant seats. 'Such a shame the rest of the family – our loved ones – can't be with us. My son, my wife . . .'

He ceased speaking. Knives cut, forks jabbed, mouths chewed, lips worked to keep the food from spilling. In turns, they waved their hands to deter two or three persistent flies. Dan folded the bread back into its plastic wrap. Fat coagulated on the meat. The salad wilted. Conversation stretched thinly across the silences. Gerrard tried, 'Paddocks look dry on the way down.'

'Yes.'

'We saw lightning. There was a spot of rain.'

'I doubt there'll be rain in it for us. You live in the city? Gerry? Gerald?'

The brothers nodded. One spoke. 'Yeah, mostly. But this is home. This is my ancestral country.' He glanced at his brother and Tilly. 'Our ancestral country.'

'Yes. Well, we've lived here, my family, for . . . must be five, six generations now.'

'They've moved away, your kids I mean? You have kids?'

'A son.'

His listeners nodded. One of the twins sat back.

'Yes. I don't see him, really. He lives in King George Town, I think. I tried to get word to him about his mother's funeral, but . . . He's changed his name, I hear.'

Dan Horton was not yet on Facebook. He thought he'd seen his son once, a young man with a shaven head; a man who shone, was suited, seemed scented and glossy. A man pleased with himself. He'd had a young woman with him, a very young woman, Dan had thought, who did not hold herself well. Something wrong with her. It was but a glance, he turned away, looked back and they were gone.

'It's no life for a young man, farming. Not now, not here.'

'Salt? Overclearing?'

'Oh, all that. Both. The same. And the changing economy.'

'And climate?'

'Oh, I don't know about that. We've had good rains of late. For this district. We like to think the country is recovering in fact. My wife went to her grave regretting how much we've cleared. We had to, no real choice at the time, but . . . Came to regret it.'

'She passed away not long?'

'Not long.' He didn't specify the time, and they did not press him.

'You must miss her.'

'I do. We were fifty years together. She loved this bush, loved this country. We all do.'

'It's powerful country. Special. Felt it again today.'

'She was a conservationist, you know. Not at first, of course. But late in her life, especially, she was very passionate. She must have replanted thousands of trees, jam and sandalwood and york. Like I said, the country is recovering. Mallee hen, bush turkey . . .'

Gerald said their names in the ancient tongue.

Dan looked at him. 'I see them on the paddocks sometimes. For a long time you never did.'

'I wouldn't know one if I fell over it,' said Tilly.

'You speak your Aboriginal language?' asked Dan.

Gerald gave him the old word for 'yes'. He was so proud of himself. 'It means hello too,' he said. And then said the word again.

'Used to be a lot of them curlews, when we were lads, before all the clearing. Someone at church was saying, just t'other day, they heard them again.'

His three guests exchanged glances.

'Used to see their eyes at night-time, when we camped. Just their eyes, shining in the firelight, in a circle around us. Only their eyes. Never hardly see them in daytime, because they camouflage themselves so well.'

Tilly wondered how they might appear if someone was to peer through a window. The dark corners, the dogs worrying the shadows, the coagulating meat, the four people huddled at the large table with its vacant, set places.

'Gerry was telling me about them, just today, at the farm,' she said.

'You just never even know if they're there or not,' continued Dan. 'And that call.' He shivered.

'Emus around the place?' asked Gerald.

'Emus! They're nesting now, you know. It's the male that sits on the nest.' He was addressing Tilly. 'It's the father that cares for them.' She looked away.

'Funny things, emus. They run in a straight line when you chase them.'

'You'd never catch an emu,' said Tilly. 'Even I know that.'

'But you can bring them to you,' said Gerald. 'Whistle and

lie on your back with your legs moving around in the air. They'll come looking. Curious, see.'

'I meant when you go after them in a car,' Dan continued. 'They stick to the track and you can get right up close behind, so you hear their legs knocking on the roo bar. They can't turn away and so . . .'

Dan held his knife and fork upright in his hands.

'Vermin, we used to call them.'

Tilly grasped a small, sharp blade.

Dan put his knife and fork on either side of his plate. Straightened them. He had not eaten much at all.

Tilly got to her feet and began to clear the dishes. When she left the room, Gerald said to Dan, 'This is very good of you, Mr Horton . . .'

'Please call me Dan.'

'Ok, Dan. Thanks very much for your hospitality. We were wondering, like Tilly said today . . .'

'You'd like to spend a night at the homestead?'

'Well, maybe. No.'

'Yes, let's,' said Tilly as she returned to the room, wiping her lips.

'Well, we do wanna pay another visit, a group of us, that are here for the workshop.'

'For the Peace Park opening? I'm so pleased.'

'It's a chance to reconnect, to face up to and heal the history, the massacre . . .' Gerald ground to a halt.

'The Peace Park . . .' Dan hesitated. 'It's for the town, for all of us really. Janet was very involved.'

They sat in silence for a moment, gazed at the floor.

'A lot of Aborigines say it's taboo,' Dan said. 'They don't like it.'

'Not all of us, and lots have never had a chance to . . .'

'Personally,' interrupted Dan, 'I hate the word "massacre".' He put both his large hands on the table, palms down. 'It hurts me. I don't know . . . Janet started all this; she wanted a plaque to acknowledge the terrible things that happened, and . . .' His gaze flickered to Tilly. 'Just let me know when you want to come. We might have a barbeque . . .'

'Let's stay there tonight. I'm not scared.' Tilly smiled at Dan. He blushed.

'Well,' said Gerald, looking up from his phone. 'The bus is running late.'

'So let's stay then,' said Tilly, insisting.

'Let's help with the dishes first.' Gerald grinned, and turned toward the kitchen sink.

'No need. There's a dishwasher,' the old man said.

'Yes, I've stacked it,' said Tilly.

'It's wonderful how you've grown,' said Dan, admiringly.

'You know,' he spoke to the two men now, 'if you did want to stay at the homestead, where it all started, the killing, I mean . . . You could. It'd be fine. There's no electricity but there is water, and it's fine to stay. We were thinking of a bed and breakfast. It's ready to be used.'

Walking from the house to the cars they could hardly see one another. Dan's voice could have come from one of the trees, any one of the figures barely distinguishable in the darkness.

'Did you find the well today, the bubbling spring?'

*

How very dark it was, the darkness congealing around them as they moved away from the old house. Trees barely discernible, a patch of star-glittering sky above their heads, wisps of cloud; then leaves and twigs closed again, concealing the stars and sky, and they flitted, the clouds and Tilly and Gerrys too; were wispy, shifting, insubstantial among trunks and limbs, among a tangle of leaves and twig and thorn.

Dan's voice reached them from a little distance. Tilly stopped. She heard the light crunch of other footsteps on gravel.

She saw the old man, framed in the light of his open car door. He looked like something preserved, an exhibition piece.

Looked like Dougie. A man framed in door light.

Tilly had been floodlit in a high-walled backyard. Tied up with the dogs. A man walking at her. Dougie. Son of God, he said.

Tilly in the night, chained at the neck to a dog kennel. Looking back at the house. A bright globe spilling light on the porch. One window light-rimmed. A wan and tired moon.

The man leading her on a leash away from the kennels. Tilly bent at the knees, stooped like an ape and just as naked. Her goose-pimpled flanks, her small breasts pointing down. Dougie did not make her go on all fours, not on this occasion. Dougie stumbled on the steps, bumped against the doorframe as he entered. He tugged on the leash around her neck. Tightened his lips, focused his loose and sloppy-mouthed smile.

Sat her on the floor at his feet, himself at the kitchen table. Began that little ritual with flame and the pipe, with needle or vial or pills. She closed the door, closed the door and turned away.

*

The old homestead leapt in the erratically sweeping headlights as the two vehicles approached. Dan's taillights died.

Motors off, doors having slammed, it was very quiet. Thunder rumbled in the distance.

'The toilet.' Dan indicated a small outhouse as they walked tentatively in the darkness to the house. 'There's a bucket in there to flush it with. Tap just outside the door. Daylight, you'll see it.'

The four of them stood close as Dan fumbled with the door key. The door swung open, creaking.

'There's a torch,' said Dan. It was very dark.

Tilly felt the twins close. As if there were more than two of them, more than just they and Dan. She felt reassured somehow. Then, revealed in the wavering spear of torchlight, fragments of the interior of the house. A steel sink, a chair, cupboards, a candle in a bottle.

'There should be a few candles, somewhere.'

Another flash of lightning showed a number of bottles with candles exclaiming their unlit existence.

Four candles moved through the dark house, their reflections wobbling, floating in window glass.

'I think you'll be comfortable, though it's noisy if it rains in this little house.'

A strengthening breeze tousled hair as the three watched Dan's taillights retreat into the scrub near the bottom of the slope.

'I dunno,' began one of the twins.

A bank of clouds covered half the sky, closing in on the moon.

'Dunno about staying here, you mean?' asked Tilly.

'Don't tighten your hole over it,' said his brother.

'Well, it's not taboo for no reason,' said Gerald, and he gave them one of the old words. 'Spirity,' he translated, 'is not just bad. It can be good too. For us. Our old people here. Gotta be pleased to see us back. Bringing the language back.'

Shreds in advance of a solid bank of clouds moved quickly across a moon that was like bone in an X-ray, a shadowy crescent.

A gust of wind. Something slammed.

Inside the house again, and shadows jumped and merged in the candlelight, sprung apart again. Shifted.

'All in one room, unna?'

'You boys in one room, I'll have the other.'

'Tilly . . .'

'I'll be alright. I'm not frightened. You two look after yourselves. I believe you; the old people will be glad to see me back.'

Tilly stood by the bed, holding the candle. The house was neat and clean. A blanket tucked in and tight. Surfaces shone in the candlelight. Leapt at her as lightning flashed again. In the window glass, lit only by the candle, her melting reflection waved a greeting. She might be a ghost herself.

She lay down, saw the face of some small spirit creature rising over the windowsill. It reminded her of the twins, though older, wizened and shrunken. It grinned. Was gone. She dreaming?

Somewhere outside, something clanged in a gust of wind.

*

Those two named Gerry lay side by side on a double mattress, fully clothed, only their shoes removed.

'She really our people?'

'I dunno, Ger. She might've been away too long, brought up wadjela way and all.'

'We're all coming from the same place, from here, the same old ancestor way back.'

'DNA's pretty diluted in her.'

'The same place, Ger, thousands of generations before us. You seen those places today. Gotta mean something.'

'Don't you gotta draw the line somewhere, though?'

'Shut the fuck up.'

'She never been with us, Ger, she never really lived with black people.'

'Shuttup.'

The world outside grumbling.

'But I think about these things, Gerald.'

There was no reply.

Tilly flat on her back. Eyes open.

The brothers turned and turned in their sleep. Moved closer together.

Tilly slept calmly. Her eyes opened, but she did not wake. Eyes closed again. Her breath came deep and slow.

The wind died. The sky grumbled and muttered. Lightning. Among the many animal prints in the creek bed, the marks of their shoes from earlier in the day. And of many small, bare feet.

Thunder.

Lightning.

Gleaming eyes all around the creek bed.

And this truth: a curlew screaming.

*

Gerald opened his eyes and saw the back of his twin's skull; the thin tousled hair, the skin beneath. It could be his own sleeping self. We age, he thought, and here I am back inside stone walls again so soon. He raised himself to his feet, and the simple act of walking out of the room elated him.

He stood pissing, and the wind moved from the creek up the slope, over brittle yellow stalks that, bent and broken, whispered of the crumbling earth.

When he returned to the room his twin brother had a needle in his arm. Looked up, his gaze scarcely registering Gerald's presence.

'Where'd you get that?'

Gerald listened to his brother grinding his teeth as they walked to the creek. Let him stumble, moving that way in fits and starts.

They found Tilly sitting on rock spread like a sheet or a blanket amid the banks of coarse river sand. She was at the edge of the rock, beside a pool of water itself surrounded by tussocks and ribbons of grass. A tree leaned over her. She was making those small footprints with her hand, clumsily. Beyond her arm's reach there were more perfect examples.

*

The car went through the creek; drops of water were flung from the tyres, landed in the sand and disappeared. Coming up the bank, leaving the water, a mallee hen walked out of the jam trees and stood on the track, facing the vehicle. They pulled up. Bird and people stared at one another through the windscreen.

A second bird joined the first.

Tilly stepped from the car. The birds, unhurriedly, walked away into the forest of such small trees, that company of tree trunks. There was a small path, a narrow foot trail, winding away from the road and Tilly followed it. She soon lost sight of the birds, but her feet kept moving along the curving track.

Trees stood back; a small clearing, and a diagonal shaft of light pointing to a cluster of tiny flowers, purple and blue. The flowers made the shape of a body, lying on its side and curled up like a baby. A small adult's body. A body Tilly's size.

'Tilly.'

She jumped at her name.

Looked around the circle. Stepped back from the edge of flowers.

'Tilly. We don't want you getting lost!'

She could hear the twins, but not see them.

Felt a little surge of panic.

Fingernails deep in the skin at her palms.

'Shame. Blackfella lost in bush!'

Tilly smiled to herself.

'Ok. I'm coming.' I think. She started on the return path.

*

Gerry met her and helped her find the channel of the road. They did not speak, and in the silence she heard his teeth grinding.

The car moved. The sound of gravel on the tyres. A little wind from the open window. Suddenly, emus sprang from the trees on the right as if they'd been waiting to ambush them. Gerry slammed on the brakes, and the car wallowed for a moment among tail feathers, arching necks and wide-eyed, indignant expressions. The emus' legs seized and threw large increments of space behind themselves: already they were on the other side of the road, had disappeared between the trees. The sense of them remained beyond knotted trees, filigree of leaves.

At first no one spoke, and then Tilly. 'Back there, I found like a grave. Flowers in the shape of a curved back, like a baby in a womb, you know, but grown size, legs curled up and arms around.'

'Yeah? And his brother warriors guarding him.'

Gerald laughed. 'They let us go anyways.'

'Aren't they but, these trees. Like warriors.'

'We're coming back d'rectly!'

The car approached a gateway, and an eagle sat on the post each side. The car went slowly, and its passengers made eye contact, were held in the stern gaze of the two raptors. Then the winged beasts lifted themselves, their great pinions bending as they cupped the air in their feathers, spiralled up and up and up.

A rushing sound beneath Tilly's feet; the air at her window roaring. She craned her neck, held her hair to her cheek because of the wind, leaned out beyond the restricting glass. The eagles tiny and distant now in the shredding clouds.

BUSFUL

The bus was running late from the start. Wally James driving, but being late wasn't his fault. Left to himself, he'd be early, always. Wally liked to work; liked to have purpose and structure in his day, a role, liked being useful. He especially enjoyed driving, whether bus, truck, tractor, forklift, grader . . . You name it, Wally had driven it. It may have been perversity, or a sense of family obligation, that led him to take on this particular driving job, because he certainly knew it would come with a lot of frustration.

Wally was at the bus hire company's door as they opened: he'd arranged to be dropped off, had his ID ready, and a list of the names and addresses of those he needed to pick up. Had already filled in all the forms.

Thus began perversity and obligation.

'A real bunch of characters,' was how he later shaped the anecdote. 'A bus full of characters,' he'd say, time and time again. Though, mind you, plenty of passengers from other trips would tell you he was a bit of a character himself. Didn't put up with any shit, Wally. A previous bus trip had become a nightmare for at least one of his passengers. Wally usually didn't allow anyone to drink alcohol when he was driving, but this one time they had, and it got so that there was a toilet stop every ten minutes. Eventually, Wally had refused. One woman was jumping around, screaming at him to stop, but he refused. She pissed herself. She never forgave him for that, Wally would tell you, laughing the whole time: at himself, or her distress? It was hard to tell.

'A bus full of characters. If you aren't on your toes they'll make you their private taxi. Then who gets the blame for being late, for leaving people behind?'

'Just call in on so and so. Just drop into the shops – I need smokes, a drink, a pie, the newspaper. Come on, Wally, brother.'

First person picked up was Wally's ex-wife, Ruby. Least, that was what he told the later passengers. But really, he'd stayed the night at her place and they'd gone together to pick up the bus.

She'd never been his wife anyway, not really: only his de facto. They never really married properly, although in his memory he had literally carried her over the threshold; jumped the broomstick, as people said. They'd loved one another, hurt one another and now – getting on in years – had come to an understanding. They'd never got on so well. The kids were doing alright, and they had the grannies to think of.

She knew what he was like. 'I was born a rambling man,' he'd sing.

'All you have to offer me is you,' Ruby sang in reply. She was the better singer, but not so confident. 'Shit, Wally, you and George Jones.'

'You're my number one, Ruby,' he'd remind her, adjusting the peak of his baseball cap. Everyone knew he'd stayed with Ruby – he always did in town – but not the actual sleeping arrangements. It made people curious, especially because Wally and Ruby were so secretive about it. If he was feeling spritely he might even, like in his younger days, rise up on his toes, bounce a little, even touch or tilt his pelvis. Grab his private parts and act all macho as if he was one of the kids in their falling-down pants.

Wally had worn a baseball cap for years; wore his hair long and tied in a ponytail, the cap concealing his tonsured skull. These days he dyed his hair too. Oh, he was vain, was Wally. He liked women (ask Ruby), though he was very jealous (ditto).

It was a two- or three-hour drive from King George Town to Hopetown. Plenty of time, then; they had all day to get there. The trip started with just the two of them on the bus. Ruby sat as close as she could to the driver, and kept moving back in the bus as they picked up passengers. She didn't want people getting the wrong idea about her and Wally. Wally was the one running after her, not she after him.

*

Wally scanned his list of names, looking for who he might forget to collect. He had no say in the list; most were rehab; elders and carers the rest.

This trip was different, because of the Peace Park opening. The Kepalup Local Historical Society hoped that (since there was a 'culture camp' anyway) they might provide some art, maybe a song or dance or do a Welcome as part of the opening.

Wally was glad to drive the bus.

Ruby snatched the list from him. Last night they'd agreed who to get and in what order. Methodical, see.

Her phone rang.

'Change of plan,' she said to Wally, ending the call.

He grunted, unsurprised.

'Old girl stayed with Henry last night.'

'Angela off her head again?'

'No. Dunno. Probably. Aunty says we gotta pick Angela up too.'

'See about that.'

'She's old girl's carer, Wally!'

Wally ignored her. He was thinking about the bus, he was thinking about traffic; not alcoholics and addicts.

Wally would tell you everyone in King George Town needed a car. No public transport to speak of, and not everyone able to walk where they wanna go. Those that can, too lazy. The town was stitched together with bitumen, one strip of which they now rolled along on their way to collect the first, and – Wally and Ruby agreed – the most important of their passengers.

Flinders was one of those suburbs it's hard to leave: most of its residents would have to walk, cadge a lift, or wait half a day for a bus. A few years back, after the visit of a senior health worker and activist from the capital city, the local paper ran the headline: 'King George Town's Bronx'. The paper ran the usual photos of bare-bummed and snotty-nosed kids, car bodies in weed-infested yards, packs of stray dogs, groups of people drinking in the playground park.

Wally and Ruby didn't think the suburb so bad. It was an improvement on the reserve they'd grown up on, and a lot better even than the suburb – next step up from the neighbouring reserve – it had been. A lot of the newer houses still held some of their shine and gloss. A lot of people had jobs. Most of the kids went to school, or slumped in front of electronic screens of one sort or another. The teenagers were no more restless than elsewhere. Families gathered around animated screens as once they may have around a campfire. On pension day it seemed many rose as one from behind their separating walls and, bumping doorframes as they escaped, stumbled to consummate their desires. Two or three days a fortnight the games machines were rested at the local pawn shop, and older brothers and sisters who had left school took their younger siblings on the long expedition to the school gates, handed them over, then made their way back through the traffic that moved in shoals about the school.

Wally was of no fixed address, moving between the homes of his daughters and sons, sometimes a while with Ruby, a guest in various homes he paid for. For months at a stretch he lived in camps, on mines or farms. He liked machines, and although he'd never articulated it, their use and maintenance healed him.

Nita was sitting beside her front door, one arm resting on her walking frame, as the bus pulled into her driveway. A thin and wiry woman, she raised her chin and her large sunglasses tilted to the sky. The verge was littered with traffic detritus; broken glass, warped hubcaps, various flattened cartons and cans.

Angela sat on the step beside her, smoking a cigarette with a determined ferocity, and softly holding her nan's hand. She glared defiantly at the bus and her lips moved as she told her grandmother who had arrived, then dropped her gaze as she moved the walking frame to the old woman. The frame was stacked with blankets and bags, and Nita's face seemed to float above them like something detached from her body.

Angela avoided Wally's gaze when the door opened. He leaned ostentatiously to see who was there to help Nita, and looked disappointed when he realised there was only her, Angela.

'We're on time so far, Wally, but for how long, unna? What time we gunna be there?' asked the old woman.

Wally and Ruby answered at the same time.

''Bout noon,' said Wally.

'Near on dark,' said Ruby.

They looked at one another, each with an eyebrow raised.

Nita threw her walking frame up the steps into the bus

and grabbed a rail. Ruby got to her feet and reached to help, Nita brushed her hand away. She tilted her body, lifted one hip and with her hands helped her leg position the foot on the step before hauling herself up one step more into the bus. It was a slow and clunky ascension.

Nita talked at Wally's back as he drove. From time to time he looked in the rear-view mirror to check Nita, and nodded while Ruby trilled an accompaniment to Nita's voice, reminding the old woman she was indeed well respected.

Inside, the bus was white and grey and black, with the aroma of plastic and cleaning fluids. The passengers bounced and shook within thin, resonant walls.

'Wally, any smokes?'

Wally's eyes moved to Ruby, then to Nita in the mirror. He answered firmly. 'Nah. Given up.'

Nita allowed a long silence while Wally drove with a particular intensity.

'Pull into the shops.'

'Later.'

'Angela took my last smoke yesterday morning.' Nita glared at her granddaughter. 'Pension'll be on the key card by now.'

'Aunty . . .'

'This old woman needs a smoke, Wally. This lot like the grog and that. I'm not the one on rehab, but I need my smoke and tobacco's not illegal, least not last I heard . . .'

Wally was at Nita's open door, the slam of his own bus door still resonating. There was this rule: No Smoking on the Bus.

Ruby went into the shops for Nita's cigarettes. Hardly had Angela set the walking frame at the foot of the steps when Nita alighted upon it, claws gripping the rails, slippered feet touching the ground but lightly. By some sleight of hand she produced a lit cigarette. Wally, keeping Ruby's sturdy figure at the counter in his vision, took a long drag. When Ruby returned thin, blue smoke curled around the conspirators' heads like an unkempt and collective halo.

The bus ricocheted deeper into the suburb's many right angles; weeds poked from beyond boundaries, shrubs spilled over the corner of fences. Sometimes a surprise of precisely bordered, green and manicured grass. Older houses isolated within a larger space, the huddled houses around them backing closer.

Children single file to school, tallest leading.

The bus pulled into yet another driveway and a man in his fifties, with the heavy body and rounded shoulders of a pugilist, came out of the front door, a packed bag held lightly in one hand. 'She's just getting dressed,' he said as he threw the bag into the bus and stepped back, reaching into his pocket.

Most of the party was off the bus and had formed a small circle around him before he could move any closer to the house. He looked around with bloodshot eyes, and ruefully offered an opened packet of cigarettes. Ruby muttered at them as she walked away from the bus. 'Next time dry camp is gunna mean no baccy too. Next time,' she said. 'I'll give her a hand, shall I?'

Wally had inhaled and was handing the cigarette back as Ruby disappeared into the house. With a dramatic air of resignation, Nita held out hers for him to take next.

A child in a nappy peeped from the front door and then, rubbing its eyes, retreated into the diminishing slot of the doorway, waving goodbye goodbye . . .

Wally turned his back on the cigarettes as Ruby reappeared and he had started the motor before she reached the vehicle.

Angela lifted Wally's cap from behind as she got back onto the bus, and kissed his bald dome. 'Love ya, my uncle.' She pulled his ponytail gently.

The bus grumbled past a school, past little houses spilling down a long slope to where the land flattened out and became a mix of swamp and scrubby bush, and then a blue-gum plantation. Deeper in that dense forest, a set of tall chimneys reached above the trees, spilling smoke day and night. The drains that ran underground and had for years leaked heavy metals into the harbour were invisible.

'Ate plenty of fish from there,' Nita said as they turned along the foreshore. They sniffed the salty sea and rotting seaweed. Between rusted and peeling sheds and railway infrastructure the other passengers glimpsed the ocean harbour. 'Didn't do none of us any harm, the pollution. "Mercurial", they say, unna? Well, that's not a word for my lazy bloody family, that for sure.'

No one protested. No one defended the family, or their individual selves. 'Except you lot of course,' she said, after a pause. 'You're all special.' She clutched Angela's knee. Angela lifted her grandmother's hand and passed it to Ruby, who clasped and squeezed and gently kneaded.

'Beryl's in number fourteen, or sixteen,' Nita called as Wally pulled into a large block of duplexes. Voices joined hers: 'Fourteen,' or, 'No, number ten, number ten!' Mostly, 'No, no!' There were a couple of grunts, a brighter exclamation. Beside the door marked number fourteen there was a piece of what might – but for the fact that it glowed with the colours of chocolate and honey – be called 'driftwood furniture'. The bench sat level, but each of its timbers twisted and turned in such a way that people viewing it often found themselves wriggling, firstly with the thought of trying to sit upon it, and then because it provoked them to straighten up their stance and align their own skeleton with respect for gravity. A packed bag and pair of sheepskin boots sat between the bench and doorframe, along with a faint blue haze of smoke and the lingering smell of marijuana.

'Be right with you, Wally.'

Curtains twitched and heads appeared at several of the windows facing number fourteen. The door opened fully and out waddled a short woman in a sombrero, long trousers and sleeves. She pulled at a fingertip, adjusting her cotton gloves and glared at the doors and windows surrounding her own. 'You can all go fuck yourselves,' she said, loudly. A set of curtains twitched one last time. Beryl went back through the door, and emerged swinging a small baseball bat. She tucked it under her arm, snatched the bag and boots from the chair and walked to the bus.

'Hello, Mummy,' she said, collapsing onto a seat and grinning. 'Uncle Wally. Ruby.' She flicked a hand; it might've been a greeting, might have been disdain. 'This it? This all of us?'

'Plenty more yet, Beryl,' said Wally, releasing the clutch.

Beryl stared out the window.

'Who?'

There was an old man, Milton, with the rounded shoulders of a fighter and a hoarse, whispering voice that made the others lean toward him. There were a few young men and women, a mother and child, and as they were drawn into the bus the others shifted to accommodate them. Angela's vigilance eased and she drifted from Nita's side and toward the younger ones.

The bus pulled into another driveway where Kathy Pinyan sat facing away from the driveway on a tiny front porch; a case beside her, and a box, a bundle of blankets and pillow balanced on top. The pillow wobbled and nearly fell as Kathy, hearing the bus pull into the driveway, spiralled to her feet and faced them. No longer of an age to spring and dance in welcome, she rocked back on her heels and opened her arms. Hands behind the glass waved, muffled voices reached her. The bus settled, and those within watched Kathy ascend from bleached sunlight, and some saw a pulse of light and not her shadow slip in behind her as the door hissed and closed. Her luggage went by hand to hand ahead of her to join the growing pile on the rear-most seats and floor as Kathy, hands resting for support on the shoulders of those already seated, made short, quick steps as the bus began to move.

Nita had moved to the back of the bus so that only Ruby was behind her now, and Kathy sat on the edge of the seat in front of the older woman. She turned. 'You got over us sharing that man yet?'

The two old women rested their foreheads together for a moment, then each leaned back. 'Oh, that was two husbands ago. Sister, even one of us too much woman for him!' Their upper bodies swayed to and fro with laughter and were it not for the fact that each woman gripped the seat rail between them, their arms would have moved like tree limbs in a gusting breeze. But of course they were not trees; they were aged people on a moving bus, and not quite at ease.

*

The bus shilly-shallied through drab and humble streets of this particular struggle-town as if looking for a way in, a way out, an escape. Its passengers said they were detoxing, on rehab, going to a culture camp; some, just along for the ride. A small number were regarded as repositories of great wisdom and heritage, or at the very least were respected as the longest surviving descendants of a small group of common ancestors.

It was a slow and kind of delayed ricochet through similar parts of the town. Now and then they stopped, tooted or knocked. The pile of blankets and luggage at the back of the bus grew and passengers moved closer, their attention more inside than outside the bus, and so they barely noticed the curtains of the houses twitching, the doors that would not open despite a ringing doorbell and the sound of TV and footsteps within.

Wally found Wilfred walking away from a small, corrugated iron shed around which some of his nephews and grandchildren stood, smiling sheepishly. A haze of smoke hovered about the shed, and the air was blue and funky. Wilfred was frowning.

He was a very small, stocky man with a mane of silver-grey hair, dreadlocked in recent years. A few sprouting silver hairs on his nose seemed a cultivated contrast. He had a habit of smiling as he looked away, like someone warily pleased with himself.

'True,' he'd tell anyone who repeated this observation. 'I am pleased with myself. And why not?'

Kathy had once drawn him as some sort of magical or spirit creature, playful and erratic. It no longer seemed a caricature. He'd grown his hair and beard to match the drawing. Despite his age, Wilfred had the hint of a swagger, a bounce and sway, as if he were a doll, a puppet animated by some other source. He wore a bright band on his wrist, sometimes around his head. Sometimes he applied ochre to himself, ran it through his white hair and beard. He liked the way it made people react to him, not only strangers and tourists, but even his own people a lot of the time.

'Same old Wilfred,' Wally said. 'He was at the mission with me and Milton. But look at him now.'

Despite his apparent age, the old man was shadow-boxing with Wally, feinting and moving his fists in small circles, lifting himself onto his toes and shifting his weight and balance like a dancer. For a moment he could have been a younger man; his arms darted around Wally's ears like angry snakes, fingers clicking. Confused despite himself, Wally stumbled. The old man laughed and turned to the bus, eyes sparkling with excitement. Then he stopped and looked around in the air above him; a pink and grey galah swooped and came to rest on his shoulder. He put a sunflower seed into his own mouth, held out his tongue and the bird took the seed from that soft and small slab of meat. Wilfred didn't look around to gauge the reaction of the others. No one said anything. Wilfred sat in the seat that had been left vacant for him next to the driver, Wally.

A middle-aged woman strode out of her front door as the bus pulled into her driveway. She pointed at Wilfred as she entered the bus. 'You need a haircut.'

'And a real job,' the parrot said. Wilfred lowered his head, glowering and smiling as if once again caught out in some repeated misdeed by some older authority, and once again forgiven. 'She shouldn't talk to me like that, but I can't stop it, I can't talk to her. Some people not even allowed to look at women,' he told Wally later, when she was out of earshot.

The woman rubbed finger and thumb together and looked around. Spoke a single word of their ancestral tongue. Several packets of cigarettes, opened, were held out to her. 'But no smoking on the bus, unna?' she verified, looking around her and laughing at Wally's back, his frowning expression in the rear-view mirror.

When they paused at an intersection, Wilfred held the parrot out the window. 'Know your way from here. Go on, off you go.' The bird ruffled its feathers, opening its wings as Wilfred tossed it into the air.

'Tilly be there? Jim's girl?' he asked, but it seemed the others could not hear him.

Inside the tinted windows the air conditioner's fan roared. They ate thin, salted potato chips and sipped water. Tasted the plastic air, although some thought the bus a limousine almost, as the road curved and dipped, rose from a shallow river valley and began a gradual descent. Speed signs slipped by, the numbers upon them increasing. They headed away from a falling sun, gathering momentum, and would cross several small rivers before their destination, Hopetown: a town named some years after all the killing. That's what the Peace Park idea was all about.

When the bus pulled into the caravan park it was dark. They stepped out into a strangely charged air and Wally later said he saw, far inland, a bolt of lightning connect sky and earth.

HIDDEN THINGS

The twins and Tilly passed the speed signs where the highway from Kepalup became the main street of Hopetown and kept driving straight for the sea. They could see it. There, the street faltered, became a gravel car park, a rock groyne reaching out from the shore. On the right, as they slowed to what seemed walking speed: holiday chalets, a police station, houses; on the left, a school, a few shops and a stand of petrol bowsers marooned almost at the street's end outside a little super-market. Between it and the sand, a little park; opposite, an old pub. 1905, it proclaimed. Tilly had wondered if this was Hopetown they had entered; the pub's name told her it was. They turned right just before the gravel car park and, around the pub, found the entrance to the caravan park, bordered on its ocean side by a grove of peppermint trees through which led a thin sandy path.

They pulled up near a hire bus.

'This'll be us,' said one of the Gerrys. It was still early in the morning. They watched a hunched and tracksuited wraith walking stiffly toward the ablution block. Tilly thought she recognised them; the figure returned her wave indifferently, kept on track.

'I gotta go,' said Tilly.

When she came out of the toilet the twins had disappeared.

She walked through the campground and saw a group – oldies – around a little pile of smoking rubble. Campfire? It was nothing but a busted barbeque. Another person was walking back from the toilets. Her hair was damp and pulled back from her face. She had the loose, upright walk of royalty. She smiled. 'Tilly?' And Tilly was so glad to see her, this woman who'd agreed to be her guardian back when Gerry was helping her get her life together. They had never met until then, and even now had spent very little time together. They hugged. Kathy pointed out the breakfast chalet.

When Tilly got there the twins were head down over breakfast and watching TV with the volume turned very low. They nodded as she came in, but kept eating.

Tilly took some cereal. Toast. A woman seemed to have taken on kitchen duties.

'Hello, love, I'm Beryl. Aunty Beryl.'

Tilly thought she was bossing more than helping.

Beryl's gaze went everywhere, even as she talked. She jumped from one to another. Turning this way and that, indicating what to do, what direction. Got in the way of anyone moving too fast and straight. Was in constant motion; at the kettle, the fridge, the stove. Brushing away crumbs after Gerry burnt his toast. Putting the lid back on the jam. Wiping the counter. Huddling over a mug, dark eyes this way, that.

Tilly went back to the toilet block. Waited in a cubicle until the room was empty. She moved a small blade, made small slices on her secret skin. Calmer, she washed her hands. Not much of a mirror, but enough to confirm it was still she. Just a little hurt.

*

Tilly recognised the old woman sitting alone by the fire. Nan Nita, wrapped in smoke, seemed so still she might have been asleep or dead. But then Tilly saw her hand move to her mouth. Smoke drifted from the cigarette in her hand as she let it fall, and smoke marked her exhalation. It rose, disappeared. She was bundled in layers of clothing, scarves and a woollen beanie in bright red, yellow and black.

Tilly slid a chair closer to the fire. The old woman turned her head and lifted her dark glasses; Tilly dimly saw lizard eyes that did not focus but moved about, away. She nodded, and Tilly returned the gesture. Smiled.

'I'm blind, you know that,' the old woman said. 'Makes it a bit hard for us to get to know one another better. Best if you sit close,' she patted the chair beside her, 'and talk. That's how I know people.' She waved a hand in the direction of the breakfast chalet. 'Ask any of them. My eyes were good once. I've seen plenty of things; enough for my lifetime and yours too I reckon.'

Tilly wondered if she'd seen someone like herself, naked, and on all fours and eating from the dog's bowl. And a bastard, the no-name called D . . . Tilly wondered if she'd washed her hands.

'Like your breakfast? Or you one of them that don't like to eat?'

Tilly looked around. Maybe she could just get up and walk away?

'You Jim's girl?'

Tilly nodded. Then, 'Yes, Jim's girl.'

'Tilly?'

'Yes,' Tilly said.

'We met, at the funeral.'

'Yes, Nan.'

'Jim was my brother's boy, my nephew. We love you, Tilly. I'm glad you're here.'

Tilly twitched, smiled. Wanted not to cry.

The old woman kept her face lifted to Tilly, as if she was indeed studying her.

'Spent more time in than out since he was a man. In prison he was a hero. He was a hero in prison.'

Tilly had not known until less than two years ago who her real father was – had been relieved that it was not her mum's boyfriend. She had visited her father in prison.

'How long were you together?' she'd asked her mum.

'Not long. Too long. You're the one good thing that came of us being together, my daughter. The rest I leave behind. You meet him, I'll tell you my story one day. Not now, please.'

Tilly had left it at that.

'Not long,' her father also said when she eventually met him. 'It didn't work out, Tilly. I've made a lot of mistakes. Is why I'm here, full-up to my eyebrows with sorry. But not you, not about you. You're my best thing, Tilly. My best.'

Next he was in solitary, and . . . Best not to think about that.

Tilly reached across and touched the back of Nita's hand. The old woman jumped and shrieked.

'Oh, cold!'

Nita turned her wrist and held her palm open waiting for Tilly's hand to return. It did. The old woman clasped Tilly's hand in her own.

Tilly felt the bones within the loose skin clasp and hold her tight.

'Tried to hang himself one time, your father. You know that?'

Nan Nita seemed to have gone into a reverie, but her grip did not loosen. 'His boy saw him, shamed him. Your brother, Tony. You met him?'

'No,' Tilly said. 'Some. Not him.'

'I'm glad you've found us, Tilly. Lovely name, that. Tilly. I'm glad we found you.' She took her hand away and gestured over her shoulder at the camp. 'We're a mess. I don't know . . .' She hesitated.

Tilly was a tiny self. A doll within many layers. She felt herself huddled in her own filth, and in the filth of others. A receptacle for their . . .

'Hey, Nita, my sister. You leave the poor girl be.' A hand gently squeezed Tilly's shoulder. Tilly stiffened.

'Coffee?' the voice said, and a cup arrived in Tilly's hands.

'Thanks. Yes.'

It was Kathy. 'You met Nan Nita then?'

Tilly nodded quietly, her hands wrapped around the mug. The way people did. It was a comfort. She looked into the fire they sat around, itself hemmed with small walls of brick. A heavy bed of ash. Large red coals, veined white and grey. Tilly tapped a long stick once; a tongue of flame leapt and danced. Tapped again, and the glowing coal collapsed on itself as the fire chuckled, wheezed, gave a puff of smoke.

Kathy swayed like a dancer, though so elderly, so heavy-breasted and grey-haired.

Nita said, 'This one wants her father back.'

'I'm fine,' Tilly snapped. 'Really I'm fine.'

'We all do, bub. You had a tough time.'

Tilly was angry and Tilly thought she might cry. What did they know?

'We all have our bad times. Bump into mad bad bastards.'

'I'm at boarding school.'

'One of those scholarships?'

'Yeah.'

Did Kathy raise her eyebrows?

'You know your dad blew 'em away at the prison last year.'

Tilly's heart leapt.

Kathy laughed. 'No, not that way. I mean, impressed them. Made them look again and think. Laugh too. Big NAIDOC thing. Public event like. Community invited, elders and councillors and politicians and big bosses too. Boys put on a dance, bits of the stories your father and his father – rest in peace – put together. All in language. Your dad spoke. People couldn't believe it. Too deadly.'

No, Tilly hadn't heard. He wouldn't be doing that again.

'We all miss your father. We could do with him here, for this Peace Plaque opening.'

An old man had appeared among them, as if he'd materialised from the air.

'Peace Park, isn't it?' he said. Then turned his attention on Tilly.

'Hello, bub. You're Jim's girl.'

The man swept back his mane of silver hair in one grand gesture. He closed his eyes and lifted his face. Look at me, he might well have said. Look at me. His hair and beard were tinted red; there was red powder on his skin too.

'Pa Wilfred,' said Kathy by way of introduction.

'Yeah, we met. Hi.'

Wilfred was glad of their attention. 'Yeah, your dad was great at the prison. But should've done a Welcome to Country. They don't like you doing Welcome to Country in prison, unna?' Wilfred smiled. There was a silence. Wilfred acted it out – a speech, then clicked his heels – 'Ok, now you're all welcome to stay, but I've gotta be going. See ya.' He mimed a stylised escape. Lifted a foot, as if about to step over a small wall. 'From the frying pan . . .' He opened his hands, his arms, in a universal gesture of resignation.

Nita took back the thread: 'Crims and thieves, all round him. Our boys, and the pollies too . . .'

'And half the screws . . .'

'No way out.'

'They were all clapping him and the boys. No one ever knew they had it in them.'

'Gerry was inside then too, helping Jim. They got hold of some of the stuff your pop did with the land council. Things your pop never learned your dad, what everyone wants to know now, half of them making it up. Used to get thrashed for some of that when I was a kid. Different times . . .'

Tilly remembered her father and all those men in green polyester. She got her father's name and went to meet him, then things went crazy. Went to see him again and he cried.

Wilfred looked into his cup of tea – it was huge, almost the size of a deep soup bowl, with a handle on one side only. 'Only one cup of tea a day,' he said, answering her attention. 'So I gotta make it worth it.' He laughed. 'Maybe two sometimes. If a tough day, you know. Hey, you sleep alright? No nightmares or nothing?'

'I only got here this morning.'

'Lucky, 'cause there's . . .' and he named various spirit creatures, 'really – round here. Little men, tease you. Grab you in your sleep.'

Tilly tightened. Fuck you mister no man gunna grab me in my bed or anywhere ever again.

'Oh, go away, Wilfred.' Kathy put her arm around Tilly. 'Don't worry about him.' She squeezed Tilly lightly, took her arm away. 'He shown you the photo yet?' She spoke to Wilfred. 'Go on then.'

'Was just about to.' Wilfred handed Tilly a phone and an image of Kathy, taken from behind, walking next to a group of trees. 'See anything there, watching her?'

You mean like us, looking at her now, thought Tilly. Wilfred's long fingernail hovered over the photo. Then: something in the trees, there. 'See him?' Tilly glimpsed a hint, a maybe-something, and then a thin-limbed creature, some Gollum or goblin clear as daylight in a tangle of branches. A little thrill of fear surprised her. She insisted disbelief. Looked away from the photo toward the trees at the edge of their camp. Back to the photo. Couldn't see it, only a hint of who might be there among the limbs in the photograph. She glanced again at the trees; they trembled and shivered, moved by a little breeze.

'You seen it!' Wilfred was delighted. He named a spirit creature in the old tongue. 'He'll be looking at you. They don't know you, see. They know this one.' He indicated Kathy. 'And they don't try anything with me. They all around us right now, looking. But you can't see 'em.'

Kathy pushed him lightly. He swayed as if he were about to fall from the chair.

'Oh, you silly old man.' Kathy laughed at him. 'Don't listen to him, Tilly. Don't take anything he says as gospel.'

'Hey. Remember I was a preacher once too.'

'Not for long though, was it? Lay preacher. Until they found you out. Lay preacher alright; laying with all your girlfriends.'

Wilfred grinned sheepishly. His jaw moved constantly, as if chewing.

'I can see them now,' said Nita, turning her head from side to side.

'Watch out, Tilly, he'll stick out his false teeth d'rectly,' said Kathy. And Wilfred did just that: a small bridge of teeth came between his lips, retreated again.

'Ha!'

'You'll see, Tilly, we Wirlomin we're lovely people, once you get to know us.' She stared at Wilfred. 'Most of us anyway.'

'We all got our problems.'

'Our little weaknesses.'

'Secrets.'

Hidden things.

Another voice. 'Boss wants us together.' Beryl joined them, swinging her baseball bat. 'Got this to make sure you all hurry up,' she laughed. 'I love to hurry you up.' Noticing Tilly's interest she said, 'Left my shotgun behind, fuck it. Stick with me, Tilly, and you'll be alright. Enforcer, that's me. I'm the discipline and the backbone all these jelly-bones not got.'

'Ha! So you say,' said Kathy. The old people unfolded. Once upright, Wilfred gave a little jump.

'Where's Angela?' said Nita, pushing Beryl into motion and grabbing at her sleeve so that she herself would know which way to go. Trees leaned into the space as they left; limbs stirred and reached after them; sap rose, and leaves whispered.

Tilly detoured to the ablution block. She had her bag on her shoulder; toiletries, pencil case, the little knife, toothpaste and breath freshener too. Already, it seemed to Tilly a slow day. She pined for her phone, but there was no reception. She sat in a toilet cubicle for a time. This supposed family of hers, so friendly. They didn't even know her.

She thought she was gone a good time, and that she would enter the room – if at all – late and unnoticed. She planned to loiter by the door but, despite Beryl's warning, they had waited for her.

A PILE OF STICKS

They moved along with the cloud shadows, Nita easily swinging the walking frame with the rhythm of her stride. It was a cool morning. Their destination was a single room, thinly walled, with an annexe of striped canvas and plastic and, to one side, a pale canvas wall or screen a couple of metres tall and perhaps three or four metres wide. At its further end was another screen made of recently gathered, and still green, bushes. The annexe failed to completely stop either the sunlight or the breeze which, shepherding clouds from the ocean, also moved this little crowd of thirty or so people, words bouncing between them like beads as they spilled into the room. Wilfred planted himself in one of a number of chairs haphazardly arranged near the back of the room. A corner of the room held an urn, cups, jars of coffee, teabags and sugar, an opened packet of biscuits, three deceased teabags in a saucer. Bags and coats were piled in another corner, and the walls held a picture of the Queen along with one of some seminal scoutmaster.

'What, we in a scout hall . . .'

'Bit of kiddy-fiddling.'

'Shuttup stupid go on.'

Tilly stumbled. One of the twins was beside her, hand on

her upper arm. Knuckles touched her breast. She pulled away, sat on a seat somewhere near Beryl and the baseball bat. The twin moved away. Did not sit with his brother.

They waited, ready. What next?

Kathy went to help Nita to her feet, but Nita brushed her hands away, and so Kathy stood and waited while the older woman levered herself up. The room fell silent. Someone poked a keyboard, and a series of images of people – including some of those in the room – was displayed on the screen and, a little fractured, on the wall behind. Were the images taken at a meeting? An exhibition? Some slow, warm party? A small group, arm in arm, beamed at the camera: Nita at the centre of other elderly individuals. Tilly saw one of the twins behind the group, frozen in the act of moving out of the frame, and looking some years younger than either of them did today.

Nita had reached the front of the room. She stood beside the screen, peering at what to her must have been only a vaguely sensed block of light. She held an open hand toward it, and her face expressed struggle of some kind; was frustrated and determined as she searched for words. She turned to the small crowd, lifted her face as if smelling the air or straining to hear. They could hear the hum of the projector fan. The tiniest of fingers tapping on the roof. Tilly glanced out a window: misty rain, so fine she would not have expected to be able to hear it at all.

Nita leaned into her walking frame.

'Some of you with us now like usual just for rehab, come along to dry out or straighten up or get in touch with family or whatever. Just like usual on these camps, but this time we got to prepare something for this Peace Plaque thing,' she said. 'Is that what they want? Peace Plaque? Peace Park?'

'Park,' said a voice.

'Plaque,' another.

'Police Park?'

'Please Plaque.'

'Stop it. Don't get distracted.'

Kathy moved to stand beside Nita, hands folded below her breasts. She was smiling, yet frowning a little too. Nita began to speak again, and Tilly assumed, from the very little she knew, that it was something in Aboriginal language. Noongar language. Her language, but not her mother's tongue.

Tilly was weeping softly, seeping it seemed. It made no sense. Beryl put an arm around her.

Then Nita moved back to English.

'This trip . . . Well, lot of us never been back to this area, not our parents and grandparents even, not since the killing. The old people been waiting for us I reckon. I hope they're not disappointed. We're all Noongars here. Wirlomin Noongar. Those that think they're not, well we claim you. Alright?' One of the older and fairer women blushed. Someone's hands flapped at chin and breast.

'Should be doing a Welcome to Country I suppose. I can't but, because it's your place here too – our place, unna? Even if most of us never been to this part before. Can't help that. How could we? Our old people were first here, and here forever. We're back here now.'

'In the caravan park,' said one of the twins.

A little ripple of laughter.

'Trailer park, if you gunna be in the movies, Gerry.'

Nita turned to the voice.

In the silence the waves fell upon the sand just the other side of the peppermint trees; shush, shush, shush.

'We black people in the hood chase all them wadjelas away, sweep the trash outta the trailer park.'

'Shut the fuck up fuck you,' another voice hissed. 'Listen.'

Nita began talking again, nudged by a still beaming Kathy.

Shush. Shush. The cry of gulls, the deep sea swell, if Tilly and one or three others were to drift to sail to be out of her depth and die their bones would return picked clean, would fall whispering and pockmarked upon the beach. Bones worm-eaten, turning grey, eroding to grains of sand along the ridges of these wind-blown dunes, to be gusted away . . . To rise and fall again, to stay like those muted staves in the lines of barbed wire fencing.

'Now, a minute's silence for those that can't be with us today,' said Kathy, gesturing at the elderly people shown on the screen. 'Sit in yourselves now, let yourself breathe and just be.'

Such a hippy, Kathy. Black hippy.

The breeze continued from the sea. The peppermint trees fidgeted. Tilly wondered who she was, running to hide all the time. Schoolgirl. Child. Outsider. The one who thought she was too good, but never good enough. This drug-addled fuck-up booted around by some shithead with all his drugs. Just a schoolgirl. She wished they could start talking. Moving. Doing things. She was going to run outside, slam the door. See who'd chase her . . .

Nita straightened herself. 'Wilfred.'

Kathy stepped forward, looked around. 'Where is he?'

'He?' The little crowd rippled, folded itself around the voice. 'He? I'm here. Stuck.' A couple of people helped Wilfred rise from the deep canvas chair which had sagged and folded, trapping him. Two young men – one of the twins and another Tilly hadn't met – held him by the elbows, but he shook them off, and pretended to jog the last steps to the front of the room.

'Sorry to keep you waiting, my Wirlomin . . .' Everyone smiling. 'For a minute there I thought I was one of those you all being quiet for. Took the life right out of me.'

He had their attention. They saw him notice the pink and grey cloth on his shoulder and, as if surprised, pluck it away. Folding it on the way to his pocket the cloth suddenly sprouted feathery wings, and there was the pink and grey galah he'd let fly when he boarded the bus. Struggling determinedly, he stuffed the squawking parrot into his pocket. It was cloth again. He gave a little resigned shrug and made brief eye contact with each of them, barely suppressing his glee.

'Seriously but. Lot of our family, our little community trying to get clean; get off the gear, grog, whatever. Fix ourselves up.'

Nita said something in the old language, then, 'What we're gunna do . . .'

Wilfred continued, 'Yeah, bit of language, some songs and stories. What the old people used to do. We all belong here. Make some instruments – artefacts, people like to say. Visit the old campsites. Re-introduce ourselves to the place. Massacre country, they say; lotta people reckon it's taboo; bad spirits everywhere, you know, they –' Here, he performed a quotation, using a high, whining voice: '"roll up their car windows while passing through Kepalup, and not even stop for food or petrol. The whole region has bad associations and an unwelcoming aura for them. It is a place for ghosts, not for living people . . ."'

He paused, then continued in his normal voice. 'And now they've got this Peace Plaque . . . Park . . . thing. They grown up, been living here a while themselves. Sorry for the history, they say. Know it's our country, our ancestral country. They're not gunna give the land back, but know we're the right people.'

One of the twins interrupted, 'Least not that other mob, dunno nothing they . . .'

'You the big culture man now?'

Wilfred waited for them to finish, went on, 'They wanted Nita to speak at the opening, but she said no. Only a few survived that massacre. Lot of us now but. She wants a few of us to be up there, in front. To be a presence.'

Milton's hoarse whisper came from the back of the room. 'What about paintings, exhibition or something.'

'Dunno, artefacts? A song?'

'They want us to do something, the white people.'

Wilfred nodded. 'Like to give 'em something good. Not what they expect but, not just pat themselves on the back and a little nod for us. Like to sit 'em back in their socks . . .'

'Up to us to show them what we are, who we are, how we link up to before the town, before the massacre and all that,' added Milton. 'Make it a Wirlomin place again.'

They stopped speaking.

Some of the little group, now and in the future, the drunks and addicts, the old people and their carers and all those otherwise lost but wanting to help and our old people in the past too, were wiping their cheeks. A general weeping had begun, it seemed, at just one fissure and then spread. The few children and teenagers wrinkled their brows and tried not to see the adults crying, wringing their hands, wriggling in their seats. Tears, tears rising around their feet and flowing down the steps.

Tears seeping, weeping, moving to the sea.

Shush. Shush.

Nita held herself as erect as a stooped and drying body will allow, nourished maybe by the unseen tears at her feet. Kathy touched her arm so she turned to face most of the others. 'I lost one brother this month, another brother not so long ago. Milton, he's not gunna be long.'

'Still here, Nita.'

She lifted her face to the sound of his voice. The old man sat in a chair against the wall, elbows on his knees, hands clasped. He was staring at the floor, and shook his head ruefully.

'Our sisters, our brothers, most of our cousins, they've all gone now. Hard workers, all of them. Slaves maybe. But you lot . . .'

'Oh, Nan . . .' someone behind Tilly started.

'You listen to me.' Nita's anger gave her energy. She straightened, stood a little taller even. Kathy put her arm around her, and her eyes shone with tears, a smile twisted her face. No tears in Nita's eyes.

'Hard workers. Hard times they been through. None of you know the things we learnt when we were kids. Noongar things, proper Noongar things, not museum made-up stuff. And not this . . .' She mimed drinking, she mimed injecting her forearm, then dropped her arms to her sides and shook her head almost imperceptibly. 'Maybe we coulda done things different. When I went to school I only knew Noongar talk, and they called me heathen. Give me this.' She mimed being caned. 'Punished and made ashamed. And scrabbling around the boots of the white man.' She put her head to one side. 'But there's good white people too, you know that . . .'

She seemed to lose her train of thought. She dropped her head and shuffled her feet, resettling. Listened. Raised her head and spoke again. 'Not so much bush tucker now, not so much bush either. We can't go all the places never again. But still got the lingo, unna? We found things written up that some of them used to tell when I was a kiddie, and I'm coming up to ninety now.' She cupped her hand to one ear. 'You still out there listening?'

'Yeah, Nan, we listening.'

'We Wirlomin,' someone said.

'We Wirlomin,' whispered here and there in the room. The audience held her blind gaze, wanting to communicate that way.

'Gotta hear you. Coming up ninety now and not gunna be here much longer,' she said.

Kathy, still with her arms around Nita, said, 'Only get together at funerals these days, but we . . . Gerry?' Kathy turned. The light had shifted; it must've been a cloud moved from the face of the sun, because for that moment their figures seemed shadows on a screen, moving toward one another and gathering at the front of the room. Then the light was as before, and one of the twins who had been leaning against the wall by the window beside Milton joined the two women at the front of the room. He ran a hand across his face, pulled down his dark glasses. Weeping?

'Our old grannies lived here with white people. Give us this life, hard for them. We got the stories someone wrote down for them, and words of our daddies and uncles long gone, and from Milton and Wilfred and me . . .' The old men were nodding agreement as she spoke. 'Been working it out, putting it together, so we can, what we need to do . . . And Jim, too, him and the boys inside . . .' Tilly felt a little thrill of pride at her father's name. Nita continued on, 'And Jim's girl, Tilly, she was taken away but she's another one come back too.' Less thrilled now. Mortified maybe.

Kathy nudged Gerry. Jump-started, he began speaking. 'Wadjelas, all Australians, this is what they're gunna want to know. Some of them do already, the good and clever ones. Blackfella stuff, it's not just up north in the desert, it's here and we're the ones to be passing on how to really belong here . . .' Gerry seemed transformed. He might almost have been an evangelist; you could see the passion bubbling in him, bursting out.

'Can't stay away from here. If we're connected to all the old people killed, they'll be happy we're back. 'Cause in the old days hardly anyone was able to get back, and if they were here, well . . . But we can bring back the language and the old stories, here, to the massacre town.'

Tilly saw the little cross on that pioneer's grave. The creek bed, the banks of sand, the brimming well.

'Before he passed away, Jim got off the gear. He said this is who he really was, Wirlomin, not the lock-up and the violence and the gear and the kids he never looked after properly . . .'

Tilly was impassive. Like a rock not weeping.

'We gunna do any fishing the next few days?' Beryl was still carrying her baseball bat.

Gerry kept going. 'Maybe. But we gotta work out what to do at this Peace Plaque opening.'

'Reconciliation,' someone yawned.

'Peace Park,' said another.

'Cup of tea now,' Kathy said. She, and Nita now too, with their cheeks wet.

Moving toward the urn and the packets of sweet biscuits Tilly heard someone ask Beryl, 'So, we all getting paid? Or just the special ones again?'

'Oh fuck off, Angela, or I'll learn you.' Her baseball bat twitched.

Someone moved next to Tilly. She turned. No one there. Then one of the Gerrys moved into the very space she'd thought already inhabited. Gerald? She clenched her hands so the finger-nails pushed into her palms. There would be crescent marks, her young skin broken.

The twin stood near her for a time. She didn't look at him, kept her attention on the front of the room. It was a long time before he spoke.

'You ok, Tilly?'

She turned. For a moment was seeing double. Except the clothes were different. Long sleeves, and no tattoo to be seen.

Tattoo to be to be taboo.

Someone wanted a cigarette.

A hand brushed her shoulder as the men left.

She took a biscuit. Nibbled. It was filled with what was meant to be jam and cream, a disk each side. The disk was patterned with tiny rectangles and circles. It was like mud in her mouth. She took another tiny nibble. Chewed and chewed.

She looked around for cups. Spat into one she'd found. Now? She wanted privacy. Where could she run to? She studied the room; it needed tidying. A biscuit had fallen to the floor. Was broken, had been stepped on. She went to look for a broom, a dustpan and brush. Something.

Next thing there she was, patting at small bleedings. Washing her hands, studying her reflection. She couldn't see a resemblance to any of them. She looked like her mother, everyone said. What would they know? Call them family? She was an orphan.

*

Wilfred was explaining the piece of cloth, once again neatly draped over his shoulder.

'Wear it all the time,' he said. 'Bird shits on your shoulder, doesn't even think about it. So, when he's with me this protects my shirt; but when he's not with me, I miss him and this helps,' he said. He twisted, reached to this shoulder and suddenly the parrot was in his hand, flapping and squawking. 'Hello, sweetheart,' it said. Then spoke in the old language, asking, 'Do you understand me?' in that old tongue. Not able to understand, Tilly stepped back.

Shamefaced, she realised the old man had somehow animated that piece of cloth and, with the semblance of a beak and eyes and voice, brought it alive. He'd done it earlier today, but this was even more realistic, and she was not the only one deceived.

Wilfred was pleased with the reaction, pleased with himself.

'Words, see. It's language brings things properly alive. Got power of their own, words. Some more than others. You'll see, you'll see proof soon enough.'

Wilfred carried on like this a bit too much for some, the older women told Tilly. That's from all that time he was a pastor, lining up his girlfriends.

*

The little crowd gathered on one of the chalet verandas. Well, they would have, except they didn't all fit, and so some stood on the ground and, arms parallel to their shoulders, leaned against the veranda railing. Others were on the steps. A few more were inside the chalet itself, just the other side of the connecting door. In one corner, standing on timber flooring, Ruby and Kathy gave instructions.

They'd all be kept busy; a range of activities had been planned, Ruby said, trying out some things we'll do later, led by some of our community people, and we'll develop a program for camps for school kids, and for rehab and other groups. Culture and Community Development, she said, the capital letters loud in her voice. She repeated this phrase many times, along with Funding and Program of Activities. Plus, a lot of the mob just need to Keep Busy. One day, she said, we'll have workshops on art, making artefacts, story and song. Try some of those things ourselves, then tomorrow, or maybe the day after, she said – like promising dessert after you'd eaten your vegetables – we'll be visiting some Significant Sites.

This was a Special Occasion, she finally said. Main reason we're here is the opening of the Peace Park. It'd be deadly to do a presentation, you know, she said once again, a Cultural Presentation. Reconciliation, someone said. Acknowledgement.

'Milton, you'll speak, won't you?' Milton nodded noncommittally. 'Wilfred?'

'Mmm.'

'We've planned some lovely walks. Some of the boys slashed paths. Lovely walks. Our old people used to walk everywhere. No diabetes, no heart disease, no mental health issues with them.'

'But, we can't do all that.'

'We're planning for the future. Culture and Community Development,' and again she said, more emphatically, 'Acknowledgement. Reconciliation.'

They moved away, coalescing in little groups. Ruby and Kathy, with Wally a less enthusiastic recruit, shepherded them from place to place.

*

Tilly hoped to hide away, but it meant so much to Gerry.

They sat around the fire in thin sunlight. Cups of tea and instant coffee. 'Breathe in the smoke, 'cause no smokes or nothing allowed unless it's a break and you walk way to fuck . . .' The fire burned slowly, the wood blackening, red and grey, reshaping . . . The ash was so very fine. A thin line of smoke rose. It was sweet, that smoke.

Someone started singing. Someone in the group? No, a little further away. Softly, one voice. Some song, Tilly guessed, in the old language. A couple of voices joined the first. Tilly glanced at Gerry, who only raised his eyebrows.

A stick landed on the edge of the fire, near the centre of their circle. A little puff of ash hung in the air.

They turned toward the sound of a voice calling in what Tilly assumed was the same tongue. She was getting to her feet. And then, more familiar, but nevertheless strange.

'Toodle-oo. Tiddle-pip!'

A hand – waving, rotating at the wrist, isolated and

disconnected – was hovering above the white screen that had been set up next to the annexe. They could discern a rough human shape behind the screen, beneath the hand. And then it was this figure that held their attention. The hand disappeared, and the dim figure on the screen bent to pick up something from the ground. Straightening again, it seemed so much taller, and seemed to have too many limbs to be human; limbs that moved and bent strangely. The creature kept moving right to left, and then, as it appeared from behind the screen, they realised it was Wilfred, and that he was carrying an assortment of sticks and artefacts under each arm.

He walked to them nonchalantly, as if he was not in fact performing; sat in a chair Beryl had vacated and, while looking around at their faces, kept glancing over their shoulders as if there were other listeners behind them.

He turned to the woodheap beside the fire.

'This?' He held out a small branch. 'Jam tree they call it.' And he gave its name in the old language. 'Not just firewood.' He gestured at the woodpile. 'Go on. Grab a piece yourself.'

The little group of people circled a heap of limbs, broken into lengths easy to handle and burn. Some leaves were so thin they might have almost been lashes, and grey and flaking bark had the texture of mud that has dried to a crust that thickens, clutching and puckering as you pull something free of it.

The circle pulled back to a centre. People sat down again, turned to Wilfred. Who ostentatiously ignored them, staring into the fire, rubbing a smooth piece of the timber, breathing its scent.

'Smell it?'

Again, he gave them the old word for this tree and its timber.

'Scrape it you smell it better.'

Wilfred pointed to an old knife, a few pieces of broken glass and stone gathered at one end of the woodpile.

It was something to do. They scraped, picked away at the wood. Threw chips and fragments into the fire, and little tongues of flame leapt and danced, greedy and grateful.

Wilfred kept talking. It might even be said that he droned on and on about how that sweet timber's scent opens your sinuses so that you feel the cathedral spaces behind your cheekbones; go on, breathe it and see how deep.

Told how our old people danced with fire. Made tentative tongues of flame, great walls of fire race across a plain, fire-balls roar through a forest canopy, leaping crown to crown. They trained fire to make the grass grow soft underfoot, and so they would know when and where the animals would be. Kept the bush like a park, easy to travel through. Takes something special to get that clever. He ran his hands over smooth wood; only grows one place in the world, this timber.

A different grass was under the soles of our old people, once upon a time. The soil was a light ashy skin, from the fire they made year after year, and the soles of your feet broke through its crust. It absorbed the rain, didn't let water cut so quickly. Our old people, our great-greats, they made it like that so don't worry too much if we good enough for this this Peace Park thing.

Tilly had peeled the bark right back from a piece of wood, scraped it smooth and fresh. Secret and quick, she nicked the flesh at the base of her thumb. The little bubble of blood was absorbed, smudged, darkened the sappy timber.

Tilly was surprised how everyone was so polite; they didn't interrupt or talk among themselves while Wilfred was speaking.

Our old people, he was saying again, they sat in the smoke same as we do now. Smelled this same sweet smoke.

He poked at the ash so that flakes lifted and settled again, fine and light and obliging.

Used this ash on the babies, like talcum, unna? Made an ash-bed grave for a body before pulling the blanket of earth over.

Gerry's leg was bouncing again. Someone was gnawing their fingernails, rapid and rodent-like. Beryl swung a small branch in the air, testing its weight.

'Make a good bat this one. Hurt.'

'These are bits of the same wood,' Wilfred said. He gave them elaborate pieces of the same timber, smooth and well handled.

'Artefacts,' someone muttered.

'Devices.' Wilfred smiled.

He told them the names in the old tongue, and the words started coming to life with their tongue and their mouths and their breath as they handled that timber.

They made the sound for the device with which a spear is hurled; for the kangaroo tooth at its end. Spoke the word for the tool to lightly dig the earth, and for how you stoop when you use it as if creeping up on strangers.

Smooth, imbued with oils and with handling, the crafted pieces of timber lingered in passing from hand to hand. Were warm.

One shaped and weighted for throwing, for striking. Another made to curve in flight, and say a flock of ducks see it coming they lift their wings, rise from the waters and, well, it turns to follow them. It will come back to you, land in your hand.

The wind shifted the leaves of the little fence, and a shallow ripple moved across the white screen behind Wilfred. Gerry straightened the leg he'd been bouncing since he first sat down.

'How long would you say the piece you've got there is?'

'Thirty centimetres.'

'Fifty.'

'Use your body to tell me.'

'Long as my arm: this bit, my forearm.'

'Two of them joined together.'

'Long as my thigh bone . . .'

Wilfred swung a thin cord woven of sinew and hair, at its end a small, carefully shaped piece of timber. There was a moaning, a throaty wailing. A song.

Wilfred slowed his arm and silence returned.

'Can we make that?'

The old man looked at the woodpile; in the firelight they seemed human limbs. In the fire, the coals were bones.

Tilly squeezed a piece of timber.

'Fence post an artefact too. Device, whatever word you got.' He was hauling on a long piece of timber buried in the pile. Gerry got up to help.

They balanced the post on its end; taller than Wilfred, not quite so tall as the younger man.

'Corner post,' he said. 'Jam tree, trunk,' he explained. 'Our old people had to cut 'em down with axes – all them empty paddocks, you see – and put 'em up again around the empty spaces. Later on bulldozers, big chains and sand and fire and smoke.'

The post was grey, rough and weathered. The grain had opened to the air, but the lower parts of its length might still have been moist. A curved length of fencing wire, and a short stab of its barbed companion, were stapled deeply into the surface. A patch of hardy lichen marked one side.

'Only need an axe to make a fence post,' said Wilfred. 'Putting them together for a fence is a bit more work, of course. This post here come from a riverbank. Fence busted and washed away in a flood. Half buried in river sand it was. That's where we used to bury our bodies, on the riverbanks.'

'Fuck off.'

Beryl had poked one of the young ones in the ribs with a digging stick.

'Have a go, see what you can do with your piece of jam tree.'

There were chisels and planes, axes and sharp blades of stone too. The old people used glass and steel soon as they saw it, just like they saw the use of ships and rifles, and would shin up a telegraph pole to see if they could listen in. But sometimes it's good to know how they did things also; to put these things in a line, to go to and fro.

And at this workshop today they talked, the old and the young, as they heated and mixed various things that belonged here: the gum, the kangaroo droppings, the different timbers and stones and sinews and sounds. It was all there, ready for them. They weaved sinew and timber, fused stone and bone and tooth, mingled their breath and the old and the new shapes of their thinking. 'Remind ourselves of the little things the old people did, the words they used.' He never stopped, Wilfred.

He told them more about firewood, and curlew. When a few black cockatoos thrust themselves across the sky in that jagged rhythm they have and the sunlight caught their flaunted tail feathers, Wilfred spoke their old name and of how, once upon a time, there were so many of them they blocked the sun when they flew, and other things came alive in the strange and feathery light. He gave them the old word for curlew. 'Never see one, only ever hear them. Camouflage itself, the curlew, and stay still and you never see it. You can pick it up, and it still won't move. Just like a piece of wood.'

Wilfred poked at the fire. 'Need some more here,' he said. A couple of people walked away and came back with their arms full of wood.

Timber in their hands, the heat and the blades, the sap and oils and ochre and sweat and the smoke moving, the timber burning and the shredding clouds, the sun in the sky above. It lulled like the murmur of voices.

Wilfred walked away from the fire. Stood with his back to them.

'What's that smell?' And turned back to them.

They continued working at their pieces of timber.

'Smell? Feathers in the fire?'

The fire suddenly exploded, and something jumped up out of sparks and coals; eyes, a beak, smouldering feathers, long legs ran from the fire, past Wilfred across the caravan park and disappeared into the scrub. A thin trail of smoke showed the path it took.

They looked, one to the other.

'Ha!' cried Wilfred. 'That's what I was gunna tell youse!' He used the old word for curlew. '*Wirlo*, you might pick him up, think he's just another bit of firewood!'

'Someone did!'

Tears in their eyes from laughing. Excited talk.

'Thought they were endangered.'

'That one was!'

'Our totem, that it.'

'See it?'

'Jumped up like a genie . . .'

'Took off.'

'We might make something like . . .'

'Something like,' Wilfred continued. 'Something that jumps up from a pile of sticks. Life not just in us, you know. Not just flesh and bone, but something sparks us. Call it spirit.

Gotta be more than just very clever to help something like that grow.'

He said they might take their work with them, their bit of tree. Or throw it on the fire or woodheap.

Flame licked Tilly's piece of timber. She stayed long enough to watch its transformations. Dead timber coming alive. Coals and bones.

Wally and Ruby suggested a cup of tea, a feed. Then they'd move on.

RECONSTITUTING

Gerald, at the centre of a circle that included Nita, Milton, Angela, Kathy, Wilfred, Beryl . . . There would have been that number twice again and Gerald, at their centre, might have been a sacrifice, something being tortured. He twisted, he kneeled, he crawled among strange words writ large on sheets of paper spread across the floor and spoke them aloud. All words seem strange if put like this, and at first the sounds fell into a vast silence. But then, like small echoes, they began to emerge from within the bodies of those listening.

Beyond, at a little distance again, even those pretending their attention was elsewhere began to move closer, drawn. Shivering in resonance, the little group became instruments of an ancient sound, were bringing an old tongue to life.

'Yeah, this . . .' Ruby smiled. They were watching from the doorway through which people kept coming to join the circle which had some kind of small, contained energy at its centre.

And it was not just words and books written on the paper, Ruby whispered, and it was not just paper. Milton had said, 'I'm gunna take these songs to my grave, and I don't want to. I wanna give it to grannies that aren't born yet.' Now some of them had those songs on their phones. Once upon a time,

Milton's brothers and sisters and parents would have been wild with him. They were punished for speaking that. And jealous they never learned. 'It was hard. Even I wasn't so interested then.'

'All that Native Title evidence, what our family give,' said Ruby.

Fragments of story and song, wordlists and genealogies, maps and photos and . . . They were working out how to share and grow. Ruby gestured toward Tilly's phone, then paused.

'That NAIDOC thing at the prison. Your dad, Jim. You go?'

No. Tilly thought of her father as she'd last seen him. Large head ponderously balanced on thin neck, shoulders broad and thin above the ribbed barrel of his chest. He was propped up in bed, legs folded beneath the blankets. Might have been a puppet. Except the head had turned, the eyes caught hers.

Ruby said, 'Something like that NAIDOC thing would be good for the Peace Park opening, but I think your father was the only one could get people doing it.'

Her father danced, his bones rattling an accompaniment to Gerry, soulmate and brother, who writhed on the floor; spoke, listened, wrote.

Gerry led them through an old story, though sometimes it was a song. Bits of language, then he'd explain. Human bones laid out in ash. Burnt, he said. Burnt and eaten, maybe, but this story starts here, with the bones laid out just so, in the ash, a perfect skeleton. There must've been a tongue, or something, because a little willy-willy, a little whirlpool of ashen air formed just above the mouth. He sang the refrain. Then the head is there, hovering just above the ash. Sang again. The head, and then shoulders, and bit by bit, singing bit by bit, body part by body part, the skeleton rose, ash become flesh, and came alive again . . . Gerry sang the refrain nervously the first time, but each time more joined in. Tilly would've liked to, but she was shy and didn't know the song anyway: not the words, not the tune. Not at first. Kathy's voice joined enthusiastically the second time through, and Gerry sang like he was in one of the American churches on TV. Speaking in tongues, maybe they were in a way. There were many refrains; the whirlwind of ash, the air moving and giving body. Wilfred sang with abandon, buoyed by the many voices. Beryl moved her lips, was smiling, looked defiant and proud. Everyone was singing and the body hovered above the ash, upright and swaying, finding its balance in their attention. There were more voices than you could see.

Kathy took over from Gerry. She was a teacher, and so she gave a language lesson but there was a story in there too, and of course she translated as she went, else none of them would have known what she was saying.

'Key Words,' said Kathy, and they said the words after her. It was embarrassing; like a kids' schoolroom, but for adults. They even repeated certain sentences. She had books. She had a computer, and images to help her. Even so, Tilly found it hard to make sense of it. It was almost like a children's story that began, 'Once upon a time . . .'

Anyway, there was a young man . . .

'Can we make it a woman?' Tilly interrupted, surprising even herself.

Kathy paused.

'You're right, this woman . . .'

She was polite and curious, this girl, this young woman in the story and really it comes down to this: she trusted herself and her instincts, and found and followed some barely detectable trail that no one else could even see . . . It leads her among spirit creatures, among powerful strangers, among resentful and jealous family. She learns more of herself with each encounter, finds her talents and abilities, learns and grows. Might rise into the sky and orbit home, or be carried on the shoulders of her clan, celebrated.

'Not likely any of us.'

'But there are stories, too,' Gerry joined, 'of when you fail, or falter, or die like that body in the ash, and the river . . . The river?'

He made the word a question, and looked to Nita and Wilfred. They nodded, yes, we will be visiting the river sites tomorrow.

'We got a lot of problems, we're not so strong.'

'Close the Gap.'

'Racist . . .'

'Sticks and stones will break my bones . . .' began Angela, chanting the old rhyme.

'Sticks and stones will make my bones,' Nita spoke over them, and Wilfred finished it off, 'and words will animate me.'

'The right words.'

Wilfred whooped with delight.

Nita smiled. 'Not just Close the Gap,' she said. 'Poor fellow me.'

Yes – paraphrasing still – these stories of when you fail, have been defeated and die, and the slow old river floods and finds the body or maybe just bones neat in the ash, and lifts them gently on rising waters, carries them across the plains, leaves them in a drying pool in the dunes, in damp sand. Sun-blistered mud and damp sand coats the bones, the figure snug in its imprint in the earth.

Someone recognises him.

Her.

They touch you, pull you from the clutching mud, from the branches and reeds, and hold you in their arms – no breath, no blood, such clammy skin. Someone will put their mouth to yours, and breathe. A voice will fill you.

Gerry said, 'The eyelids roll back and show just white globes.'

The body sits up. Even though it had seemed dead, it sits up. Is. A monster? Can it speak?

'The mouth opens,' said Kathy, 'and . . .' She gave the old word for hello, for yes.

'It is hard to not step away,' said Kathy, 'even when a loved one comes back alive. But someone needs to cradle the body, listen to the voice return.'

'Story like this really about all coming together, healing and making ourselves strong with language,' said Gerry.

They all looked around, stepped back from one another, suddenly shy. Where did that come from?

'Too deadly,' said Wilfred softly.

'True,' Milton offered.

'Yes, we will go along the river,' said Gerry. It was as if he was trying to cool down, tightening up again. 'There is the massacre site, the farm.' They had planned it, he and Milton and Wilfred, Kathy and Nita and Wally and Ruby, too. Jim, when he was still alive . . .

They would do it in sequence. One place, there is a rough and boulder-scattered gorge, its steep sides strewn with grasses, with everlasting flowers and ferns brushing the rocks, and jam trees and yate trees towering over them. Parrots and parakeets call and call, their voices bouncing above pools of water. Sometimes a small waterfall calls a journey to a halt. There was a skull there for a time, a human skull jammed in a deep stone crevice; too deep to retrieve, too deep to see the bullet hole.

But we will not dwell on the skull, the bones and bodies and bullets.

Further along, the river changes again, and high above the banks of the dry and rocky river bed there are clearings surrounded by old and dying sandalwood trees where the earth will drum with footsteps, and voices carry across a distance to nestle in the ears of each listener. And in each clearing Tilly will see a few stones in a small hollow in the ground and agree it is a grave. Those clearings are because of the many feet, because of the thousands of years plucking, because of the fires and the compacted earth.

There is an ochre quarry, and some springs near the river mouth, inland from the dunes.

Tilly will sip from a pool of fresh water in the bed of a creek which, when it flows, is salty. Small fires will be lit. People will say this is a culture camp and a rehab thing and it is family and Tilly is welcome.

It will be men and boys, mostly. No, it will be women too. Mostly young ones, Tilly's age is good. Families, the ancestors and the children, walk among the trees, take sand paths, paths of leaves and reeds and tread the stuff of time even, the occasions merging, the many many feet.

Gerry walked on reeds, recently slashed.

'Would've burned it old days,' said Gerry.

Young ones throwing stones, sticks. Hitting their targets: tree, rock . . . It was hunting, showing your skill. Come here with rightful anticipation.

But the twins, the young men and boys, they'd hardly seen a living thing yet.

'Won't, noisy like that. Nothing let you get close.'

Older men leading them – Wilfred and Milton – and so they move at a slow pace.

'How far we gotta walk then?'

'See if we can get close to kangaroo up ahead.' Wilfred used the ancient word for kangaroo, and it was repeated. 'But you gotta keep quiet.'

'Got a rifle?'

'No.'

'We heading into the wind, unna?'

'That's right.'

'See how close you can get.' Again he used the old word. 'You say it. Might catch him with your voice, your bare hands maybe.'

'Like that old story?'

'No spears.'

No spears.

Anyway, need a spear-thrower.' At a look from Milton he used the old word. 'Like that one yesterday.'

'But no spear?'

'I got a . . .' A hesitation, then the word for a throwing stick.

'Good,' said Wilfred in the old tongue.

'Probably never see nothing, not get close, racket you mob make.'

The boys quietened, sensing some purpose, and the long walk beginning to quell their energy. The wind and lay of the land helped them along, and the two old men kept near the shelter of trees. From a small clearing high on a slope they watched a mob of kangaroos grazing, maybe a hundred metres away.

'Reckon you can get close enough, maybe get 'em with that thing?' The old man pointed to the throwing stick.

A Gerry uttered the old word for kangaroo, continuing, '. . . gunna die, boy.'

The older men settled themselves down to watch. The kangaroos were grazing, regularly lifting their heads to scan their surroundings, scratching themselves absent-mindedly.

The old men watched their charges, men and boys, move through the trees like noisy shadows. The kangaroos became restless, a number of them kept their heads up. A stick sailed through the air, bounced off the ground beside one of the kangaroos, and then figures were racing toward the animals, throwing stick and stones . . . The kangaroos nonchalantly bounded away. The old men began walking to join the rest of the party; some of the hunters had resumed their pursuit of the animals, incited by the way some of the kangaroos had stopped at a further distance and were looking back at their would-be killers. Pursued again, this time the animals went in among the trees and disappeared.

Wilfred lit a small fire, and they waited for all to gather.

'Old days they used fire, eh, to get them.'

'Well, mainly so the new grass would bring 'em close next time, yeah.'

'Everyone uses a gun now, so why you only giving us stick, expect us get them with our bare hands?'

Well, it was because it made them think how to get close, notice the world around us.

'There'll be one just up here a piece, anyways.'

Where a fence emerged the other side of the next copse of trees a kangaroo hunched with a cord tight around its neck.

'Snare.' People use wire, but Wilfred still liked to use sinew.

The animal was weak, agitated.

Milton approached the animal, and then moved so quickly they hardly saw the knife. Blood spurted, the animal's head hung loose.

'Someone wanna carry it? We'll have to dress it too.'

Some of the boys untied the snare, studied it.

'Made that from the tail, sinew there,' said Wilfred. 'Show you later.'

They were not back at the car when someone saw a racehorse goanna. Startled, the reptile scurried up a tall, very thin sapling. The sapling bent a little, and the animal was silhouetted against the sky. Milton motioned the group to sit. He whistled, walked a little closer. Whistled again. The goanna began to make its way to the ground again. Not quite back to earth it sidled along a horizontal branch, ceasing its movement altogether now and then, and came to a halt next to Milton. The old man stroked the reptile's back with a twig.

'Reckon we'll let this one be, what you reckon?'

'Got plenty of them already.'

They were in separate cars, travelling single file on a narrow, thin track through plain country, with occasional clumps of trees and taller shrubs. The front car pulled up near just such a clump, and they waited. After long minutes, Milton got out on the driver's side. He walked toward the other cars, grinning. Finger to his lips to indicate silence he had them get out of the car on his side and walk some twenty or so metres away from the track. Then he stopped and turned around. The shrubs had concealed what they now saw: two kangaroos, one close behind the other among shrubs up to their haunches. The one in front stared at them, clearly aware of their presence but not prepared to move away. She reached back over her shoulder and caressed the head of her partner behind.

Milton used the old word for sex.

'Couldn't shoot them like that, unna?'

Quietly they walked back to the cars. Quietly, they drove on.

*

Late that same day they all, women and men together, went to the ocean's edge, west of where the river waits way back in the dunes. They walked through a gap in the thinly veiled mounds of sand, along a soft corridor of peppermint trees, finally emerging at a small beach made not of sand but – in this portion of its long curve – of rocks and pebbles.

Milton's hand on Gerald's arm brought him to a halt. Milton picked up a rock and turned it over to show Gerald a bird's footprint imprinted in the stone.

'One rock on this beach,' said Gerald. 'How did you know?'

'Best place to keep it.' He put it back among the countless other rocks, footprint down.

A flat, walkable reef extended toward the waves, and within it a narrow channel where the water moved more forcefully. The channel was replete with small rocks and many, even this close to shore, moved and jostled against one another, compelled by the swell breaking onto the distant edge of the reef.

Gerald balanced awkwardly on his haunches at the water's edge, and watched stones sliding together. Reaching for one, he slid partly into the water, and scrambled to avoiding falling in. He clasped the hand Tilly held out to him, and turned back to the water and seized one, small, hand-sized rock.

Smooth and cool, it sat neatly in his palm. Fingers curled around it.

These were human-sized rocks. Rocks people carried, held in a hand. They found those of a size or shape that called them; those that were beautiful, useful or, if very lucky, both. Carried one away, took a special one with them. Here, now, the pebbles rattled, moved at delayed intervals by the distant, crashing waves.

*

That evening they viewed film of earlier trips and camps in which the old people, most now passed away, were singing. Old songs, all of them; traditional songs, mission songs, karaoke. There was a didgeridoo, a piano accordion, quite a few guitars.

Ruby and Wally were forcing things a little at this late stage of the day. It is always hard when people are missing the familiar rubbery structure and brittle bones of their everyday existence.

Ruby and Wally sang, some country and western song translated into the old language. 'Was easier charged up,' Wally said, and then sang one of their very oldest songs unaccompanied.

Their inhibitions began to break; bit by bit, one by one taken by surprise, they began to sing.

*

Late in the night, by the fire, one of the twins said, 'Tilly, come here.' He led her into the darkness. She believed it was Gerald. She looked back to the fire and saw Wilfred watching them walk away from the light. Gerry put his arm around her, his face beside her own, and pointed up among the stars. She was sure it was Gerald. His cheek was all but touching hers. She felt his warmth.

'Look between the stars,' he said. 'Not at them, at the dark patches. See that long skinny space? That's the neck. Upside down, he's upside down tonight. Be better soon when no moon.'

Tilly's ankles seemed to have fused, and the soles of her feet curved around a planet grown so tiny or herself so large that her head went orbiting through the stars even as the world so slowly pivoted beneath her.

Tilly did indeed see the emu in the sky, caught for a moment as if in some slow cartwheel, but then it was gone and only the cold and glittering stars remained. She was as before, her own shrivelled self.

Here came the partial moon rising.

*

Gerry asked Tilly, 'You got blankets and that?'

'Yeah, sleeping bag.'

'Kathy or Beryl will help sort a place to sleep.'

They were walking past the bus, and Tilly went to the bus door and, in the dark, leaned against its cold glass. 'Could sleep here,' she said. The door opened suddenly, and she flinched at a steadying hand on her shoulder.

'Sorry,' he said. Was it Gerald? 'Come with me, Tilly, I'll find where they got you.'

She followed, a few steps behind.

He stopped, turned. 'You right?'

'Yes,' she said, curtly.

He called at the open door of an annexe, softly. 'Aunty Kathy? It's me, Gerald.'

'Hang on.'

'Got Tilly with me, Jim's girl.'

Kathy was in tracksuit and long gown, grey hair spilling wide and down past her shoulders.

'Tilly, love.'

Tilly found herself in the older woman's arms, held. She leaned into her, despite herself.

The twin slipped away.

'Got you a bed here.'

A single bed, blankets tucked and sheets folded back. A pastel pillow. On mattresses on the floor around it, bodies were curled and deep asleep already.

She inserted herself into the blankets of a small folder bed, but she could not sleep. She listened to the older women shifting in their beds, breathing. Pulled her blankets back. The school logo on her tracksuit chastened by the night. Tilly folded the thin mattress and blankets and went to the bus. Once inside, she locked the doors, stretched out in the aisle and slept with the bus seats around her like guardians.

She dreamed of Kokanarup, but this time she travelled alone.

The same gravel road breaking from the highway, the same trees, but this time closer, more densely bunched, looming as if in the headlights of a car (but there were no headlights, and no car). They reached for her from each side. Tilly glimpsed faces in the gloom, and in her dream she moved upright, gliding, her feet trailing behind. The road curved right and left, rose and fell. Never a long view. A narrow path was opening before her, and then the grave. A small boom gate rose at her approach, admitted her inside its picket-fence enclosure. She shied away from the headstone, and suddenly all was parkland: copses of trees, the walking easy. Footsteps crunched in burnt, brittle-crusted earth. She smelled the old, sharp smoke. But they were not her footsteps; she was gliding still. Then it was soft grass, green and newly sprouting.

Tilly felt the cool earth under the soles of her feet. She was motionless, might have been a statue or a puppet, discarded. Snakes slowly curled around her ankles as, unperturbed, she studied the old house from a little distance down the slope. A house of bone with hooded, blank windows, and an iron roof raking down very low, its corrugations making fine lines of inky black and moonlight silver.

There was someone beside her. She turned, and turned, but the companion stayed just beyond her vision, must have taken a step each time she twisted. She heard joints clicking, perhaps bones creaking. Someone old, she thought in her dream, but still sprightly enough to escape my gaze.

Tilly woke, and it was dawn. Closed her eyes. Opened them a second time, and the sun was bright in her face. Soft conversation. Fire and tobacco smoke. Tilly felt unusually refreshed, but for that dark star within; that constant, central shrinking; that memory and shame she must fight to extinguish.

WHAT WAS LEFT

Light expanding, a new day: there was a fire, with two small walls of brick each side and a metal grate across the top. Daylight growing. Thin fire smoke becoming blue. The old people sat around the fire, a great many of them, looking into its centre.

Ping of a microwave.

A crow.

A cough.

An outboard motor grumbling across the water.

The sound of waves.

Caravan park guests moved to and from the ablution block. A woman with her towel across her shoulder. Hands in front of her, like a kangaroo, holding her toiletries.

The moon in the sky fading to a piece of bone, to less than that; a shred of skin.

Thin stem of smoke, rising. The fire hissed, crackled, its many small tongues licking the wood; hummed like some animal relaxed and breathing in the throat. A lot of white ash for so young a fire. Ash rose at any footstep, and then settled again, claiming.

'Boy still on holiday?'

'Do him good in a way.'

A prison was named.

'Yeah. They still doing those classes, Jim was showing them?'

'Dunno.'

'Jim was teaching them?'

'But he never knew nothing special, did he?'

'Old girl. Milton. His dad made some tapes too. Some old paperwork, from way back I think. They were doing same sort of thing inside like what we doing here.'

Wilfred pointed with his lips at Nita.

Nita felt their attention, turned her blind face to them; it was as if she smelled their intention, heard them thinking.

'Well they got plenty of time in there, unna.'

'Wordlists and language. Paper and computer. Family trees. History and policy and that, when we not allowed in town, and the kids dying like flies. Stand in a shop and wait until last. But I don't think they spend too much time on that; plenty still to tell them all that stuff. They mostly do language.'

'Heard they got a prison officer helping them.'

'What we doing today?'

'Stuff.'

'Better get everybody up.'

'He up, himself?'

'Oh yeah, he up himself alright.'

'Ha. I mean awake, out of bed.'

'Well, this one is.'

'She Jim's girl?'

'Yeah.'

'She know about her mum and dad?'

'Just met her dad. Only ever known him inside.'

'Shame.'

'Know about him and her mum?'

'Dunno. Ask her, why don't ya?'

'What we doing today? Going upriver?'

124

'That her?'

'Tilly? Yeah.'

*

At a distance, Tilly smiled at them. No one would have seen the smile. She was walking from the showers. Wearing long sleeves, leggings. Gave a wave, the movement mainly from the elbow, the upper arm close to the body. Hand moved away, then snapped back like it was held by a rubber band. Her hand flapped like something trying to escape.

Tilly had been to the beach in the early morning and, entering the thick copse of peppermint trees, her feet following the sand trail that wound raw between them, she'd realised there was someone behind her. Unseen, she stepped among the trees. Hid. Two people walked by. Husband and wife, she guessed. Old biddies. She followed them, then. They never even knew.

Yesterday's footprints dimpled the fine white sand. Seaweed in squiggly lines, brushed back and heaped a little at the sea's edge. The lacy edge of water went to and from. The man and woman went onto the rocky groyne, unspooled their hand lines over an unsettled, blue-grey sea. The sea shifted about; was ruffled by a breeze.

Walking back, Tilly crushed a peppermint leaf. Cupped her hands around her nose and mouth and breathed in deep.

Old man and wife together, like they were old friends. Fuck them the fuckers fuck them all.

Tilly began to jog. Saw the old people sitting by the fire. No escape; no privacy for her anywhere.

*

Gerald was awake. Was he?

'Gerrard?'

125

'Fuck off.'

'Fuck you too.'

'Shuttup you two.' A third voice.

There were four in the room. Two bunk beds. Another two beds in the room with the TV. Gerald saw that his brother had undressed. Sometimes, men sharing a room like this slept clothed. He put on his shoes and went out the door.

A little dome tent floated on a scrap of lawn beyond the veranda. Tent was zipped, someone still sleeping.

A thin column of smoke grew at the centre of a little group of people, shifted like a friend with each movement, and their cigarettes seemed as if they were weaving, repairing the column between them.

The girl. Tilly. Not exactly marching from the ablution block, but very nearly. Limbs moving very stiffly. Clutching herself. Maybe realising this, she seemed to suddenly concentrate on letting her arms swing free.

Gerald found a private spot where he could see anyone approaching. Took out a little pipe, fondled it. Nothing to burn; he admired his own willpower. He went along a little path, the white sand like a scar. His feet stepped between tufts of grass, droppings, marks in the sand left by . . . He let the old names move through him.

Yesterday, just saying the words. Tilly had believed in him.

The sun broke its link with the horizon. The sea breathed again, drinking the light, you'd think. Leaves turned on their vertical axis.

Gerald went up on his toes, swung a leg over the fencing wire. Blossoming from the trees the other side, he saw Tilly . . . On her way to the ablution block again.

She must really like that place.

*

They were going to visit some places along the river. There'd be the bus, and one car. Come with us, Tilly, Nita said. Since they'd got to the camp, Angela had strayed away from Nita. One of the Gerrys – Gerald, Tilly thought, same clothes as yesterday – was with her, jangling the car keys. The other twin arrived with Wilfred.

'River mouth?'

Although in this part of the world, river mouth is a misnomer. An ancient coastal plain, the rivers are small and meandering and have distributaries more than tributaries. In flood, some places just spread shallow over a vast area. On occasion, at such a time, they will break through the sandbar blocking them from the sea, the waves rush to meet them and there is such a surging, salt water meeting fresh, a turbulent mingling, and fish moving from ocean upstream and vice versa too.

'Fish move from ocean upstream,' said Wilfred. 'True. I seen big fat bream in the tiniest of river pools. Wiggle your finger, and they'll jump out of the water into your campfire.'

All that life right there and you'd never think it.

*

The little bitumen road became gravel, became sand, then they were driving the long sandy curve of the beach toward a granite headland and a little island a short distance from its tip, like some sort of punctuation point. The beach widened, and the sand squealed. On their right, the turquoise, wind-ruffled sea folded and bowed at its edge, again and again.

'Used to light a fire here, and my daddy sing the dolphins in, bring the salmon for us. Leap onto the beach for you.'

The beach was hard, and Gerry drove fast. The car rose over small undulations, lurched when it reached softer sand in between.

127

'Easy, Gerry,' said Wilfred.

The driver laughed.

'Slow down, Gerry,' Nita said.

'It's alright, Gran. Trust me.'

The old woman turned, her blind eyes faced the driver. 'You in the back, Gerry?' The twin beside Tilly said something in the old tongue, then, 'I am, Gran.'

Nita opened her door. 'Slow down, or I'm getting out.' The wind rushed into the car, it tore at her hair; they could hear the tyres in the sand. 'Stop the car, Gerrard, or I'm getting out.'

The car kept on.

Nita swung her legs around, both her feet by the door.

The driver swore, slowed. He stopped the car.

'Change drivers,' the old woman said. She slammed her door shut as the driver got out. The twin next to Tilly and Wilfred opened his door and the two men pushed at one another on the sand for a few moments.

'Move over, Tilly,' said Wilfred. He now sat between her and the twin, Gerrard. The persistent sea reached toward them, and became silent again as the doors closed, the car moved off slowly, the windows were again sealed.

*

They drove close to the sea, on the harder sand, and started to make a wide curve back toward the dunes.

'We nearly there, Wilf?' Nita said.

'Yeah,' he said. 'Feed it.'

'Give it a kick in the guts,' the old woman muttered, and as they made a wide arc toward the dunes sand sprayed from the tyres like a breaking wave. The vehicle slid and bucked, the motor roaring like some great beast as it shook itself and bounded up a mound of soft, white sand. Tilly was terrified, thrilled.

The going was easy again, a sand track winding through the old, shaggy dunes. They approached some paperbarks, crowding at this edge of where the dark water paused, pooled, consolidated itself. Skirted the flaking trees that leaned together in conspiratorial shade and ankle-deep shallows.

Then, a thick mass of weeds and rushes.

'The springs. Old people would've burnt to get to them I guess. Snakes everywhere through there.' Just the other side of this expanse of rushes, a little hill with a humble building on top.

'Café. You can see a bit of the spring, the water itself, from up there.' Unseen, water continued to issue from the earth at the base of the hill beneath their feet, ran gurgling through rocks and reeds and mud to the brimming pool. But they had no time to stop, no time for the café or the restful river pool, not now, because they needed to be further inland to meet the others.

Driving, driving, and although Tilly had been long awake and had moved through tea and coffee and gossip around the campfire, through breakfast and cleaning and discussion about the coming day, visited places along the river and dozed in the car, inexpressibly tired from who knew what cause, Tilly only really came awake – felt she came to consciousness – after they had been driving for quite some time.

They drove away from the coast where the wind shifted restlessly, and the jostled ocean tilted its many facets away. Seated behind the driver and Nan Nita, Tilly instead imagined herself in a chariot – this car made invisible. Better yet, in a litter, and carried on strong shoulders back to her people. She leaned back and jiggled the foot of one leg, compelled by a slow wind from the frozen south and supported by sisters and brothers and cousins and . . . by angels, since they were surely flying.

'This place, Tilly, where we are going,' Gerry began, but Tilly was not listening, and he let the words die. No one took up the conversation.

Seen through the insect-smeared windscreen: scarcely undulating, dry and bleached ground; fence lines beside the road and dividing, at wide intervals, a mostly bare landscape. A fence is just the posts holding hands, thought Tilly, and such long arms between them. Trees grew in scattered clumps, in eroding crevices and gullies, in the corner of fences and on the rocky crowns of worn hillocks. Trees grew among spills of irregularly shaped rocks; slabs, blocks, flattened and broken spheres. Trees, isolated at the roadside, flailed their limbs and tossed their crowns as the car rushed past.

'Look, daytime moon.'

Tilly ducked her head to see beyond the window frame and out to where the old woman was pointing: a partial and trembling moon, forever dissolving in that vast blue.

'Fingernail moon.'

Nita's quivering finger pointed, the hooked nail could've been bone or ivory or that same moonstuff itself.

How could Nan Nita – blind old woman that she was – even see the moon or know where to point?

Nita laughed. 'What, you think I'm that blind?'

Gerry only shrugged in response to Tilly's expression of enquiry. The old woman tilted her face back, and the curve of her large sunglasses made a protective prow, a Cyclops visor.

''Course I know where the moon is; still had my eyes when I was older than you lot. I know where the moon is.'

'*Kaya*,' said Tilly, using one of the words from yesterday's language workshop.

'This place we're going, where I'm taking you, best go there when the moon's in the sky. Moon in the rock too, like drawn there. My daddy showed me when I was a little girl and now I show you.'

They pulled up on the road verge. The bus was already there.

Look how far they had come already.

'Our old people here.'

The wind was cold, and dry. The road, no longer so black or smooth as when seen at speed, was textured with small stones. Rough timber fence posts and the horizontal strands of wire might have made a crude musical stave for the call of a crow. The plants around them rattled like small bones shaken together, and grains of sand hissed.

'Show you this, Tilly. Kangaroo and the moon story, in the rock up here.' He gave her the old names for kangaroo, for moon.

The old woman threw her walking frame over the fence, while Gerry held the wires low enough for her to step through.

Gerry reclaimed the walking frame, handed it to Nita and became her guide as the old woman, thrusting the walking frame into the crusted sand, began her long journey up the bristling, stubbled slope. The others joined her, moving barely an arm-span apart and so slowly they might have been a search party.

A small bulldozer squatted a hundred metres away among soil and rocks still dark and damp from having so recently been uprooted and laid out beneath a sun and stars they had never known.

Tilly saw the old man – Pa Wilfred – veering toward that very place. On an impulse she followed him.

Wilfred leaned against the brightly painted bulldozer, his back to Tilly. He must've sensed her approach. He didn't look around.

'Cunts. They've ripped it up.'

Tilly had never heard him swear. As he turned to her she saw both his surprise at her presence and that there were tears in his eyes.

A voice, faint on the wind: 'Wilfred. Tilly. Come up here. Tilly, Wilf, it's here.'

The others were waving from the top of the slope. Come here, come here.

And so, lifting heavy feet from the soil, they resumed their journey.

'We gotta keep going. No tears, her up there tells me. She'll kill me if I go weak.'

Despite their slow tread Tilly thought she might rise, and skim above the lifting grains of sand as if something was lifting her, buoying her.

A very small crowd stood on the granite that capped this worn hill. The wind handled them, tousled their hair. In the distance, the corrugated iron roof of a new homestead shone brightly in the sun, and the creek bed was a dark line curving by collapsed and rusting iron sheds, and the old stone house they'd visited yesterday. From here they saw Dan's place also, the other side of some trees, further around the hill.

'He dunno this place, even his granddaddy never knew this place.'

'See where the kangaroo lay.'

Gerry pointed with his lips, nodded his head; he widened his eyes, looking pointedly at the sheet of rock upon which they stood, and not far from their feet.

Tilly looked for the leaping silhouette of a kangaroo, expected to see something like the image on Qantas planes and tea towels but saw only a shapeless, dark mark on the rock.

Pa Wilfred sat down on the ground. He leaned over on his hip and one elbow, scratching his chest with the other hand, and with his head held peculiarly upright.

'You alright, Pop?'

'You ok?'

'I'm just resting, my dear ones.'

'Like a roo, unna.'

Nita snorted dismissively. 'And somewhere here,' she said, walking away a few steps. 'Look. Tell me what you see.'

They saw a series of circles waning, and waxing again; lichen-encrusted, flaking a little at the edges, exfoliating as granite does. One small, shallow pool of water within the series shivered in a sudden gust of wind.

'Know this story, Tilly?'

Nor did most of the others.

The homestead and assorted sheds and machinery seemed like toys so far away. The creek bed snaked across dull brown and stubbled earth, disappearing as it reached a remarkably straight line marking where farm land became Forest Reserve. The old burial ground was along that creek bed.

Nita spoke a little in the old language, the words and sounds of which Tilly was only beginning to recognise. Impatiently, the old woman pushed a strand of grey hair away from her mouth and said, 'Kangaroo and the moon.'

It must've been a little wind that lifted grains of sand from the ground around them, but not from that dark patch where the rocks had been ripped from the earth or from this sheet of rock upon which they stood. At their feet, circles in rock.

'So the kangaroo says to the moon, I'm gunna die. I'm gunna die.'

And so would Tilly and Wilfred and Nita and Gerry and all the rest. Their bodies might be splayed on this sheet of grey rock; flesh suppurating, picked at by the birds, flesh lifted and falling away. The sinews and tendons, at first tightening, would slowly allow the bones to ease apart. Released, and neatly ordered in some semblance of what they had been, those bones would crack and turn grey in the sun as the earth rose around them.

'But the moon don't die, see? Comes back all the time, young and strong again.'

'Like us,' someone said.

The moon was a sickle, sickly. Sick. Almost not there.

'See, Tilly?'

Gerry pointed again at an irregular, dark patch near the series of waning circles in the rock and beside where Pa Wilfred had earlier so ostentatiously rested.

'That's the mark – the mark exactly – roo leaves in the dirt when he been sleeping a long time. When he come back same place every day to sleep.'

Pa Wilfred had been teasing her when he sat on the rock that way.

'He wanted to help you see it.'

'Not a cartoon kangaroo.'

No, no, of course not.

Someone suggested they visit the homestead. Nita and Wilfred knew of the man there, remembered from when he was in nappies and they were themselves children. He was a boy when they went away to the mission. Maybe they would go knock on his door. The twins and Tilly had met him, and they'd stayed at the old homestead.

They began to walk back to the vehicles.

'Tilly,' Wilfred called after her. They were left alone.

Ahead, they saw Gerry lean to the ground. Pick something up, or did he leave something there?

The old man held out a hand, thumbnail up. He pointed to the partial disk at the base of his nail; the white crescent showing clearly against his dark skin.

'Moon rising in you too you know.'

In Tilly's thumb; like the daytime moon above, but growing.

Wilfred showed Tilly what Gerry had left in the paddock: a stone from the ocean.

The engines grumbled and sighed, gravel crunched and popped under the tyres. A crow called scornfully at their backs.

WELCOME

Dan exited his doorway – our doorway, he would have preferred to say – the hushing, reluctant screen, its baggy mesh billowing with the movement. He stepped just far enough to avoid the arc of the door's passing, kept his back to it, waiting for the sound of it clicking shut.

Forty years he had been going through this door. And the house before that, at Kokanarup? It was here that he and Janet had made their life together. Nurtured children. Made the farm a business. Children gone now. Janet too.

By the time the door closed he'd usually be halfway to the shed, boots kicking up dust. The dogs stood ahead of him, waiting, stranded, enquiring heads turned back over their shoulders.

Dan held out his arms, and the little dogs ran back and leapt, one two, into his embrace. He smiled, gruffly; not quite begrudging the smile, but surprised and not trusting the circumstances that triggered it. Janet's long absence, he knew, had made the dogs anxious. He patted them with callused hands. Stiff-fingered and sun-splotched hands. Rough hands, Janet used to say.

Janet's skin was smooth and unlined beneath her clothes. Touched by his young man's hands.

The little birds in their cage. They chirruped and tut-tutted him. Where is our woman?

The dogs pressed into him.

They might die of the absence, he thought. It happened. Separation anxiety; it was real enough, he could vouch for that.

He felt her presence behind him and turned. Could see nothing.

Janet would have been thrilled to see Tilly. And to have Aborigines coming onto the other property, for them all to talk, to share their minds and to see if they might find their way forward together. She'd been the driving force for the Peace Park, the plaque and all that . . . For their children, she said. For the town. For us.

Us.

Their son did not care to return.

What did his son do? He thought of the young man he'd once seen in King George Town, how he'd recognised something in the body language and, overcome, had looked away. It may have been an apparition.

Dan never used to think about history at all, even though he knew of the family's association with the . . . killing. He'd always known about that. Massacre? There were so many lies. He never really thought the Coolman family – Tilly's family too it seemed; such a coincidence, or was it God's will? – he never thought of them as linked to all that. Except, perhaps, if he looked close and deep, he felt that they should be grateful they were spared. They had fitted in well enough. He remembered the old women, sisters. They were midwives, good mothers. Keep to themselves, people used to say, as if they were relieved. We made them keep to themselves, Dan realised. There was an old couple used to help with the shearing, when he was a very young child.

They must've all been related to the people that were shot and killed. Stranded, marooned at home.

Janet would not have been surprised.

The door clicked, set him in motion and, as if on invisible rails, he went to the shed. The smell of diesel and gravel so familiar he rarely noticed it.

The sky was stark and blue. The moon barely there.

Was that people on the hillcrest other side of the creek? Tiny, stick figures because of the distance, barely seen against the sky. They could be drawings. Blackfellas . . . He looked at the ground, and stayed that way for a little while.

Looked up again. One figure, maybe. A tree? He dropped his gaze a second time, looked up again. Nothing.

He was staring at his workbench and thinking about driving to Hopetown, might even see how his recent guests had settled in, when he heard a car pull up; it was Tilly, those twins from the other day.

'Hi Dan,' the twins did the talking, 'thanks for letting us stay the other day, and sorry we haven't got back to you – bit too busy organising this camp, and getting ready for the Peace Park, of course.'

'That's fine. How's it going?'

'Great.'

'It was great the other day.'

'Yeah, thanks.'

They were all beaming at one another. But what next?

'You know, Dan, apart from being here for the Peace Park, we got some old stories – a researcher with us, got creation stories recorded with our old people, hundred years ago . . . We wanna reunite them with the landscape, bring the sounds back too.'

'Oh yes.'

'You said you knew some sites, on your property.'

'Yes.'

'Someone told us there's one, about the moon . . . got circles in rock of the moon waxing and waning . . . Do you know that one?'

'Nah, sorry . . . Gerry. But I'm happy to show you more old waterholes, and anything that I do know, that might be interesting.'

'That'd be good.'

'We thought you might like to come back to camp and have a meal with us, meet some of the others.'

'That'd be lovely. What, today?'

'If you like. If it suits.'

*

Daylight seeped away. Tilly had her face against the glass of her door, was looking up to see the beginning of the night sky, a moon or perhaps an emu among the stars. She sat behind the driver, sealed within windscreen and rubber-lined doors, and the headlights of Dan's car behind cast shadows within their own vehicle, showed the hair on the twin skulls before her, but their faces were lost in darkness, hers too, faces lost in the darkness where they stared. The radio droned quizzes, opinion, stale music. Tilly would have reached for her phone, used her own soundtrack against this night, but something stayed her. Now and then space opened up beside the road, paddocks touched with the feeble light of the moon as it tore itself free of the clouds. Then it must have been trees, because the darkness closed again, pressed up against the glass and made a tunnel and each side there were Cyclops' eyes, red and white in a row. Tilly realised she was tiring. Tense around the shoulders and neck. They were running a gauntlet, pushed from behind, malevolence each side.

Freed again, Tilly saw a light – a blue light, shapeless – in the paddock on her side of the car. It was some distance away. Curious, she stared. What? Tractor? No. It kept parallel, moved at the same height above the ground with no bump or even jiggle. Constant, equidistant, parallel. Yet they were travelling – she glanced at the speedometer – at 120, 130 klicks.

Clicks.

'Gerald, Gerrard,' she whispered, not caring which one answered. Neither responded. She did not reach out to touch them. She spoke again. Nothing.

She watched the light for what seemed a long time. Then, it disappeared. An indistinct darkness moved close once again.

Figures leapt up either side of the road ahead, shone in the headlights. Ghostly. Insistently waving, their palms open and up.

Gerald spoke something in their ancestral language, startling her. Then he gave the common name for the plant. 'Tallerack.'

'Same?'

'Yeah see, belongs here, like nowhere else.'

'Like us,' said his brother.

They were back, together again.

A red glow at the driver's lips. Smoke twisted in the green, the red, the blue of dashboard lights. His window went down. Air roaring, smoke gone.

Tilly wanted some of that. Some obliteration, she thought, savouring the word in an unconscious denial of its meaning.

The moon might have winked, was an eyelid closing.

Gerry offered her something to smoke. She refused.

She thought of the creek bed at Kokanarup, the smooth surfaces of water reflecting these stars. Embraced in stone, the water brimmed, and brimmed again. All along the river, scattered here and there in the gloaming sand, pools of stars shone and in a full moon light would be oozing everywhere. But not today, not yet.

The car jolted, hit something. Startled, she glimpsed a kangaroo upside down against the stars, ghostly pink in the taillights of their car and the headlights behind.

The warm body spasmed on the cold, starlit bitumen road edge.

They drove on. Who would have thought they'd drive so far, so long? Tilly remembered coming up the steep hill that formed the main street of Kepalup: the school, the supermarket, café, the little park next to the old town hall, the hill crest and the fork in the road. So warm and cosy in the car. Tyres humming. She remembered crossing the dry riverbed, and going through a gateway of two towering trees that leaned to one another from either side of the road. They will touch one day, though likely be chainsawed before then because what if a truck it is a safety thing the government must do those things and the glass was between her and the outside, the glass and the two men why did she think them boys the two in front of her driving why had one of them which one done that and then the other there was a fly or something buzzing puzzled you'd think by the glass and maybe the outside world rushing by so fast yet it had its feet firm on solid air it could not breathe . . .

She could not breathe, and then he had loosened the leash and she did what he said, opened her mouth and one time it was dog biscuits, she leaned to the floor and took them in her mouth straight from the bowl or lifted her hips and begged and then so long as he gave her more and then with that it never mattered so much . . . He was so sweet at first and once upon a time, so sure of himself and the world and so strong could move like a dancer despite the bulk of him and his smile no hair on his head never liked it when the stubble came he had to shave each morning she saw him looking back at her from the mirror over his shoulder but straight ahead too and then he would bring her a cup of tea and open his hand and she took it and it was all good again she hated herself she loved him but it was not love but need for what he gave and withheld so she begged whatever he wanted. He dressed so well. His shining shaved head. His great bulk such a big, glossy man with a ring on his finger and he held her down and she would've killed herself . . .

She awoke. The caravan park. The twins were opening their doors, leaving. She thought for a moment that as their feet touched the ground they would spring into the air and take flight, but no. She heard footsteps crunching, and then Dan walked past her car door, not even seeing her and all his attention ahead of him.

And there, in front of the car, framed in the windscreen: a big, bald man, stepping out of her nightmare memories. Tilly wanted to crouch on the floor, hide behind the front seat.

*

'Doug! My son, my son, who would have thought . . .' That was Dan's voice. The two men were shaking hands. And then quick as that the bald man whose name she did not want to form was at the car, opening her door.

'Tilly. Tilly. Long time no see.'

Holding out his big hand. A hand she knew so soft and smooth and strong it could hurt.

Behind him, the Gerrys, watching. Puzzled. 'Arsehole,' one of them muttered, and stepped forward.

Tilly waved them both back, waited, got herself out of the car. Then stood, thinking of running but no she was going nowhere. Tilly, Dougie, his father Dan and the Gerry twins: there was much silence, except for Dan. Dan was delighted.

'But, you two know one another? Why, that's wonderful. I would never have believed. Of course, back then, but Tilly, you were too young to remember . . .'

'It's good to be back, Dad.' Dougie stepped forward, clasped his father's hand. He smiled over his father's shoulder at the rest of them, and his gaze held Tilly.

Tilly looked to the trees beyond which she knew the ocean lapped the sand, and beyond again a continent of ice from where arrived this wind on her cheeks mingling with her own stale breath and the festering inside that was Dougie was Doug was something not easy to tell or remember. And her dead father Jim Coolman alive at the centre of it. As if she did not have enough to do, without this monster turning up.

*

Several hours later Dan sat in his car at the caravan park. The hire bus, large and white in the thin moonlight, some logo marking its flank, gleamed indistinctly. Behind it, caravans, chalets and tents filed among the shadowy trees. The motor ticked as it cooled.

Doug had disappeared almost immediately after they'd met – some business, he told his father, someone to see, they would catch up tomorrow or the day after, soon – and Dan had remained at the camp to share a barbeque meal of . . . goanna, they said, and he saw it taken from the fridge, whole. Kangaroo too. Pleasant enough, but his mind was on his son, Doug. It was probably rude of him to keep bringing up the name of someone they did not know, and so of course they nodded politely and moved on to other topics whenever he did so. Something had upset one of those twins.

Tilly was unwell, they said. Headache, or something. It was all rather disappointing.

144

He made his excuses as soon as he could, and drove around the few streets of Hopetown, foolishly looking for Doug. He had driven back as far as Kepalup, and driven around that little town also, looking for his son's car, Doug's car. And then – inexplicable really – had returned to this caravan park. He sat in the car, momentarily awed by the night; its stars, its space and silence after the confines and rushing wind of the cab. Was he going mad? It was very late, around 11pm – hours after his usual bedtime – and it seemed that everyone had gone to sleep.

Then he saw a phantom, an apparition in a gown or some old dress, take Tilly's hands and lead her gently toward the ablution block. Beside them, a tall lamp – its halo of light dissolving in the moist night air – seemed a tall flower of steel and glass and electricity.

Dan watched them walk across the rectangle of bleached, dew-glistening grass. The lamp fizzed in the damp air. Vague human forms hung in the air. Laundry.

'See you later, Mr Horton. Dan,' she had said the other day. For a moment he had thought she was going to say 'Dad'. He watched the two women – young and old – disappear into the building.

The peppermint trees stood silent, waiting for him. Hush said the sea, and hush again. Dan got out of his car, kept walking in the darkness. He knew the band of trees on his right was very narrow, beyond it the beach sand. But say you didn't know that? He listened to the waves caressing the beach. The sea sighing. The windows of the old pub on his left were lit up like movie screens, but there were few customers to be seen. Music, throbbing softly. He looped around the trees and back onto the beach. How many boots, working boots like his own, had crossed these sands? As against bare feet. Holiday makers. Natives forever before and, they said, forever after.

Sand gleamed silver. The sea's ruffled presence, whispering and sighing; was trying to tell him something. Did God speak to us this way? The sky above. A shooting star. It was surely vanity to feel so special.

And now his prodigal son had returned.

He drove back to his home, his humming regularly broken by long sighs. When he arrived home he sat for a long time in the car, looking at his house. Waiting for a light to come on, a door to open. Waiting to be welcomed.

II

MUM N DAD

'I never tried to keep you away from him, Matilda.' Tilly's mother, Ellen, braced herself against the steering wheel and stared straight ahead, but she was not really looking at the cars parked all around them nor at the towers and walls topped with barbed wire. Ellen wore trackpants, t-shirt, scuffs; as she had already told Tilly, she was not going to be visiting anyone in prison. She turned to Tilly and – perhaps it was the result of being about to meet her own father for the first time – Tilly saw her as a stranger: the sloppy clothing, the sunglasses so large they might have been designed to hide behind, the dry and freckled hands on the steering wheel. 'But,' her mother continued, 'he is in prison. He's spent most of his life there. He said himself, he didn't want any of his children to see him in "lock-up".'

'Other children?'

'Well, yes. Not with me, Tilly.' Her mother sniffed disdainfully.

'I have brothers and sisters?'

'Apparently. Tilly, he has asked to see you. I can't . . . I would have told you, I guess, in good time, and I'm sorry they got in touch before I had a chance to tell you.'

'How long were you going to wait then, Mum?'

'Well, perhaps I did wait too long, but count your blessings, darling – you've been lucky enough to have a good man be a father to you. While you let him, Tilly.'

'Mum. He's your boyfriend, not my father.'

Ellen had brought Tilly up on her own. Tilly had never known her biological father, and certainly hadn't known he was an Aborigine until recently. A Noongar, they said. Tilly's first thought was it made her really Australian, but of course it was more than that. Then she realised she knew nothing, not even herself. She hadn't met many Aboriginal people. But then again, it seemed you couldn't necessarily tell, not by looking at them. Herself, for instance? Was she?

Tilly had not been to a prison before. Her mother again said she'd wait in the car. She and Tilly's father had not known one another long, she told Tilly. It didn't work out. He went to prison soon after they met. Her mother kept looking away from her.

'What did he do, Mum?'

'Best if you ask him that, don't you think, Matilda? Wouldn't you want it like that, if you were him? Not me telling you?'

Tilly said, 'Shall we go?'

It had been arranged that an aunty of Tilly's – aunty on her father's side, of course – would accompany Tilly to see her father, since she was still not yet eighteen years of age.

'Yes, you go, Tilly. You don't need me.' She accompanied her daughter until they reached a roofed but otherwise open area with a few timber tables and benches, just outside the Visitors' Office. A woman was waiting at one of the tables. Aboriginal woman, Tilly reckoned, and quite young.

'I think you'll be right from here, Tilly,' her mother said, turning back. 'I'll wait in the car.' Tilly dropped her gaze until she got close and, as she looked up, saw the lone woman was looking directly at her.

'Tilly Coolman,' the woman said, leaping to her feet and giving Tilly a hug.

'Smith,' said Tilly. 'Tilly Smith.'

'Yes, of course. But, you know what I mean,' the woman said. 'You're a Coolman.'

Tilly felt overawed by the woman's beauty and the way she was dressed. Most of the people she'd seen moving from the car park were dressed very casually, as was her mother. But this woman – Cheryl, she had introduced herself as – wore clothes you might see, thought Tilly, at an art exhibition or a big horserace or something. Not that Tilly had ever been to any of those things, but she'd seen pictures. Cheryl wore a hat (that was what brought horseracing to mind), a short skirt, strappy shoes and a lacy top. Tilly thought she looked gorgeous. She felt proud to be seen with her, though ashamed of her own appearance. It wasn't fair.

'Look at you,' Cheryl said. 'You got your dad's good looks alright.'

Tilly felt more sophisticated, just being with Cheryl. It was impossible not to notice the attention that came their way. Tilly walked beside Cheryl, taking her cues from the other woman's confidence. Cheryl walked up to doors as if she expected them to be opened for her, and looked right into the camera when they photographed her eyes (or whatever it was they were doing). She threw her little clutch of objects – phone, purse, keys – into the locker and confidently answered the uniformed staff's questions. Tilly tried to look like her; as if she had nothing to fear and was ready to take on the world.

They were led to a room full of small tables around which prison inmates and their visitors sat, and Cheryl chatted to the officer the whole time. Flirting with him, Tilly realised, and he wanted to please her. The prison officer pointed to a seat at an empty table and Tilly felt many eyes on them. Were they thinking two pretty young women? Or one beautiful woman and a fat little girl?

Her mother had no photographs of Tilly's father. Nothing. It was a one-time thing, she said.

A fling?

'I suppose some people might call it that, Matilda,' she had said. 'I'm sorry, love, it was a long time ago, I don't like to talk about it. You judge for yourself. He wants to see you now. They say he's dying. He hurt me, Tilly. You make up your own mind. Be careful, my darling.'

The prisoners all wore a green uniform; it was as if they were all in pyjamas. Of course, Tilly had seen this on TV and the movies. It was a prison, after all. But still, it was a shock; the loose, unstructured clothing made their limbs seem knobbly levers, and their uniformity focused attention on their arms, hands and, of course, their faces.

Perched on a plastic chair attached to the floor and at a similarly fixed table, Tilly tried not to stare, but it was hard; she did not even know who her father might be, until Cheryl beamed at an approaching prisoner and prison officer (the officer's uniform was belt and buckles and creases, buttoned pockets and pleats and epaulets). The prisoner, seemingly unperturbed by the situation and his costume, came to a stop and held out his arms. It was an invitation to hug, not insistent. Perhaps, the gesture seemed to say, if she liked, they might embrace. Tilly held out a hand, and he took it in both of his own. He was quite small, and lean. Like she should be, if she was not so greedy and weak-willed. She resolved that she would fix that again soon enough. And he was lively, walking not with a swagger but with a sort of loose bounce, as if he might leap into action at any moment, might spring in some unexpected direction. She noted he quickly scanned the room as he held her hand, and gave small nods of acknowledgement. She thought he seemed proud to be seen with her.

He said something, performing the words like a declamation. Tilly did not know the words, it was a language she did not understand, and so she did not immediately know that he told her she was beautiful and his daughter and that his heart was smiling. But then he told her the same, in English. They faced one another, separated only by the length of their arms. He was clean-shaven. His eyes bright. His thin hair was cut very short and growing grey.

Cheryl had waited silently, and now he turned to her. They embraced chastely.

Her father turned to the officer who had been glaring at them, but kept his eyes mostly on Tilly even as he addressed the man.

'My daughter, Mr Daniels.' There was pride in Jim Coolman's voice. He sat down and arranged himself so that his back was to the officer, who looked away disinterestedly.

'They'll be thinking,' he said, tilting his head toward the rest of the room, 'that you're both my girlfriends. I know we just met, Tilly darling, and I'm a silly old man, old enough to be your father and of course that's exactly what I am. But know this: if there is anything worthwhile I can do for you in our lives, please let me. I know it's late, and I've never been a father to you . . . I wish I could teach you a little bit of our old language.'

He must have seen she looked disappointed, because he laughed a little, to himself, perhaps about himself.

'You are cool, Tilly. Ha. In the old language I might say *yoowarl koorl* which, if you wrote it down might look like "you are cool". But it means, "come here". You are cool, Tilly, and you came here.'

Tilly thought no one had ever paid her so much attention. 'Sit down,' he said. 'Now, I want you to tell me all about yourself.'

'What did you do to my mother?' Tilly asked.

Jim Coolman straightened. 'I was young and silly and I hurt her. I hurt her, Tilly. I was selfish, jealous, violent. Drugs . . . It's not for me to say how much I hurt her or what I did, Tilly, it's for your mother to tell you. I don't want to. It's gone, can't be changed, all in the past, but it means you are here. You and me. Father and daughter. Now.'

*

Her mother was standing by the rear of their car, and there was a man on his knees beside the back wheel.

Their faces turned at her cough.

'Matilda.' Her mother was excited. 'We had a puncture.'

The man hammered the hubcap into place with the heel of his hand. Even on his knees you could see he was big. His head, completely bald, gleamed with a sheen of sweat. It must be his coat – an expensive-looking leather item – that her mother held.

'It probably happened just before you got to the car park,' the man said, his eyes moving from Ellen to Tilly.

'Doug Harper, this is my daughter, Matilda.'

The man rose to his full height. He was even taller than she'd thought, and heavily built. Younger than her mother, older than herself, he was dressed in a white shirt and blue jeans. Doug wiped his hands on a cloth Tilly's mother pulled from under a car seat. He smiled. His face was mobile, and glossy, surprisingly attractive; the eyebrows – the only hair to be seen on his head – were expressive, constantly moving squiggles. When he smiled the skin around his eyes formed deep creases.

'Lovely to meet you, Matilda, but we'll have to shake hands another time.'

He held out his hands, palms up. They were marked with dirt and grease from changing the wheel.

Tilly was disappointed. She didn't think his hands were so dirty.

He turned his back to her mother, and held out his arms.

Tilly's mother helped him into his coat like she was his servant, and Doug clenched his hands as they entered the sleeves. Such big fists, Tilly thought, almost as if she were in a fairy tale.

She thought it must be hot with that coat on.

Her mother drove in silence, but for the radio. It was news, often a single voice: Tilly's mother could not abide advertisements.

'So what'd you think of your father?'

'Oh, he's . . . It was good. Said he made a mistake not staying with you.'

Ellen snorted. Tilly was not sure if it was amusement or contempt. Her mother lifted her chin like she did when pleased with some achievement or perceived victory.

'And that Doug. Lovely man, don't you think, Matilda? Works with the parole board, I think he said. Helps the prisoners.'

*

Tilly's grandfather – her father's father – passed away. Tilly never knew him. Her mother said she wouldn't go to the funeral. No way, she said. I'm afraid no way not me.

Aunty Margie gave Tilly a lift. She was another relation Tilly had recently met. They were late to the service.

She saw her father at the far edge of a sea of dark clothing and lightly bobbing skulls; one of a raft of prisoners, each with a uniformed office beside them. Nearby, more centrally, bodies in the front row of seats leaned into one another. A keening voice rose above them, and the little crowd pulsed with sobs.

The man at the lectern asked if anyone Wished to Say a Few Words.

Tilly's father got to his feet and lifted his shackled wrists, tightening the chain that held him to the officer. The officer got to his feet, and Jim turned his back and began to walk to the lectern. Wife and sons and daughters milled around him; two girls had their arms around him, almost hanging from his neck, and he and a son hugged strongly, somehow, in the midst of all those bodies. They were a little younger than Tilly, this brother and sisters; they were a cluster, the father the nucleus and the mother kept at the edge. Jim Coolman held his head high on the swaying column of his neck, trembling ever so slightly. A small man, he had grown taller and now seemed at the centre of what was almost a dance, his children circling close, touching him, and backing away, clearing his path. Of course Tilly wished to be with them.

Jim Coolman held his arms out before him, wrists closer than even the handcuffs demanded. His body language insisted the audience notice the shackles. At the lectern, in the space it gave, he held the chain between him and the officer taut, moving his wrists in a little circle. The officer stepped closer, stood just a step behind, in Jim's shadow.

Her father enjoyed the little power, enjoyed suggesting he was in control despite the way it might appear.

The other prisoners remained in the front rows, officers stiffening at the spectacle unfolding before them.

Jim Coolman commanded the attention of the room and, varying the volume and rhythm of his voice, went through a list of names. 'All the boys,' she heard him say, and mention Comancheros and Mixed Bloods and God's Garbage. Brothers in prison. He talked of family, of his now departed father, of identity and heritage.

'What I had never had the chance to learn, because history, because we been just black people in King George Town.'

Tilly felt a swell and summoning of spirit in his audience, was buoyed on this sea of occasion.

'And Gerry, my brother, Dad loved you. Loved you for your interest in the old ways, and what you and him were gunna do, our people's history, our old language.'

The sea was calm, but you felt its depths.

'And what we been doing in the prison, me and some of the boys, we couldn't've done it without you and him, what you sent us. I disappointed my father, I know, my drugs . . . violence. I got that from him too, same as what I know now. But what we really are. It's not what we've been, not even what we are now.'

'He's good,' someone near her whispered.

'High as a kite.'

'One of his girls must've slipped him something.'

They made eye contact, Jim Coolman and his daughter Tilly, and across that dark sea of strangers and skulls turning to her, open-mouthed, he called, 'Matilda, my daughter, my lovely, I'm only sorry you never got to meet your grandfather.'

Connected by their shared gaze, she and her father floated above the crowd, and other daughters and sons they stood back, arms at their sides, acknowledging her while some long leash stretched and looped and pulled them all together.

*

Cars streamed past the entrance to the cemetery.

'That was lovely how he mentioned you, Til,' Aunty Margie said.

'He was . . . deadly,' one of the other girls said.

'Special.'

At the cemetery Tilly stayed at the outer perimeter of a crowd of men in dark clothes, some with ties so tight they kept turning their heads like discomforted and wary tortoises, and women detouring between graves who lifted their feet high to pull their stabbing heels from the soft ground. A grey day, and the sheoaks leaned in the wind and murmured. Her father was at the crowd's centre, by the grave, and a group of mostly young people milled about him, the stooped mother at their edge. Call her Aunty?

The pallbearers were all men. Tilly wondered who among them had rung to say her father wanted to meet her. Now, sudden as thinking it, his own father had died.

Her grandfather. All these people here for him.

An old woman was led by the arm to a chair beside the grave. She seemed to be blind, was weeping. Despite her misery, her age, her likely infirmity, she moved to the chair with conviction, limbs like levers and spine upright. Long grey curls spilled past her shoulders, and at the one side were tucked under the collar of her thick coat.

A little old man stood nearby, his mane of silver hair tied back on his skull. The scarf around his neck was the same colour as the pink and grey parrot on his shoulder.

After the burial, Aunty Margie took her to these very two people in the wide hall where the wake was held. They were sitting near the centre. 'Pa Wilfred and Nan Nita,' Margie said to Tilly. Then, to the old couple, 'This is Matilda.'

'Matilda? Jim's daughter?'

'Yeah, he said you at the service.'

'Your mum come?'

'No.'

'Oh.'

'She took me to visit him – Dad – in prison. They said he was dying.'

'But he looks ok don't he?'

'Met that woman of his? Any your sisters, brothers?'

'No.'

'Oh Tilly, you got the price? Got the price, Tilly? Lend us a dollar, sis?'

These last questions, fired in quick succession, startled Tilly, and so did the little being on Wilfred's arm that had voiced them. It was Cheryl in miniature exactly – bright red hair tied up into a high ponytail.

'I never seen her that way,' said Tilly.

Then it became someone else, something else, was gone. Tilly, at first so startled, was laughing still.

Wilfred smiled shyly. Slyly?

'How you do that?'

'Do what, Matilda?'

'One of his puppets. Don't mind him, Tilly. That's just your Pa Wilfred. Thinks it makes him special.'

'Well, I am special, sister.'

'So you are, Wilfred. But my brother Lenny whose death we mark today was special too, and so too Jim his son. And Tilly too, who we gotta look after and put our hopes in.'

'Need one of them.'

'Yep, need one of them to step up.' Another voice, another little being, one Tilly didn't recognise, emerging from . . . somewhere in Wilfred's clothing. His sleeve? Pocket? No one else seemed concerned.

'Summoning up them spirits, what you reckon, Tilly?' He laughed, turning his scarf, maybe it was his sleeve too, into a puppet. It was a big loose jacket, nice scarf. Light, but even so must be warm. And – Tilly was trying not to study him too obviously – he had some sort of red powder in his hair. A red band on his thin wrist too.

'C'mon then, Matilda,' the old man said, and held out his arm so she could place her fingers in the crook of his elbow, hand on his forearm. Nita had his other arm.

The two old ones had someone set up chairs at the end of one of the food tables.

'Here,' Wilfred repeated for the next half an hour or so, 'this is Matilda.' And as she was shaking hands, or sometimes hugging someone, he or Nita would add, 'Jim's daughter. You know. Coming back to us.'

Then Aunty Margie was beside her. 'Time for us to go, bub.'

Someone else was beside Nita, and Wilfred had disappeared. Nita had her face lifted, as if she were listening for something.

Outside, people gathered around parked cars as if at a caravan at some poor oasis. Cars close together, doors open, bottles clinking; people talking through car windows; drinking, gesticulation.

She saw that man, Doug, slide into a car at the far corner of the car park, and two of her father's other daughters – sisters, Tilly might have whispered – hurrying away with their mother.

One of Wilfred's puppets had shown the mother exactly, now animatedly talking to her girls. It was something about the way she held her head.

'You know them, Aunty Margie?' Matilda gestured in their direction.

'Who? Oh them. Yeah, but . . .'

'But?'

'Nothing, bub. But nothing; you'll meet them soon enough, no need to rush.' Margie's attention was on her driving, she was looking for a gap in the traffic. So busy; it too obviously took all her attention.

As they moved into the rushing stream of cars, Tilly couldn't help but smile. How did the old man do that with the puppets?

*

Tilly wanted to visit her father. Her mother would not take her. What could she do? It was easy enough to escape her mother's watch. After all, Tilly was nearly a grown woman. She thought of how Doug had looked at her, and treated her mother like a servant.

She caught a bus. It was still a long walk to the prison, but that did not concern her.

From the outside the prison could have been a factory, perhaps even a stadium. The barbed wire and the high fences might have held something valuable; been there to keep people out, not in.

She didn't want to know why her father was here, and for so long. Didn't want to guess.

The sun hammered her skull, heat rose from the bitumen and sunlight glittered on chrome and glass as she walked through the car park this summer's day.

No rich or powerful person visited prison. There was a young woman, probably not so many years older than Tilly herself, with a toddler in tow and a baby in her arms. Another woman drew Tilly's attention, flesh spilling from her too-tight clothing.

Tilly sat on a bench in merciful shade and with a view of the office where visitors began the process of visiting family and loved ones who had not known their touch for a long time.

A vending machine rumbled, and cans of soft drink snapped and fizzed as they were opened. The packaging around various snacks rustled, and the trees shading rustled also, though more softly.

The breeze lifted her hair, ran along her skin. The walk back to the bus stop would be long and hot. Having got this far, she acknowledged she had no ID or any idea of how to get through security to visit her father. She had known this all along, but only accepted it now. That was ok. It was enough to know she could get here. That must satisfy her. Go back to the bus stop.

A couple of men in flannel shirts greeted her. Their ungroomed hair, low-slung jeans and bellies marked them irrevocably, to Tilly's critical eye. Bogans, she'd say.

Doug's dress sense was as out of place here as it would be in her own suburb. For all that, he had had no trouble changing a tyre, which didn't fit Tilly's expectations. And he was so bald. Did he shave his head? Did his skull develop stubble? How might the skin of that skull feel? Tilly was looking at her phone, not texting or surfing, just gazing upon the blank screen, her dim reflection.

'Matilda.'

Was thinking of him, and now he appeared. Some magic she had? Cheryl was close to his side, her shoulders bare, her skirt short, and thin straps of leather twisted up from her feet and ankles. With her hat at an angle on her head, and those bright, bold hoops shimmering above her shoulders she might have been someone on TV, or some celebrity come from champagne and bubbles of laughter and money. She must be not so much older than Tilly herself, and her bright smile shone across the shrinking distance as if they were friends or sisters. Tilly, thinking herself a chubby schoolgirl, sat up, blinking, and brought her knees tightly together.

Smiling, Doug sat down beside Tilly. Cheryl continued toward the office, walking tentatively, walking almost as if she could not quite trust her long legs.

'You want to see your dad,' Doug said.

She nodded. Of course. She made herself look boldly into his eyes. 'I caught the bus, but . . .'

'And you're on your own?' Doug looked worried for her.

Tilly nodded.

'Tilly, can I tell you something?'

She nodded once more.

'Your father and me, we had a falling out a long time ago. A silly thing, about a girl – oh, not your mother – it was after him and her split up. I've got a lot of respect for your father, but . . . Best you don't mention me. Not yet. Later maybe.'

Tilly nodded again. 'Sure.'

*

'Long time no see,' her father said to Tilly and Cheryl. He seemed very pleased and eager somehow.

'Got something for me?'

Cheryl and her father kissed each other on the mouth, and the kiss lingered. Her father was grinning as they pulled apart. He swallowed.

'Miss that more than Facebook?' said Cheryl.

He was a good-looking man. Tilly looked for herself in him. She was a little jealous of Cheryl. Again, she sat opposite her father.

'Good that you could come with your Aunty Cheryl.'

'How are you, Dad?'

She saw he knew she knew.

'You can beat cancer.'

Cheryl was studying her fingernails. Voices hummed around them. A man walking past nodded at Tilly's father, who dipped his head, but when Tilly looked back to him it seemed his gaze had never left her.

'I never wanted any of my kids visit here, see me like this.'

He must've seen her expression: 'But don't get me wrong. I'm glad you came.'

Tilly said she had met her brother and sisters. 'Some of them,' she added, reading his expression. 'Facebook. We're gunna catch up.' Jim Coolman was pleased, she could tell.

'I never knew who I was, Tilly,' he said. 'Drugs mixed me up. I been too violent. Stupid. I never knew. Didn't understand. And once you been here . . .'

He was very talkative. Kept pulling the fingers of his left hand as he spoke, one after the other, in sequence from the smallest. He switched hands, started from the smallest on his right.

His attention turned to Cheryl. 'You still with Doug then?'

'See him sometimes. When I was coming in here matter of fact. But we past all that, trust me.'

Her father resumed: like he'd already said (so why say it again?) he was leading classes, culture classes, with some of the young boys, their fathers never taught them nothing. Everyone needs the language and the old stories, to know their family and their family trees and where they are from, who they are. That's what you need to know. You need it. Like what Dad was doing. 'We are special people, Tilly. You and me, we're one of the first families this part of the world.'

She did not say much. There was no need. When their time was up he hugged Tilly briefly, then he and Cheryl kissed again. The officer's voice brought them apart. Her father did not meet Tilly's gaze. He turned to the prison officer.

'Back to the cell then.' He seemed almost cheerful.

*

The music in Doug's car was something she would never otherwise have heard, unless perhaps in a movie. They wove through the traffic. No one spoke.

'Drop you at the corner, Matilda?' Eyes met in the rear-view mirror. Doug understood she would not want to explain to her mother.

'Thanks for your help.'

'Be in touch now.'

Outside the car, she bent down a little to ask Cheryl, 'What did you give my dad, when you kissed? Was that drugs or something?'

Cheryl turned. 'Oh Tilly, bub.' Then: 'Would you like some?'

Doug scanned the street. 'Not in the car, not the street. Not now.'

'Yes,' Tilly said.

'Give us a call. Come pay a visit.'

Cheryl's hand moved in the glass as the car shot away.

*

I feel great.

Did she say that?

Cheryl and Doug. Aunty Cheryl, but Doug said just call him Doug, because he was white. They beamed her smile right back at her.

'Think of it like medicine, but you're not sick. So it's a bonus.'

Her whole life made sense. It led to this. She'd never met anyone like Cheryl, so generous, so much a big sister. So beautiful. Cheryl said something Tilly could not understand, then explained. 'That's our language. It's culture,' she said. 'It's your culture.'

Look how late. Where had the time gone? 'I got school tomorrow.'

'Yes. Good. We'll drop you off, bub.'

When Tilly returned to her mother's house the walls moved in on her. She saw how small her mother was, how faded and tired.

Most of the time it was just the two of them, her and her mum; sitting in front of the TV. Washing the dishes. Wiping the counter. Her own little girl's room made her ashamed.

Cheryl worked part-time, and then only in the afternoon. It was perfect. In hospitality, she told Tilly. Business functions, making sure everything ran smoothly and no one got too stressed.

Tilly's mother shouted. 'You'll ruin yourself, Matilda.' She tried locking Tilly in, but couldn't lock herself in at the same time, could she? She had to go to work, to pay the bills, to la-de-la-de-dah. Tilly felt sorry for her mum, really she did.

Tilly came home late one night and the door was locked. She knocked, waited. Nothing. She called Cheryl, who came to get her. Tilly spent the next few nights with Cheryl.

Mum's boyfriend tried talking to her. He started off smooth, but was shouting at her soon enough.

'Your mother is worried, Tilly.'

She doesn't need to be.

'Cheryl? She's a prostitute. Fuck knows what he does for a living, maybe he thinks he's a big-time drug dealer . . . He's not.'

They were jealous. Plenty of people lived a good life that never kept at school, never went to uni.

'Yeah? Like who?'

Plenty.

And even if he was a drug dealer, so what? He had plenty of other business interests, that was where the money came from. The parole work was community service; giving back, he said. Look at people with their beer, wine. Smokes. They're the ones bad for you. Stuff she took didn't do any harm at all, only was a crime in some people's eyes.

It didn't cost her anything. Doug and Cheryl just gave it to her.

*

They went to a boxing match: Tilly, Cheryl and Doug. Though it was not really just the three of them because they met so many there, men shaking Doug's hand, shouting so that they seemed boys, and Doug nodding his shiny head, and looking past them to the next person and yet they were so pleased, mostly, to have been with him. Or they held him, tried to detain him. And women that were almost as beautiful, Tilly thought loyally, as Cheryl. Cheryl was so exotic, Tilly heard people say.

'But not exotic at all, am I, Tilly? Not exotic at all are we, you and me? We're indigenous; we're at home here. Beautiful black women.'

'That's right,' said Doug. 'My beautiful black women.' His palm on the back of Tilly's hand.

'A bonus. That little extra.'

Cheryl helped with her clothes and make-up. 'Exotic and erotic.' She looked years older. 'The perfect age,' said Doug.

A contender in the ring shadow-boxed as if no one was watching him. But of course most everyone was, in between – Tilly saw, observing in turn – determining who they knew in the crowd.

Almost naked men, stalking one another. Up on their toes, dancing; crouching, sweating, testing their reach and the other man's power and speed. A dance, but for the malice; the want to hit and hurt. The slap of knuckled leather on flesh, the spattering arcs of blood and sweat, the faltering eyes. People rose from their seats, baying. Baying all around Tilly and in her too. Her hands at her mouth. Tilly tried to look away, but could not. Cheryl smiled at her once, a tiny, private space in that crowd.

'You ok, bub?'

But turned away before the answer.

Driving home. Cheryl's head against the glass, snoring a little. She had stumbled into the car.

Tilly asked, 'Did you ever fight, Doug? You're big, you're fit. Did you?'

Doug smiled. 'You flatter me, Tilly. No, I let people do my fighting for me.'

Neon lights, police lights flashing. Doug's eyes in the rear-view mirror. But the police never pulled them over.

'Got a boyfriend, Tilly?' he asked.

'Nah, not really.'

Thinking of one boy, and how her own desire surprised her despite his clumsy way.

'I'm surprised.'

'Nah. No time for boyfriends – I want a man.'

Cheryl snorted. She not asleep. 'Tilly! You sound hungry, girl.'

'Well, that last fighter was a hunk.'

'Fighting's one thing; you want a man who knows how to please you, not hurt you.'

'Maybe some do both?' Doug offered.

'If you like being hurt, maybe,' Cheryl countered.

Boxing match, football match, concert. One after the other, then begin again. They had a good car, but usually it was taxis, limousines even.

Doug had money, friends. People came to him. He paid people to cook, catered meals for friends. Tilly's friends now, too. Despite what Cheryl said, it was an exotic life. Tilly was so lucky.

*

'You a virgin, Tilly?' Cheryl asked. Like sisters, they talked about everything.

'Been with women, Tilly?'

No. You?

'Yeah. With a woman, with a man, women and man. Lots of times. The best. Old days, our old people; women would share a man. Old woman, young man; other way around too. No hang-ups like now. That mission mob, them stolen generations and born-agains.'

*

Tilly's mother nagged her. Treated her like a child. 'I need to know, Tilly. You're . . .' Her mother lost it; shouted and cried and then gave up so quickly. Was worn down, inside out.

Tilly said, 'You're nothing.'

But she thought Doug Harper was somebody. Aunty Cheryl too.

*

Cheryl had a good friend who worked in welfare.

'Your mum locked you out? Her boyfriend shouted at you? They locked you in the house? Of course we can help.'

Tilly filled in the forms. Unable to live at home due to extreme circumstances. Family breakdown. Abusive men. Risk.

Cheryl told her she didn't want to make the mistake of relying on welfare though. 'Look around, Tilly. All the women with no man, and lots of children. That sort of money doesn't keep you living a life you want, not one I'm happy with, that's all I'll say. I don't wanna live like that, and I never will.'

*

Tilly thought she would keep going to school when she moved out of her home and into Cheryl's flat. And so she did, for a time. But there was so much to do, so much new. Never just sitting around with TV. Never.

This rush her father must've known so well.

Doug knew everyone, and he so quiet and polite most of the time when the others brayed and strutted, tried to show power and influence. Little sister, Cheryl said, and always made sure she got back safe from wherever they'd been. Cheryl was called away with work. Tilly found herself at Doug's house. Her own room, own en suite.

'Yes, you do need to be with your people,' he would say. 'Cheryl can help, but doesn't mean you have to be down in the gutter, Matilda. You're better than that.'

Her mother never let her use candles, but Doug had no such rules. He had food delivered. Proper food. Tilly was happy to help keep the house clean. It was nothing. She felt important.

And a surprise: Doug had three large guard dogs he kept in the backyard. The rear door was separated from the living areas and, having wandered the house one time in his absence, she stood by the heavy glass door. The dogs stood the other side of the glass, not barking, only quietly snarling and slavering at her. They followed her every movement. The backyard was such a contrast to the front, and the interior of the house. It was almost all concrete, with what she assumed were kennels in the far corner. Tilly retreated, and heard one of the dogs give a short bark.

'Security,' Doug said when she asked. 'Don't go out there, whatever you do. Unless they're chained up. They'll get used to you in time.'

*

170

Her father's skin was tinged with grey, and his face more lined than she remembered. He was thin. He looked old and sick.

He turned away when Aunty Cheryl went to kiss him. 'I'm my own man.' Hugged Tilly; his skin was clammy. He glanced around the room before he sat down, and held the gaze of the prison officer before he turned his attention to Tilly.

'You ok, Dad?'

'Better for seeing you, Tilly.'

Her father licked the corners of his mouth, clicked his fingers at the end of sentences. Stabbed his index finger for emphasis.

'No good. Kids don't know who they are. Gotta get the language back. That's it.' He pounded his open palm against his chest. He said some of the old words.

Tilly had heard all this before.

She may have felt the air shift at her back, or more likely it was the prison officer's body language, a change in his expression.

Her father's other family – the woman and children she'd seen at the funeral – had arrived. They were a dishevelled group, and hadn't dressed up for the visit. The mother's hair was tied back, her clothes rumpled and stained. Tilly didn't recognise any of them from Facebook. They glared at Tilly. Doug seemed to have ushered them in.

'There must've been a mix-up, Tilly. With the visits, I mean.'

Doug was talking with the prison officer who had accompanied the family to the visiting room. They smiled together. Doug was calm, complacent and satisfied. The officer and Doug seemed not to look in the direction of Tilly and her father. They stood between the entry and the door of the office. Other prisoners and their visitors glanced at the mild disturbance; this bubble of ill-feeling. It amused them.

No wonder her father felt proud of her, look at them. The boy tapping his thigh.

'Perhaps you should go, Tilly.'

She reached across to him, but he did not get to his feet. 'Look after her,' he said to Cheryl.

Cheryl stood up. She spoke to the prison officer nearby, 'We'll leave now.'

Her father muttered, 'Doug.' Or was it 'Dog'? Turned his attention to his other family who remained near the prison officer and Doug even though the space between they and her father was clear. They could have approached; but they waited. The prison officer took Cheryl and Tilly wide of Tilly's other family; her siblings, she reminded herself. Only then – was it Doug gave permission? – did they and the officer move toward Jim Coolman. As Tilly reached Doug, she looked back. One of the girls mouthed, 'Bitch.'

The officer put his hand on the mother's shoulder, helped her decide to sit at Jim's table. Doug put his arm around Tilly's shoulder and they left.

It was very upsetting. Stressful. 'Tilly,' said Doug, 'you know what makes you feel better. You know who you really are. You're wonderful, Tilly, you are very, very special.' He gave her so much; clothes and pills, music and dainty little pipes, broadband and subscriptions and needles and rituals of preparation to confirm the truth of his words. 'For being you,' he said, offering again. 'Bonus.'

*

Next time Tilly saw her father he was in hospital; a chain between bed and wrist. In hospital, there was a prison officer in the room or nearby, but they let her see him. Doug helped arrange that.

She missed Cheryl. Live in the moment, Cheryl told her. The moment. No longer segments of day and night; school and home. Tilly had never felt so good about herself. She was living in a state of exultation, she told herself, savouring the word.

It was a shock seeing her father. Like walking into an invisible wall; the world withered and shrank in the instant it took to recover. Her father was dying. The prison officer stayed in the room, but tried not to be. He was looking through a women's magazine; Tilly was touched by his courtesy.

Even now, despite the obvious and aching sadness, she felt proud of herself. She was the hero at the centre of her life, as must be; had left her mother, found her father. She brimmed with strength, growing into what she would become.

Her father treated her like an adult, an equal. 'You're special, Tilly. We've got thousands of generations before us, living in the same country,' he said. 'First People, we are. Ancestral country, but it's massacre country too. Hardly any of us have; stole our country, killed us off, made were laws so we couldn't go back, those of us left. Some don't even remember. But you been there, Tilly. You lived there when you were a baby. I was in all sorts of trouble and your mum was sick, she had to foster you out. Must've been meant to happen. She's a good woman, Tilly, your mother. I didn't know where you were, but you was home, it was our old people's country you went to. Not just co-incidence, that. Taboo, they say, but nothing happened to you, Tilly. Spirits of our old people looked after you I reckon.'

He held her hand. He was so calm, Tilly thought, had so much love.

'I'd like to see your mother, Tilly. I want to apologise to her for all I did. I was a weak man, wanting to be powerful. She's done a wonderful job bringing you up.'

Tilly squeezed his hand. Said she would bring her mother to see him.

'I'm different now, Tilly. I was mad before, that's why I'm here. But getting back our language, learning our history and that . . . I only knew the anger, the racism. Nothing worth passing on to you or anyone really.'

Tilly was nodding at him. Tilly wanted to learn. What could she do?

'Go back there, Tilly. Go back with some of our people. Not everyone is scared. We'll take the language back, the stories that belong there and tell us who to be, what we can do. I can help make that happen, even if I can't be there. But we'd need you I reckon.'

*

Doug understood the stress she was under, the change and challenges she was facing.

He listened to her, Tilly thought. He really listened.

'Oh, so that's where you're from.' He seemed very interested. 'That's your dad's country. And you were fostered there.' Doug gave a snort of laughter.

'What's so funny?' Tilly said.

'Oh nothing, nothing. I know that area, that's all. Pretty rough. It's funny to think you'd be fostered there.'

'Yeah, that's what dad said. Sort of.'

They talked about the trouble with her mother. 'I'll get in touch with your mum,' he said. 'I'll arrange it so she can pay your dad a visit. With you one time, that'd be best wouldn't it?'

He massaged Tilly's shoulders. Her feet. He gently moved her hair from her face when tears came or when she'd been sick. Supported her when she became a little confused.

On a later visit Tilly saw that her father had shrunk. His

head – his completely hairless skull – seemed huge and precariously balanced at the top of his spine; it tilted a little, and turned slowly. Although weak, he was able to sit upright in bed. Shirtless, she could see the ribbed detail of his barrelled torso rising from a tangle of sheets, towels, various cloths to absorb and not stain. One leg was folded beneath him, the other foot dangled at the side of the mattress from beneath the sheets. A prison officer sat just outside the doorway.

Her father needed to be moved to another room for some tests. He'd had them before, the procedure was familiar. There was some confusion among the staff; the wheelchair, the stretcher . . .?

'You take me, Tilly. Fuck 'em.'

She stood in front of him, he put his arms around her shoulders, and she carried him on the curve of her back. So tiny, her father. She hunched her back, leaned forward, and his useless legs dragged on the floor behind them. Cheek to cheek, near enough; his arms around her shoulders and neck, their hands clasped. They were one; she carried him easily and he was no burden.

*

Jim Coolman was in intensive care. Tilly studied the large doll her father had become, quite still now but for the shallow rise and fall of his breath. Cables connected him to machines and screens where coloured lines and lights wriggled and blinked. The room was at the very top of the building, surrounded by windows. Outside was the unreachable and implacable bright blue sky. Sunlight shone in rectangles upon the floor, and no dust no particles no motes bounced in this air. It occurred to her that her father might be providing power to this whole building, this medical complex, this city.

He recovered. Tilly rarely encountered a visitor; only the prison officers still stationed (ridiculous, since he was now so feeble) outside the door. And even they disappeared. Her father was not much more than a skeleton, the skin stretched over him, but became intensely alive. He sat upright in his hospital bed: the barrel-ribbed torso, the hands so large at the end of stick-thin arms . . . The span of his bony shoulders reminded her of a coathanger. He slowly turned his head, and fixed his bulbous eyes upon her.

'I'm a Noongar man, Tilly,' he croaked. 'Been mixed up, what that means. Noongar warrior. Ha! Snared. Until just lately, and . . . Too late. Say sorry to your mum if you can, I never meant . . .'

His jaw clenched, relaxed, clenched again like something mechanical. He might have been a puppet, but the fire of life burned ferociously. He was staring over her shoulder. Tilly turned. Doug stood in the doorway; glossy, leather-jacketed, smiling as if deeply satisfied. His head needs shaving, she thought, incongruously.

'He and you?' her father enquired.

'Dougie?' even though it was obvious who he meant.

'Dougie?' her father repeated, as if hurt by the intimate rendering of the name.

'He's been helping me,' Tilly continued, defensive despite herself. 'He said it was best you didn't know, since you were sick. Because of the mix-up you'd had, one time. He said you'd been very close, and . . . Nothing really, is what he told me . . .'

'Know her mother, too,' said Doug, from the doorway.

Tears in her father's eyes. He leaned back into the pillows heaped around him, was slipping away from her.

She touched him. Stood up. 'Call the nurse,' she said to Doug.

But Doug did not move. He remained, leaning against the doorframe, studying her father.

'Nurse!' called Tilly, louder this time, she who was usually so quiet. The nurse brushed past Doug and into the room. She felt Jim's wrist, checked the machines. He was ok, but perhaps needed some rest? It might not be long now.

Doug had Tilly's arm, and was moving her along the corridor. There was a small waiting room, and her father's other children were there with their mother. They looked at her blankly. A boy, one knee jumping up and down as he picked and scratched at the skin of his face and arms. A daughter with headphones, fingers clicking. Another concentrating on her phone, her jaw working.

'Got your dealer man, have you, darling? Boss man. Or he got you?' The boy looked to his mother, as if for instructions. Her lips curled; it might almost have been a smile.

Doug paused. 'He's all yours.'

The woman looked at him, mouth open, jaw hanging. 'And after,' he said, 'if you can keep your children civil . . .'

'Children? We're not . . .'

'Shuttup,' the woman hissed.

'If you can control your children, go see Lindsay. He'll have something for you.'

Tilly could hear their voices rising as the doors closed behind. She might have been a patient herself, and Doug her protector; or a prisoner, and he her jailer.

'Here,' he offered, almost as soon as they got back to his house. Home, is how she put it to herself these days. 'A bonus.'

*

Tilly's phone wanted her. It made Tilly almost nostalgic. Like Cheryl said, she had real friends and family now, face to face friends, not just Facebook friends. So she had been breaking the bond between her and the phone. But the phone gave that little buzz – a message – and she remembered the pleasure. Silly.

Call me. About your mum.

It was from her stepfather. As if she wanted to talk to him, especially after all the bossy shouting she'd put up with from him lately. Nothing new there. She had a good idea what that would be about. She ignored it.

He was persistent. She was determined not to give way. Tilly switched off the phone, put it away from her.

Later in the day when she turned it on again, almost without realising what she did, the habit still so strong, she was pleased to see a message from Dougie. This was unusual. He might not be back until late. And there were a few repeats from her mother's man. A little wave of worry lapped at her. If Mum really needed her, she'd call, wouldn't she? The wave receded, clutching with feeble fingers. Tilly put herself at ease.

The doorbell called her. Now? It was dark already; the day had left her behind. Peeping through a narrow tunnel, a figure at the other end, distorted by the lens that let Tilly see through the door. Cheryl?

'I lost my key,' Cheryl said, hugging her. The embrace lingered. 'Tilly.' What was it? Tilly wondered. Cheryl went to the fridge, took out a drink, gestured did Tilly want one also? Cheryl stood in the fridge door, illuminated by it. Like a character stepping from between the pages of a book. But no, Tilly didn't want a drink.

Cheryl seemed nervous about something.

'Tilly, darling. Doug . . .'

'He'll be late. I had a message.' Tilly knew already. He'd let her know first.

'He's with the police.'

So? He was hurt?

Tilly's face must've shown more than she realised, because Cheryl was quick to reassure her. 'He's alright. He's alright. Some trouble with some prisoners. They took the car. Escaped. The police need to talk with him, that's all.'

And then, before the details, before the story. 'They crashed it. Your mum was in the car.'

That was a surprise. How come?

'They took her to hospital. She's passed away, Tilly.'

It played through her head for many days to come, getting the story straight, coming to terms with it. Cheryl stayed that night. Went with her to see the body. It was just the two of them. And a body. Tilly couldn't believe it was her mum.

Doug was suspended from work and, despite all the pressure he was under, he was so very helpful; he supported her.

Doug might be too nice.

He wasn't even officially working, apparently, when he gave two prisoners – well, they were on parole – a lift. He knew them. They were in his care. Tilly's mum was in the car. Doug said she'd wanted to talk about Tilly, that was why she was in the car.

The prisoner behind Doug had overpowered him at some traffic lights. Got the seatbelt around his neck, pushed him out of the car. He'd almost blacked out, and might have been run over by one of the cars behind. Twenty minutes later they'd crashed.

'Your mum, Tilly. She was gone by the time they got her to the hospital. One of them died too. They were both high as kites, the prisoners I mean.'

179

They must've both grabbed Doug then. He wasn't sure, he could hardly remember it. But he was a big man, Doug. The prisoners were boys really. The seatbelt around his neck was what did it. That's how they overpowered him. They must've been high when he gave them a lift. Her mum was already in the car, and he saw the two men in the street and gave them a lift. Too helpful. He was too nice, and it might be that he was in trouble because of it. He'd lose his job maybe. He'd be under suspension for a time.

A LONG WAY

Tilly never went to her father's funeral. Never heard until it was too late. The days flipped by. She thought of something she'd seen in an old film; a paper calendar, the pages flipping quickly one after the other, but she couldn't even make out the numbers.

Her mother's funeral would be delayed, Cheryl told her. Because of the accident and everything.

Again and again it was like she was slapped awake: an orphan. She collected her things, the bits and pieces of her childhood. Of course Tilly missed her mother. Her father too, who she'd only begun to know. Missed her old home and school life. But when it was withheld, she realised it was the bonus she missed most of all. She was a little ashamed of herself, of how she had turned away from her old life. But, as Dougie said, it was a lot for someone as young as her to go through. And what he offered helped. He was a great help. Some people, he explained, special people, they need support. Artists. Creatives. It was self-medication, and taking responsibility for yourself. You have to look after yourself first. And he was right; she needed to get herself right. She just needed a break. For days it was just her and Doug. She needed . . .

She was glad when Doug began once again to stay away during the day. She guessed he had resumed work.

No phone. No internet now. No Aunty Cheryl. She'd been too long away from school. Doug locked the house. Security screens and sliding metal doors – she had not realised the house was so secure – there was no point even trying to break a window, and certainly no exit via the rear of the house with those dogs waiting for her.

The house was spotless. There was TV, DVDs, music. Magazines and books. He left medicine – her bonus – and the implements she preferred. Sometimes she told herself she wouldn't take it. But then, why not?

Because what difference did it make to be locked up anyway? She was safe. And once she relaxed, what did it matter if she was locked up? Good enough for her father, good enough for her. Only, when he was dying, he'd said he'd wasted his life.

Tilly padded barefoot through the big house. Shied at some noise. Something in the ceiling? Told herself she didn't need anyone. Sat on the big leather sofa and cried, loudly, her sobs absorbed by the house. Took the bonus.

No more Cheryl. No more concerts, football matches, the champagne and the lights. Just the bonus. And Doug. Doug who dressed her, undressed her, told her she made him happy, told her he needed her.

She only had Doug, and what he wanted with her.

'You can't stop me leaving,' she said. Went to follow him out. But he could. He took her back inside, crying. 'Have your breakfast,' he said. He gave her a bowl of cereal, a glass of fresh juice he'd mixed himself.

When she awoke she was naked but for underpants; too large, they weren't hers. She had a collar around her neck. Was on a small mattress on the floor.

Doug sat in a large reclining chair, his feet up. 'You're awake,' he said, turning away from the TV and swinging his surprisingly small and immaculate shoes to the floor.

He pulled on the leash, quite gently at first. Smiled; that seemed gentle, too.

'Bonus? Something to make you feel better?'

He pointed to a bowl of dried dog biscuits on the floor. Yanked on the leash again.

She knew what he wanted. She ate, kneeling. He touched her and she bent her face low, did what he said; lifted her pelvis up. Ashamed of herself, the pleasure her body took from him even with that taste still in her mouth, still smeared around her lips and how she hated him.

Remembered it later; amazed, disgusted, resigned to it happening again.

Never told anyone.

In the evenings he sometimes chained her up with the dogs. Muzzled her so she could not call, and tied the dogs so they could not quite reach her. They growled in their throats, showed their teeth, lunged on their own chains. Tilly crawled back into her kennel, kept her eyes on the back door waiting for Doug to return and rescue her. Did her best to ignore the dogs, which wagged their tails like puppies when Doug approached, so pleased to see him.

As was she.

*

If you could've seen Matilda back then, once upon a time. Our Tilly, walking through the house as if her limbs were full of lactic acid. They weren't; it wasn't exercise that was making her limbs heavy, that was making her blood stream sluggish and weighing her down. She had the medicine to fix it.

The house had a glass sliding door between two of its main rooms. Tilly walked into that glass, and staggered back with her hand to her head. She approached it again, both hands out in front of her, feeling the glass. She roamed the house grinding her teeth, bumping into doorframes, lashing out in frustration. Her eyes were vacant, her hair lank, jaw loose. Food stains at her chest. Tilly walked from room to room, muttering and singing to herself. A blowfly was trapped in the corner of one of the windows. She stood still, listening to it.

What other sound? A knocking. Thump thump.

Tilly turned, saw a pair of legs dangling from the ceiling; this became a man hanging by his arms. The man let go, landed smartly on his feet.

'Tilly, it's me, Tilly. Gerry. Gerry Coolman.'

Oh Tilly. Her heart was beating. She backed away from him. 'Tilly. I heard, Tilly. Your mum.'

Tilly's head was going side to side, slowly. No no no.

'Jim would've understood you couldn't get to his funeral. But, your mum. She brought you up, Tilly. You should be there.'

Gerry sat down on a sofa. Picked up a remote, turned on the TV. Tilly's eyes went to the screen.

'When you're ready, Tilly.'

She sat down.

'You got people love you, Tilly. Missed your dad's funeral, don't want to miss your mum's as well.'

'Gerry?' she said.

'When you're ready, Tilly.' His eyes scanned the room. 'Shit, I broke into houses before, but never had to break out of one.'

He got to his feet, gestured for her to help him. They pulled a table under the manhole from which he'd descended. Then, considering Tilly a moment (her eyes kept moving from him to the TV screen) he swung a chair over to the table, put another one on top of it.

'C'mon, Tilly.'

He stepped onto the table, then onto the chair and his head disappeared into the roof space. He bent his knees and their eyes met. Tilly looked away.

Gerry stepped back down onto the table, held out his hand. 'Tilly. C'mon.'

Tilly turned away from the game show on the television screen.

There, a million dollars was being offered. Here, a man precariously stood on a table beckoning her, and could offer only his empty, open hands.

'*Yoowarl koorl*, Tilly. *Yoowarl koorl*. Come this way, Tilly.'

Tilly fumbled with the seatbelt before giving up and slumping in the seat. In a moment she was asleep against the door, a line of saliva running down her chin.

*

Jim, Tilly's father, had said, 'Get her away from him, Ger.' But Gerald had to wait until he was himself released – that trouble his twin caused, along with too many fines from nothing but being inattentive and, he had to admit, out of his brain. It had not been easy to straighten himself up. At first, in fact, it had seemed impossible – until he started working with Jim, and found himself a different source to grow from.

He was not going back, and he would help Tilly move on too. He often felt so alone these days. He went with Tilly to her mother's funeral. There were very few people present. Gerry tried to introduce himself to Tilly's stepfather, but the man turned away almost immediately. The man was upset, of course, but he snubbed Tilly also. Gerry and Tilly stood quite separate as the small crowd watched the coffin enter the furnace.

'Thank you, Gerry,' Tilly said, as they left. 'I hate myself,' she continued. 'I keep thinking, go back to Doug.'

'Doug, or . . .?'

'Bonus, he called it. Dad was an addict too, wasn't he?'

'Yeah, that was something Doug had over him. Doug worked at the prison for a while, apparently, early on, and your dad was so proud and so angry. Played into Doug's hands, really. And then the drugs . . . Like an ambush. Doug likes that power over people. Seen that yourself now, unna? Your dad wanted to break out of that cycle, for himself, but . . .'

They went to Gerry's Aunty Kathy's house. The front door was open, the mat spelled out welcome. Aunty Kathy looked irritated, but almost immediately softened. Jim had been mad and bad all those years ago. She settled the girl, left her to fall asleep.

*

Gerry tried to explain the situation as he saw it. Yes, Tilly was Jim Coolman's girl, and she'd picked up a habit. That Doug Harper. She and her mother moved from interstate, no other family so speak of it seemed. Her mother had been in love with this man, and now she had died he didn't want nothing of Tilly. Tilly didn't know who she was, never been told she had Noongar family. She met Jim recently – her dad, you remember when he first went inside? The mother was that girl. Gerry didn't know how much Tilly knew, but she was mixed up ('Not alone there,' said Kathy). Didn't know who she was or what it meant and Dougie-boy saw that and he grabbed her. Gerry had seen it before. That Cheryl, for instance, he'd discarded her now. He seemed to have got to Tilly very quickly, broke her down quickly too.

'Doug set that up, the mother?'

'I reckon.'

Neither of them had faith in the police.

Kathy made a cup of tea. They went out and sat on flimsy chairs in the big backyard, in the shade of a big tree near where Kathy had a small campfire going. Talked.

Tilly would need a new environment, and good people around her. She had nowhere to go really. They'd seen enough addiction to know coming back to the same didn't work anyway. But it would be good for her to get back into school somehow, especially since she'd been doing her last years of schooling and was doing alright from all accounts.

'She's a state ward. You could be her guardian? If she agrees? If we can get her at a boarding school or hostel or something? Then you'd only need to have her here in the holidays, maybe?'

She might get a residential place at one of the boarding schools. Something. If she could rest, if she recovered, if she wanted. Not everyone did.

'I know a school. Not far from me – 'course, I'm at the primary school, but I do some work there; language, and Welcomes to Country sometimes even. Get her in there and she won't really need a guardian.' She looked at Tilly slumped in her chair. 'Yeah, I can help. They're good, the school I mean. And there's scholarships, to stay there and that. Bed, food, decent company,' said Kathy. 'My nephew, Ryan, he knows more about it than me. We'll talk to him.' She studied Gerald. 'You too. Ever think about study? You come a long way, Gerald.'

Gerry thanked her. He was not accustomed to this. He told himself to hold on to her compliment and appreciation; it would help him.

KNOW SO

At first it seemed to Tilly that she'd been dropped into a maze. It was easy to get lost among the rooms and people, and that was just the hostel. The classes were even more daunting, so different from the school she had previously known. Or perhaps, she was wise enough to realise, it was she who had changed. Most everyone was so purposeful and self-assured. She found herself favouring a view that was framed at one end of a corridor between buildings; a view of distant, shimmering foothills.

Kathy visited her with one of her nephews. Ryan worked at the university near the school. 'We just wanna give you some pathways, Matilda. Too many of our mob can't help themselves.' Ryan was an unassuming man. 'You have to wear a uniform all the time?' he said. Tilly said yes. It wasn't true. Then they were talking about the language classes her father had led in prison.

Kathy said it was healing. 'Fixed me up,' Ryan said. 'Got me off the gear, and your dad too, he cut back, he would've come clean . . .

'It means everything to me,' he continued. 'We need you able to stand on your own two feet, Tilly. Anything else is a bonus.'

Tilly winced.

He told Tilly the hostel – though most called it a

college – where she would stay was advertising for an Aboriginal Support Officer, and she probably should make sure she introduced herself to that person as soon as they were employed.

So, between them all Tilly's immediate future was arranged, and within weeks Tilly began to show that she might blossom in this environment. She knew habit and routine – had secretly mastered her diet and body for most of her brief teen years, and now suppressed her experience with Doug with a ferocious will. She followed schedules, did sport. She was otherwise happy keeping to herself. She knew what she wanted; in fact it was not much more than to make herself a life like this; of timetables and study; of frequent, tiny rewards.

A tutor helped her refine skills; she set goals and made plans to reach them. As for society, it was enough for her to greet the people who lived in the rooms around her and to share meals within the domestic confines of the college.

*

Gerald found a night job packing shelves in a supermarket, but the drudgery of it, to say nothing of his stoned companions, made it hard for him to maintain his resolution. Concentrating on 'structure and purpose' as advised, he applied himself to the language and other study he had begun in prison under the guidance of Tilly's father: the wordlists, the imagined dialogues, the recounting of old stories and fashioning of new ones with the old language. But it was not the same.

He turned up at the meetings his parole demanded, and went to enquire about an Aboriginal Bridging Course at the university. There was mention of a language class being held at a local community centre. He was proud that he got himself there. They concentrated on sounds, drew their own representation of spoken words with a finger, stick or brush dipped in paint.

The words were written with great care and – Gerry hesitated in saying it – with love.

He went to a lecture with his cousin, Ryan, which centred on the 'shared history' of their nation, and offered the 'fundamental truths': stolen country, the tiny minority of the original population which survived the first decades of colonisation being subject to generations of oppressive legislation into the late twentieth century.

He rarely saw Tilly. 'She's good,' Kathy said. 'Don't see her much myself. Maybe next year.'

Some weeks into term Tilly received a notice saying a woman had been appointed to the Aboriginal Support Officer position. Remembering Ryan's advice, Tilly went to see her.

'Yes, can I help you?'

'Oh, I'm Tilly.'

'Well, I'm the Aboriginal Support Officer.'

'Yes, that's why I came to say hello.'

'Oh, you're Aboriginal?'

'I'm a Coolman.'

'Yes.' Make sure you tell people, Gerry had told her, otherwise other people will tell you who you are.

'I see. Gee, with some of you it's hard to tell. Where are you from? That's what matters to Aboriginal people, did you know? That's what they always ask.'

'Oh yeah,' said Tilly.

The pin-up board behind the woman was covered with pictures of Aboriginal people. Many were copied from newspapers, magazines and from books but most were apparently quite recent photographs.

'I'm Maureen McGill,' the woman said.

Maureen noticed Tilly studying the photographs. 'I took the photos myself,' she said.

'They your family?'

'Oh no, I'm not Aboriginal.'

'Friends?'

'I just took them, you know, around the place. I thought it would make people comfortable, to have them up in my office.'

'Mmmm.'

'I've worked with lots of Aboriginal people, you know, up north. Cultural people, still on their country. I've got a skin name.'

Tilly nodded.

'What's your skin?'

'I dunno,' said Tilly.

'That's alright. Lots of people lost their culture down this way. We can fix that up. I'll get some workshops, some classes or something happening. We'll have excursions – we had one this morning, to the Aboriginal Community College.' She named the suburb. 'But it was terrible, those poor kids.'

'How do you mean?' asked Tilly.

'None of them could play didj. Some of us, some of our kids, will have to go and teach them.'

'Didj doesn't come from down here.'

'Oh, Tilly, but it's so Aboriginal. Didgeridoo means Aborigine to everyone, surely!'

'Well, I don't know.'

'You Stolen Generation, love?'

'No, not really.'

'Who's your mob? Where you from? That's what Aboriginal people always wanna know.'

'Yes. I see.'

'I want everyone to be proud of their culture, Tilly. Sit down, I want to show you something.'

She got up from her desk and closed the door. 'I thought

we'd run some workshops, you know, maybe some art, artefacts or dancing or something like that.'

'Can't help you.'

''Course you could.' Maureen played with the computer mouse. 'Look.' She flicked through a series of images of boomerangs painted in bright patterns of dots and lines. 'Googled them. I thought we could have all the Aboriginal kids teaching the other residents the traditional art of boomerang painting.'

'Nah.'

'But it's your culture, Tilda.'

'Tilly.'

'This art; it's your culture, Tilly.'

The office door was closed. The window blind drawn. Tilly thought she might get up and run.

'We're going to have a proper College Ball, at the old prison. I thought we might put on some Aboriginal dances for everyone. We'll have some dancers teach us.'

Tilly nodded.

'Would you be interested?'

'Do anything.'

'Good. I'll let you know then.'

She got to her feet, opened the door and Tilly escaped.

*

The school ball was imminent. Maureen grabbed Tilly's arm to tell her about rehearsals for the dance they'd perform. Despite the Support Officer, Tilly felt obliged to go.

Maureen called them together in a room with a large mirror on one wall. There were several students, all new to the college, and they found it hard to keep their eyes away from the mirror. Mirror mirror on the wall, Tilly almost said out loud, because of the mirror see and because she, Tilly, had been living an evil fairy tale: bitten the poisoned apple, been rescued from the ogre's castle, once upon a time. To her disappointment the mirror confirmed that she was indeed the fairest of them all.

'Don't look at the mirror yet,' said Maureen. 'Oh, and I want to acknowledge the Traditional Owners, and spirits past and present. Is anyone here,' she asked, 'anyone here a Traditional Owner?' One girl shrugged, said her people were. Maureen said, 'That's lovely, dear,' and continued on. Most of the students were from regions remote from the city. 'Then you'd know some dances,' Maureen told, rather than asked, them.

Some of the girls had dropped their heads, were glancing at one another. 'I seen them dancing, miss,' said one of the girls Tilly knew as Sue-Ellen.

''Course you have. And it's natural, you'll see, it'll come to you. Aboriginal people are all great dancers.'

A couple of the girls snorted. 'You oughta see my dad!' one said, and swivelled on one leg, giggling as she demonstrated even her father's facial expression.

'No, seriously.' Maureen frowned. She pushed her sleeves up to her elbows, and adjusted the headband that held her hair back from her forehead. 'Sue-Ellen.' She gestured to the girl. 'Let's start with you, show us your way.'

'I've only seen 'em, I never danced with . . .' Maureen took her by the arm, and brought her to the front of the group. 'We'll need some sort of music, but for now . . . Do they dance to the didj where you come from, Sue-Ellen?'

Sue-Ellen nodded, twisting with embarrassment.

'Dance then,' Maureen commanded, and began imitating the sound of a didgeridoo. Sue-Ellen looked around at the others, and lifted her arms. Tentatively she began the steps of a dance she obviously knew.

194

Still making didgeridoo sounds, and nodding encouragement, Maureen began imitating Sue-Ellen's dance. Sue-Ellen stopped, her arms hanging at her sides.

'That's great. I know that one,' Maureen said. 'I taught at Karnama for two years and used to –'

'Not from there, miss, that dance.'

'Oh, but dances are always exchanged,' said Maureen. She folded her arms and again furrowed her brow, emphasising rather too obviously the intensity of her thinking.

'I can see, I know you're shy,' Maureen said to everyone, with a special nod to Sue-Ellen. 'I can teach you. I think we can start there, with what Sue-Ellen showed us – thanks, Sue-Ellen – but maybe change it just a bit, make it more Aboriginal.' She was demonstrating movements as she did so.

'But . . .' began Sue-Ellen.

'S'cuse me, I've gotta go,' said one of the girls, giggling, and two of her companions sidled away with her. Their giggles bubbled from the hallway and through the still closing door.

The diminished group stood in silence, trying to avoid eye contact with one another. 'Oh fuck,' said Maureen, and perhaps she saw the grins or even shock on some of the girls' faces, because she continued, 'Honestly, since I've been hanging around with Aboriginal kids I've been swearing more, drinking and smoking more too.' She lifted her arms, began to stamp her feet. 'Like this, copy me.'

A girl looked at her phone. The door was still open.

*

Tilly did not go to the ball, but she saw the photographs as they came online. Lightheaded and thinly bleeding she felt pure and in control – but some of the photographs were disorientating. Gerry had been at the ball, she saw. There were images of the professional dance troupe that had performed on the evening. And there was Gerry again. As the night wore on she saw images of Gerry on the dance floor. It *was* Gerry, but he looked different somehow. Drunk? Out of his head some other way? There were some shots of him embracing one of the girls. The girl's face was shocked.

Some of the girls left early, they said, because of a ghost. The venue – an ex-prison built in the late nineteenth century – was haunted. Some left because of, as they put it, That Creep. Should have thrown him out.

Maureen called the police. But the stranger had left before they got there.

Tilly scrolled images for some days. This was the person probably closest to her now. He'd helped. She trusted him, but who was he? What was he doing? She took deep breaths, felt for the boundary between herself and the world, believed she was distilling to some essence of herself.

*

'No, not me. I wasn't even there.' Gerald held his parole officer's stare. 'I was not even there.'

'We got photographs. Statements. The man – you – the man gave his name as "Gerry".'

'No. Seriously, I was home.'

'Alone, no doubt.'

Gerry nodded.

His parole officer leaned back in his chair. Gerry tried to read the titles on the files behind the man, upended as they were and each balanced on an invisible full stop.

'We know you have a brother.'

Gerry tilted his head. It was the sort of thing Gerrard would get up to. He had a thing for schoolgirls, especially when charged up one way or another. Terrible.

'We also know it wasn't your brother.'

'You know that, do you?'

'Yes.' The voice came from behind Gerry. He spun around on his chair. 'He was with me.'

A man stood framed in the doorway, a folder in his hands. A bald man; tall, heavily built and dressed in a glossy leather jacket.

'With you! Well you got him properly in your grip.' Even as he spoke, Gerry's anger surprised him. His own brother, and Doug.

'Don't make things worse for yourself. We need trust. Even lying endangers your parole . . .' Doug began.

'You fucking dog. Crawl back in your hole before I rip your fucking guts out your throat.'

'Tough little man.'

'Gerald.' The man on the other side of the desk was controlled, but he seemed not to have heard Doug engaging Gerald further. 'Gerald. Threatening behaviour on its own is enough to revoke . . .'

*

The beginning of a fortnight free of classes, Tilly came to break-fast late to find a cluster of residents around Sue-Ellen who was sobbing and distraught. 'I can't sleep,' she kept saying. 'Every night since then . . .' The large dining room had a clinical sheen, and the space created by the girls being bunched around one table in the corner of the room unbalanced it somehow. Tilly came through the doorway diametrically opposite, and felt she was walking downhill. The sobbing girl, exhausted from sleepless anxiety since the College Ball, believed some evil spirit must've followed her home. Sympathy for her plight had grown, and other residents had also become distressed. The college might be haunted.

197

Bustling from the serving area, a metal bucket in one hand, Maureen said, 'We need a smoking ceremony.' She was, as usual, authoritative. The unhappy girl's sobbing grew louder. 'Miss . . . Maureen . . .' The students leaned toward conflict. They had become impatient with Maureen, but she was stubborn, resilient and needed to prove herself at the job.

'What you got in that bucket anyway?'

'Incense. Sandalwood incense. They used to have sandalwood everywhere in the south-west, you know.'

'I can't stay here no more,' the unhappy girl sobbed.

'Who's doing this ceremony, Maureen? You?'

Eventually, a girl said one of her family – yes, he was an Elder – could help.

The upset girl looked to her. 'Please?'

Early next day an older man visited the college. He had his nephew with him, who carried a metal bucket into which small holes had been punched, a bag of leaves and not much more. The older man was lean, and a little stooped. He smiled politely, but did not engage with any of the residents or staff. He studied the dimensions of the dining room. The boy stood by.

'Just the one room?' the old man asked.

Maureen seemed disappointed with the lack of ceremony, and that so few residents were present. She wanted an audience.

'We're doing this for Sue-Ellen, no one else,' one of the girls said.

'This everyone?' the old man asked Maureen. 'You got them all?'

Maureen nodded. Close enough.

As his younger companion bent to fan the flames in the metal bucket, the man introduced himself. He outlined what he was going to do, joked about 'occupational health and safety' and asked that all the doors be closed. He spoke for a while, and sang in what Tilly guessed was his ancestral tongue. He walked the perimeter of the room, and the younger man walked inside of him with the smoking bucket. Hands waved, and smoke curled and twisted, evading.

The staff worried about the paintwork. The smoke was surprisingly thick, and pungent.

Tilly felt particularly weak; she was studying hard, not really eating. She didn't require a lot of food.

The old man stopped beside her, smoke billowing around the two of them. Sunlight streamed through a window, spears of light among twisting strands of smoky air.

'What's your name?'

'Tilly. Tilly Coolman.'

'Oh, you Wirlomin mob?'

'Yes, I think so.' She could see Maureen behind the two men, watching.

'I know so,' he said, and kept on. 'This tree we burning from your country, down your way. This song too.' The young man waved the bucket toward her and Tilly felt smoke curl around her, gently cling, enter her nostrils, make some wispy being inside her. Smoke trailed the two men, insubstantial, shape-shifting.

'Open the doors,' the old man said in a voice too soft for most in the room to hear, but the instruction was carried. The doors opened, the smoke swirled and there was the sky. Tilly's phone grabbed her.

Hi Tilly get Esperance bus to lake grace 2moro. Someone will pick you up there for the camp. Gerry.

She had to go. For her dad, her mum even. She had to trust Gerry.

THE BONES WITHIN

Dawn. Tilly dozed, as did most of those in the rooms around her, slipping between the world of dreams and this. Wilfred and Kathy rose before the sun; tended to the fire in the gloaming dawn, their tongues moving with the flickering flames. Then the sky came afire.

Ruby and Wally moved everyone through breakfast, attentive to the schedule. Peace Park opening day after tomorrow; two more days to stay strong, sober, straight; let the old spirit fill you. Today there were visits to make. And tomorrow, first thing . . .

The campfire coughed. Its flames were thin in the sunlight, dancing nearer the edge of yesterday's ashes where the fence post from yesterday lay half-buried, as if thrown onto the dying fire but the flames had never caught.

'Leave it there,' Wilfred said. 'Don't move it.'

He looked a different character altogether this morning. Was hard to recognise at first, until he spoke. Overnight, he had shaved his beard. His hair was almost as short.

'Bit of a change?' He stroked his cheeks and chin, rubbed a palm across the short hair of his skull, the white whiskers bristling as his hand passed over them. Patted himself down while he had their attention.

'Still all me but, don't worry.'

Kathy drew each dawdling arrival into the group, and the Gerrys – on instruction from Wilfred – kept the fire away from the post that lay in yesterday's ashes.

Blind Nita and Kathy wanted everyone by the fire. They stood in the sweet smoke, nodded at Wilfred to speak.

Wilfred bent to touch the ashes at the head of the fence post. Some of the others put their hands to the soft powder, still warm from yesterday's fire.

Wilfred moved ash away from the buried post, revealing a smooth and ash-covered dome at that end.

'Lift it out.' Wilfred gestured to Gerald to lift the post, and how he should do so. The domed end swung uppermost, and there a human face rose and dipped above their shoulders, fine ash falling away from its face as it exhaled, scanning each of them from its lofty height as if it sat lightly just above their shoulders. Fencing wire, pulled tight and repeatedly around the post seemed ornamental, a chain-mail sash, and the smoke flowed and folded, made a smoky robe. Tilly wanted to reach out, to wipe the ash from its lips and eyes.

A gust of wind lifted the campfire ashes, and they clung and coated the legs of the little group.

Wilfred gave the word for the tree the fence post was born from; he gave them the words for head, for fire, for ash and for breathing.

Gerald tried to get Tilly's eye, but her face was as wooden as the one moving above them.

'This is what I'm making. Device, unna?' Wilfred was excited.

The post was replaced in the ash, again face down. Wilfred shrugged. 'Grab a piece of wood you like the look of. Take a little walk.'

'Walking today, like our people musta done. Walking. Keep moving,' said one of the men.

'Old people used to do nearly everything with a stick. Throw it, hunt. Play. Cut with a stick, bit of something else there to help – tooth, stone. Dig too.'

'Fight?' said Beryl.

'Yeah, but not just fight.'

The diminishing group walked one of the paths that led from the caravan park.

'Just a little walk, with a stick. Back soon,' said Wilfred, musing. A few turned back, some went with Wilfred, a couple strayed with Milton as he detoured from the group and most of the women took their own direction. They were they no more.

It was quite a small group of women among the trees; the young ones scraped their sticks, swung them. Sometimes Kathy pointed out some bush foods for the plucking, or they dug to get at the roots. They talked of what should be said about the massacre at the Peace Park opening, what words would be good . . .

There were other things on their mind. Needs. The desire to be some other, but of this they did not speak.

Milton and his small group had gone to a shed the other side of the park. 'Use real tools,' he said as they entered the work-space with its hand tools hung against the wall. 'So long as you smell the wood,' he told them. Again. Even Gerry was getting a bit tired of being told this. Smell that timber. Feel it in your sinuses, concentrate on that, not the other thing you think you need. We'll use some other stuff too. Resin, grasstree. Sinew, kangaroo tail. Work out what's got you by the throat while we're at it. How to make a snare, get out of one too, different sort of snare. Fire. Smoke. Your sweat and blood.

They repeated the words he gave, and made them again.

Walking beside Kathy among the peppermint trees and the hushing of the waves, unseen, as accompaniment to their voices, Beryl held her rough stick of wood in two hands, and made a short, swift arc in the air. 'Wish I'd had this when that c— . . .'

'Mmm,' said Kathy.

'All those years ago,' said Beryl. 'He raped me.'

One of the younger ones stumbled. They fell silent for a time, began a slow arc back to their campsite, the caravan park.

*

The plastic legs of Doug's chair bowed dangerously as he rested his weight back against the caravan. To a non-participating bystander – someone like Doug, for instance – roaming the edge of the campsite and peering from outside the circle around a campfire, not much of consequence was happening. This bunch of people who mostly called themselves Aboriginal – Noongar – were making artefacts. They were going for walks. They were sitting around talking, singing, sometimes painting and drawing. Crafts. Crazy-crazy, they were playing with puppets. Puppets were not Aboriginal art.

Doug knew most of this group. Quite a few had tried rehabilitation before. Some several times. He sold to a lot of them.

Sometimes they met in a sort of tent, or in one of the chalets. They'd held a 'workshop' (he'd heard them use that very word) under the sky, out in the breeze. Had moments of intense and enthusiastic discussion, in which he thought they were scarcely recognisable.

When no one was around, Doug went close to their campfire. How come they were the only ones allowed it anyway? A short screen – call it a fence almost – ran not far from the fire to the building where they ate and met. This fence was star-pickets woven with thin branches, twigs and leaves. There was a rectangle of white sheet near the middle of the construction. Like a projector screen, or something.

Doug walked here and there, found new vantage points for himself. He prowled the camp. He'd wait, they'd weaken, come begging. This bullshit wouldn't hold them. He reckoned they wouldn't make it to the Peace Park opening, and if they did they'd afterwards be feeling so civic they'd have to celebrate.

He had already talked to the local police, and informed one of them, a friend, that he'd unfortunately booked a few days at the caravan park at the same time as an Aboriginal community group were staying. A few of whom, he told his friend, might harbour some resentment against him – almost unavoidable for a parole officer, really, he explained, and they understood completely.

The police made a very ostentatious visit. Told him they'd make sure they were a presence.

So when Doug bumped into the twins he was glad they were out in the open. 'You following us around, Dougie?' He didn't reply.

'Don't let me catch you when there's no one else around, Dougie-boy.'

'Fuck off, Dougie.'

'It's a free country,' he replied. 'Call the police, Gerry; reckon they'll listen to you?' The police car drove slowly by the entrance to the caravan park, and then the group of women were returning; Milton's little group too. Doug moved away and Tilly saw none of this.

*

That which had been a fence post and which Wilfred had earlier made hover at the campfire was now in the room with them. Upright, the impassive face stared just above their heads and shoulders. It had been rubbed smooth, and glowed in deep streaks of dark ochre and honey. Beside it a human spinal column – more likely plastic than bone – was balanced on a pelvis made of some other carved timber and shallow, concave stone.

Wilfred and Milton were leading the men through some exercises. The men and women remained separate for the dignity and comfort of both.

'Lot of strength comes from your hips and your upper legs,' Milton said. He had been a tent boxer, and now he bent his legs and pivoted.

'This what we're doing, like yoga,' Wilfred said.

'Like in boxing,' said Milton. 'You gotta know yourself properly.'

'Not your soul, just now.'

'Only your bones and flesh. Your breath. The sinews and the little muscles under your skin, they all connected up hanging onto your bones.'

'So make it easy for them. Relax. Know what that means?'

The men, as with the women, were not a particularly athletic group. Some were skinny, some overweight.

They lay on the ground. 'Means let the flesh melt, feel your bones on the floor, the bones within. Go loose in the sockets, in the joints. Feel the sinews and the cords of muscle let go.'

'Feel all yourself, not just those little bits you always got your hand on.'

There was even more laughter in the women's group, enough to help even Tilly relax and feel less anxious. Kathy led them through the movements. 'Like some wadjela do in yoga,' she said. 'Like in tai chi, in Pilates and at the gym too. Little bit.'

Opened up and bending backwards from a kneeling position, lower legs on the floor, Tilly felt space opening in her chest, her skull, her sinuses. Moved into the positions they spoke, and felt spaces within of which she was unaware, and how the bones of her skeleton worked like levers. Her vertebra balanced lightly one on the other and when her head moved the body followed, like a puppet; not one of those cloth ones, but the other kind with rod and strings.

*

There was a roster of sorts, who was on cooking, who cleaning, that sort of thing. Kathy was in charge.

'Damper; it's not real blackfella food, is it?'

'Well . . .'

'It wasn't, then it was. Now it is. So are hamburgers, dough-nuts, spaghetti . . . All the things we Noongars eat, now. That's our food. Don't have the great big farm like we used to have, our own country; used to harvest with fire, that fire-stick farming.'

'So, what we having tonight?' Beryl wondered if it was kangaroo, naming that animal in the old language.

Kathy smiled. 'No.'

'The boys got one the other day, unna?'

'Yeah, but we'll use that for the Peace Park. Stew. We're catering too.'

Tilly went to the fridge. She jumped back when she opened it, claws and tails and reptile tongues!

Beryl looked over her shoulder.

'Oh no,' she said. 'Not lizards again!'

'Well, maybe we can have lizard stew at the Peace Park too you reckon?'

*

Doug walked within sight of their campfire and screen as daylight was fading. He saw the sheet was white with light, but no images, and a bunch of people sat around the fire, looking at it.

Then two hands were silhouetted on the screen, sharp shadows shifting their shape, that clever way some people knew, showing first a face in profile, then a dog, a parrot. A comical parrot at that; feathers spiky, wings outstretched, squawking gibberish.

The people by the fire were calling out a response, again in that language. Must be Nigger Lingo, Doug told himself, inordinately pleased with his secret vocabulary. Stupid Nigger Lingo. Tilly wasn't with them. There was open space between the campfire, the ablution block, the room where she was sleeping. No chance to speak to her, or grab. Bitch.

Then different silhouettes appeared on the screen. An axe. Knife? Spear. A sequence of shapeless sticks. Voices called out in some unfamiliar language as each appeared.

Human figures on the screen, walking. Puppets? One seemed familiar, somehow.

'Dougie,' a voice called.

'Dougie. It's Dougie.' Hoots of laughter.

Did they say his name? What of him did they see in that shadowy image?

Doug turned his back, walked away from the laughter.

Perhaps only the eyes of Wilfred and Kathy followed his departure.

The caravan park later in the evening was sporadically lit, TV screens and shadowy figures flickering, detached voices. That little group near the fire had gone. Their lights were out.

*

Earlier that same day, Dan had held a sheep between his legs and drawn the knife across its throat. The beast barely struggled, though it continued to kick fitfully even as the flow of bright blood slowed. Dan was an old man, he straightened stiffly, and reached for a large hook that hung near him, attached higher again to block and tackle. The hook was dark metal, darkest at the tip, and as the carcass rose into the air its head hung loose and blood dripped into the soft soil at Dan's feet.

He shooed the dogs away and pulled at the fleecy skin so that it came off in one piece, the flesh starkly white beneath. Paused, bagged the bulging, coiled intestines and the organs and his brother – it was idiosyncratic, both the way they worked as a team and their methods – then had it all within the skin ready to carry away.

'Save the liver, brain and that?'

'Do we eat that stuff?'

'No.'

'No.'

Dan was tiring. His brother Malcolm helped him move the beast to a dark and heavy workbench built against the outer wall and here they completed the butchering, separating the body into its parts for cooking . . . The swarm of flies around them grew, but the men worked efficiently. Closed the lid of a large, plastic box. The brothers' hands were streaked with blood and small pieces of flesh, their fingernails darkly lined. Together, in silence, they walked to a water tank. There was a cake of soap on the corner of the tank stand. The brothers handed it one to the other, carefully; it never slipped.

They carried the box of meat to a stone shed with a corrugated iron lean-to holding the refrigerator. The first area was gloomy, but well organised. Then they stepped up through a door in the stone wall, and into a much larger space, heavily enclosed but for a huge rectangular opening on the far wall. From one corner, a raised and fenced-in quadrangle extended

211

almost like a stage, and a long-unused shearing harness, dulled by dust, hung nearby. The two men did not notice the smell of old sheep shit, of lanolin and dirt, but it reassured and comforted them.

The brothers paused, each turning on their heel to look around the room and, though they sighed a little at the clutter and the thick layer of neglect, it would easily accommodate twenty or so people. Malcolm moved aside a bucket, some tools and a few hessian bags from a particularly gloomy corner. Dancing, sunlit motes showered him as he wheeled an ancient barbeque toward his brother.

'There's a gas bottle we can use, I know there is.'

'If they turn up. If they stay.'

'I'm pleased, so pleased. If only Janet . . .'

Their footprints remained in the dust, the pattern of the last sole clearly delineated. Voices clear in that high and stone-walled space. 'Now, this Tilly of yours . . .'

GRAVEYARDS

Today they would visit some more sites, Ruby pronounced, and meet with Dan Horton and his brother on their property, the 'massacre farm'. First, they would go to the springs near the river mouth.

The bus and utility pulled up together in the unsealed car park of a straw-bale house – or was it a café? – perched at the edge of where land tumbled away down a steep, grassy slope.

'Springs here feed into the river,' Wilfred said. 'Flows kind of inland lot of the time; our old people followed it to the main river, and up to where we'll be later today.'

Below them the water snaked away from where it pooled among gnarled paperbark trees in the ancient dunes. A profusion of reeds in the foreground, at the base of the slope, and no real edge of water to be seen.

Gerald climbed the fence.

'Plenty of snakes,' Milton said as Gerald walked down and among the reeds.

'Can I help you?' A woman walking quickly toward them. She stiffened, pointing. 'What's he doing?'

They watched Gerry pushing his way among the thick reeds, stomping his feet, hoping to frighten the snakes away.

He crouched for a moment and then, as the woman repeated the question, straightened and turned to walk back to them, almost as if he'd heard her question despite the distance between them.

She owned the café, the woman told them. She wondered what a busload of people were doing pulled up in the car park, bypassing her business, and climbing over her fence. It was not a strong fence, not a fence made to hold a crowd or keep a people away.

'We're the Traditional Owners here,' said Gerry as he returned.

'Custodians.'

'Oh, well, I don't know about that. This is my land. I mean . . .'

'Yeah, we know what you mean,' said Beryl.

The woman turned, a little startled at what appeared to be a female wrestler stepping toward her, cracking her knuckles.

'I can't have you all tramping down . . .'

'We'd get bitten by snakes in there,' Wilfred cut in. 'That'd be no good for any of us.'

'I never been in there myself,' offered Milton.

'No one much been here for a long time,' said Kathy, ''cause of the killing.'

'Oh, you mean . . . Are you here for the Peace Park?' the woman asked, brightening.

'Yeah, we're artists,' said Wilfred.

'Presenters,' said Gerry. 'Performers.'

'Tell you what,' the café owner said, 'I can't help with the land or the terrible things that happened here, but what about a cup of tea for you all, on me?'

When they got to the café, Tilly trailing behind, Doug was already seated at a corner table. He looked down at his cup.

Wilfred was telling them about a time he came here with

an archaeologist; some survey or other. They'd pulled into the car park and the archaeologist got out of the car and froze! She'd just stood there, gaping. 'Thought she was going to wet herself,' said Wilfred. 'She reckoned the car park – compacted, scraped, machines running all over it – she said the car park we standing on is all those bits of stone; you know, those flakes and whatever left by people sitting around chipping stone edges and points, yarning.'

Doug had raised his head for a moment, captivated by Wilfred same as everyone. Then looked at the floor, as if there were things might suddenly be seen there.

In the car park, they picked up little pieces of stone and showed them to one another. Doug waited a few minutes for them to leave. He scuffed his soles across the car park, and his spinning tyres made a thin hail of stones.

*

They drove for a long time, went up the hill of Kepalup and left it behind again until, eventually, the bus pulled up at a one-lane bridge crossing the river.

Milton pointed out a set of remarkably clear prints in the red mud at the road's edge, and gave them a word of the old language.

'Echidna,' said Gerald to Tilly. She saw the mark of some creature, some other, the toes like satellites of the palm, a foot-like-a-hand print.

They walked through a fringe of trees, and then in single file along a narrow path beside the river, to where a granite sheet sloped into the water.

The older ones sat themselves down on the warm rock beside the still, sky-full river, and the paperbarks stood in the shallows the other side. 'Go on a bit,' someone said. 'Round that bend.'

'Not me.'

'Not used to walking, you know.'

'Our old people walked along here, this a path for them too, heading upriver. Carrying some of those stones – remember that place the other day? Telling those same stories, these same words.'

A couple of them were singing that same old song now, weaving pieces of it together; weaving reeds and leaves too, some of them.

Tilly kept on with the Gerrys and a few of the others. The group widened, drew back into line again as the path narrowed. Tilly was happiest alone, near the back, and keeping the others in sight. She glanced behind at regular intervals.

*

They emerged onto blood-red slope that led to a cliff face marked with struggling shrubs and crumbling yellow and white rock. The solid rock under their feet had the look of something that had once flowed. Near the base of the slope, trees and shrubs waited at the edge of a tight, looping bend in the ancient river.

'Old campfires and all up there,' said Milton, pointing to groves of tall trees along the top of the cliff. 'Nice under them.'

'Heard about this,' said Gerry, and led them across the lower slope away from the river and into a wide trench that narrowed as it entered the very slope itself to form two vertical, human-sized surfaces.

Their hands moved along the walls, which crumbled at their touch and moistly clung to their hands. Tilly dug her fingers in the deeply coloured earth and stepped back, her hands full of stuff the consistency of cosmetics, handfuls that might blend with sandalwood and jam-tree smoke and be rubbed into the skin. Tilly smeared it across her forearms and hands.

'Hey.'

Dots and short lines of ochre marked Gerry's face, and he was beaming at her. He held up an ochre-smeared finger, and Tilly let him dab it on her nose, her cheeks.

Emerging ochre-patterned and lighthearted from that small corridor they almost walked into the other twin. Gerry One glared, turned his back and walked away.

White ochre on their skin, red ochre on their palms.

Light glinted in the depths of the river pool as if it were an eye, and trees and shrubs filtered small movements of air. Footprints formed in the vibrant earth.

*

Fine, misty rain; a rain that is like tears, that is like weeping, their old language says. The weeping ceased, the sky cleared and the bus pulled off the bitumen, heading for Kokanarup. This is a new word in that old tongue. It means something like 'place of sheep; sheep issuing forth'.

There was a momentary silence, a lull; a change in the sound. Fine gravel and sand clung to the tyres, and Tilly wasn't conscious of hearing two thin strips of the road's crust lifted by the wheels, but something opened and and . . .

She remembered this gate, remembered leaving behind the same crowd of trees they were now entering . . . No eagles today. Cresting a hilltop, for a moment the trees fell back and they were almost in the sky, but then it was forest again and they were falling, falling. The bus splashed through the creek and onto a dry, bleached slope. The blank, lidded windows of the old stone house stared past them, and the bus rumbled right by the house and pulled up at a much larger building, made of the same rough stone.

'I dunno about this,' muttered Nita. 'I never been here. It's a bad place, I can feel it.'

Ancient and rusting farm machinery was scattered between the buildings; spindly levers, spoked wheels, long drive shafts and circles of aging black rubber all mostly inexplicable to Tilly. She saw a graveyard, the spiky and skeletal remains marked with the colour of dried blood. Recognising a plough-share, its cutting disks wedged in the earth, she saw multiples of herself leaning chest forward into each disk, frozen in the moment before being sliced open, the blade continuing on into the earth beneath. The dry and splintering grain at one end of a wooden axle was held within a circular band of metal; the axle itself part of a tilting two-wheel cart, the horse long since departed.

At this end of the shed, a water tank rested knee-high above the ground, a rusted metal bowl of water below its tap and a cake of soap like a cuttlefish on the corner of the tank stand. There were drums, pieces of timber and rusted coils of wire; a trailer full of rubbish sat near the shed's entrance, and an old and bulbous truck rested on wooden blocks the other side of the doorway, its bonnet lifted above a dark and dusty maw.

Nita shook her head. Were such images in her rattled thoughts? She couldn't see so well, but was a good listener. 'Young ones want us to come here; why should I keep a bad sad story going? Not frightened, just getting old, that's all.'

Tilly touched the old woman's bare shoulder, and startled her.

'Oh. Cold hands.'

'Sorry, sorry.' Tilly wanted to reassure, to gift her love. Nita grabbed her hand.

The telegraph poles stood mute like soldiers; the grass hissed and the wind rushed up from the creek bed.

'I promised my mum I'd never come here,' Nita said. 'We gotta move with the times.' The other passengers were filing from the vehicle, and toward where one of the twins and Milton waited with the two old farmers beside the entrance to the shed.

Nita clasped Tilly's hand tighter. 'Tilly, dunno if I can get off the bus.'

But the others could, and were. Kathy and Ruby told Tilly to go on ahead, they'd wait with Nita. Tilly walked behind Beryl and Wilfred and so Dan did not see her until she was right upon him. His face showed surprise, then pleasure at seeing her. The two tiny dogs watched from their vantage point at the top of the trailer's pile of rubbish. Tilly stepped into Dan's tentative arms for a moment; then, when his brother opened his arms, she held out a hand.

'Don't remember me, Matilda?'

'Don't remember nothing,' she said.

The group stood in loose formation, many looking outward and away from the two old brothers, studying the sheds and machinery and ruins, and their gaze wandered toward the distant creek.

Beryl stood close with her back square to the two men, and peered intently back to the bus.

'Where is . . .' Dan began, but Beryl answered before he had finished.

'Aunty Nita's coming now.' Relief in her voice. They watched the old woman manoeuvring herself down the steps, Kathy and Ruby moving their hands in the space around her, assisting.

The dogs sprang to Dan; one leaned lightly against his leg, the other stood between his boots.

Tilly shivered; a shadow crossed the ground, and she looked to the sky. High above, an eagle.

Nita approached slowly, flanked by her cousins.

'Speak,' said Milton. 'She's blind.'

'Nita,' said Dan.

'Aunty Nita,' his brother said.

'Mrs Coolman,' Dan began again. 'Welcome.'

'Hello, Mr Horton. And thank you. I guess you don't want a Welcome to Country then?'

Dan and his brother smiled nervously, and then Dan spoke up. 'It is an honour to have you here. Sad as this place must be for you, it has been our home. Thank you.'

'You're welcome.'

Now she and Dan shook hands and, when Nita held out her other hand, Malcolm took it greedily. But she did not let go of their hands. The brothers held their uneasy smiles; they did not want to resist, but did not know what to do. They looked at the others; confused, not quite pleading.

'Come closer, Mr Hortons,' the old woman said. 'My eyes don't work so good.' Shadows flitted across the ground. Clouds. The sun was covered, then brightened again.

'I know you're not to blame for what happened here all those years ago,' Nita said. She released her grip.

'I know, I know.'

'Our grandfather prayed that God would make a property available, and to bring up his family, so . . .'

'I never been here before,' Nita said. 'This is my first time, and likely my last too.'

Milton lifted a hand in the sort of gesture used in a blessing. 'It's our homelands, our ancestral country we're reconnecting with . . . Being here, it's like an awakening, even if it is a sad place, a very sad place. But we're walking over ground that our old people . . .'

'God answered our prayers,' Malcolm said, and Dan continued, 'God wanted our family to be here. It's a precious place for us too.'

Beryl spoke up, 'That thirteen-year-old girl your grand-daddy raped was my granny . . .'

'Great-great-grandmother,' said Wally, who had finally left the bus.

'Grandmother,' continued Beryl.

Nita lifted her chin, turned her head. Listening or sensing the air? 'What about we move this way a bit. Away from – a building, is it? Maybe some shade? Gotta tree we can sit under, Mr Hortons?' The little group moved to a nearby tree and stood within its circle of shade. Beyond, light shimmered shallow over a wide span of dry, broken, intricately crossed stalks of grass.

'Your grandfather was killed because . . .' Nita began.

'Our grandfather's brother,' interrupted Malcolm. 'There were three brothers.'

'One of your grandfather's brothers was killed because he was messing around with teenage Aboriginal girls. The wrong girls. Girl. That's why he got stabbed, that's why he got killed. Assassination. That was the law.'

Dan gave small, quick nods; was impatient to speak. 'The information board, at the Peace Park, we wanted it to be worded from both sides . . . My wife was working with them, and we would like it so no one is offended.'

'This is a massacre site,' said Nita.

'That's a word that hurts us . . . There were lives lost, yes, absolutely . . .'

'Raped; and so then he had to be killed. The old people already gave them other women. Marry them in, see; they was gunna be the go-betweens, not this one . . .'

'She might . . .'

'Not her; she was wrong way for them. The other women were given, were gunna bring them together, them and their kids, see, but she was promised other way and they didn't know your people thought every woman was theirs to take . . .'

'The police came, and shot four culprits,' said Dan. 'That's documented.'

'Shot more than four!'

'Our grandfather's other brother, went out on a horse to try and talk with the people . . .'

'Went with a gun!'

'They tackled him. He fired a shot and killed one, and they kept coming, kept coming and he fired a shot and killed another one, and then they fled . . . They left the area and apparently after that there was never any more conflict . . .'

'Bullshit. Nice if you can believe it, nasty even like that. You listening to yourself, mister? They burnt the camps – there was a baby, and they took him away to be raised. That's this one's' – she indicated Wally – 'ancestor. And two sisters, one of them our old granny or great-great and . . . I know for a fact that white people poisoned the waterholes, and they took turns going out with the gun . . .'

'Can't see that gun on display in the museum *and* have a Peace Park,' added Wilfred.

'Shot down like rabbits,' said Milton.

'We took that gun down from display years ago. It's gone. I'm sorry.' Dan dropped his head.

'White people won't accept, they won't acknowledge . . .'

'My wife said that.' Dan looked at his brother. 'Janet.' He looked back at Nita. 'She was in the Historical Society. She's the one made them put the gun away, that it was wrong.'

The little group was quiet.

'All jokes aside, white man robbed the black man ever since he put foot on the ground. Ever since then black man's getting punished,' Nita said vehemently.

'There are so many stories, on both sides.'

'Yes,' said Nita. 'True.'

'Things happened, and it's terribly hard to come up with the truth . . . but we've been working on the Peace Park, and your people want . . .'

'Not our people, we never been in these talks about the Peace Park. Them ones weren't the original family, they're the pretend people,' said Milton.

'There's a lot of them about these days,' added Beryl.

'We seen what you written.'

'But you have joined us now, we know who to talk with and we'll tell them . . .' said Malcolm.

'My dream,' began Dan. He looked at Malcolm. 'Our dream is, because we're Christians and don't like bickering and bitterness . . .'

Nita snorted.

'We're all people,' Dan persisted. 'We're all descended from Adam and Eve. Let us all be together, as people . . . Like, it's history; mistakes were made, and we're very sorry about it all. We wish it wasn't like that. Let us get together and reconciled so we can enjoy each other . . .'

'Like your great-uncle did with our girl?' muttered Milton.

'My dream, and I'm dead keen,' Dan continued, and Wilfred wrinkled his brow. 'I'm dead keen for there to be a Peace Park, a memorial plaque, for us to be together to open a place in recognition of the Aboriginal folk that lost their lives here. I want to see it happen, I really do, and so did Janet . . .'

Silence.

Nita broke it. 'I said I'll never come here. But then again I do like to walk where my family been. Hundreds and hundreds of generations of them been here, until not long ago really.'

'Please feel free to have a look around,' said Dan, waving his hand, his eyes shifting from his guests.

'Well don't wanna look at the house, or that bed where the killer slept,' said Beryl. 'I'm sticking around here.'

'I'm gunna go down the creek see his old grave again,' Gerrard told his brother, and he went off alone, leaving the track and crossing the dry slope. The wind had dropped again, and if he'd known how he might have heard more than only his own footsteps crackling the grass, and felt the soil adjusting incrementally to the imprint of more than just his solid, boot-shod feet, here, today.

The group under the tree splintered, moved apart as if its holding centre had collapsed, whether that was the old brothers, Gerrard, Nita or some other altogether, and people roamed in singles, in twos and threes, around the barely groomed ruin and wreckage that represented this farm's history.

*

In the shearing shed Tilly smelled dust and sheep, long fleeced and gone. It was a very grand shearing shed, with massive, patchily rendered stone walls, rough timber floorboards and a very high roof. It was also untidy; drums, boxes, hessian bags and various implements were heaped in dark corners, and coils of wire and half-filled boxes and bins spilled onto the floor. A corner of the big room was fenced with timber railing, and a door there, if opened, would allow through only ghostly sheep. On the wall, a horse yoke hung, battered and torn, covered with a thick layer of dust. Closer still to Tilly, a large noose was suspended in the air. Light spilled through the huge doorway, dissolving its edges, and yet the corners of the building, like the distant roof timbers overhead, were hard to discern.

Tilly sensed movement behind her and, still blinded from the wash of sunlight, she turned and saw an old woman clawing toward her from the darkness, speaking in the old tongue, calling her name.

'Granny Nita, you scared me.'

'Thought I was a ghost? Plenty of them around here, Tilly, but they're not gunna hurt you.'

And then there was a crowd in the room.

*

The barbeque sizzled in one corner of the old shearing shed. The brothers had a number of chairs – plastic and canvas – and a tablecloth covered a table. A long board balanced across several tins of paint against a wall was further seating. There was salt and tomato sauce, sliced bread, paper plates and bottles of cordial. The barbeque smoke drifted out through the open doorways and window.

'Gerry,' said Dan. He had taken the twin aside.

'Gerald,' this twin said.

'Gerald, I want to present your people with some grinding stones we've collected over the years. Do you think that will be alright?'

'I think so,' said Gerald. 'I'll check.'

Discreetly asked Nita, Wilfred, Milton and Kathy. 'Well,' he heard, 'they can put what they got on the table. Doesn't meant we'll accept it.'

Gerald reported this to Dan, who nodded his understanding. They ate, together.

*

Dan stood near the doorway, light eating away at him like acid. He held up a shaking hand to gain their attention, and placed

225

a bundle on the table. Something wrapped in an old bag. They could read the faded lettering: *superphosphate* . . . something.

'I just feel it's been a wonderful time together. I'm sure my brother Malcolm . . .' Here, his voice broke. He looked at the ground, swallowed; continued: 'Malcolm feels the same. How good to chat with you, how we love you could come on our property knowing its history.

'As for me, Kokanarup, this place, it's very special because it's my whole life since I was a baby . . . I was born here – well, the hospital in town – and my family . . . Well, it's a special place for us too.

'What I've got, now, you can have a look . . . You don't have to do anything if you don't want to, but over all the years we've been here . . . No. Not here, the stones come from upriver, really, that property we bought late sixties, sixty-seven, thereabouts, since about then . . . Over the years, what we've found, what I've got right here . . .'

It was uncomfortable for everyone, how nervous and emotional he was.

'My wife was very keen on keeping them, and I'm very keen – now that she's passed on – your ancestors were the original people in the area and this is part of them.

'I feel it would be absolutely lovely if you people could take this as a memorial, back home, to remind you that your ancestors had these and so I'm going to unwrap this now and you'll be able to have a . . .'

His hands were shaking. Unwrapped, a large bowl of fist-sized stones. Smooth. Different colours: grey, brown, black, almost white.

'These grinding stones? Our family picked these up over the years, mainly along the river down at this spot. I can take you there. We loved being in the bush. Please, at least have a look . . .'

226

This circle of people moved in from the walls, left chairs scattered across the floor, became a tight group, shoulder-to-shoulder and two- or three-deep around the table. The stones had small hollows, sharp edges, so smooth and comforting they asked for human hands.

'Because my wife's gone,' Dan was repeating himself, offering variations of what he'd already said. 'She loved keeping historical stuff – I feel, in my heart, that I'd like to see you folk, because you know you're descended from people who had these . . . and I don't know if those helping with the Peace Park . . . It's up to you, they're here for you if you feel you can take them.'

They hefted the stones, caressed them, passed them one hand to another. Remembered that crevice in the ocean shallows, stones this size, rocking in the ocean swell. But these were chipped and worked by human hand, carried here. They were warm.

'I'd like you to take them,' Dan said. 'Like I said, most of these we got upriver, but there's other . . . sites I guess you call them, I'd like to show you. Easy to get to, close, you can bring the bus . . .'

Wilfred interrupted. 'We might give a couple to the town's Historical Society for the museum. You return 'em to us, we lend 'em the museum.'

The old men – Dan, Wilfred, Milton – piled into Dan's vehicle. Malcolm stayed behind, and the rest followed in the bus. They drove down the slope, back the way they'd come upon entering the property, and came to a stop only a few hundred metres away, beside the riverbed. Dan led them across the sandy bed, and onto a sheet of rock. He stood beside the little brimming well he had previously shown the twins and Tilly.

'You already know this place?' Beryl realised.

As they were about to drive off another vehicle arrived; Doug.

He pulled up beside the driver's door of his father's vehicle, and must've raised his voice because some of the passengers heard him say, 'Showing them our sites? Good on you, Dad.'

He looked at Gerry. 'Thought I'd have a look at that car of Mum's.' Dan blanched. Doug looked again at Gerry, speaking softly now, 'Not trespassing, am I?' Laughed.

Dan drove on, the bus followed on past Doug's wide smile.

The rutted track ceased after a kilometre or so at another water source, a small soak among reeds and with a low stone wall on three sides. 'Aborigines must've helped them build this one, maybe. I never thought about that until lately,' Dan told them.

He led them along a narrow dirt path that wound between trees to the base of a sloping sheet of rock. Wilfred gave the old name for rock waterholes, and asked the twins to lift each of the two slabs of stone that lay on the rock. Beneath, each deep, barrel-sized rock hole held water, clear and cool. Tilly, too, sipped from her cupped palm.

'It's symbolic,' the old farmer said, 'that we do this.'

They drove back to the homestead. It was agreed that tomorrow, before the Peace Park opening, they would visit the Hortons' other property, further upriver, where the stones had been collected. Dan had some other artefacts they might be interested in too.

As they drove away from a waving Dan, Milton said, 'Nice to get those stones, but if he give us the farm, that would really mean something!'

NAIVE

Half an hour the other side of Kepalup, they turned onto a gravel road and, after a time, a road smaller again, past a small office, and came to halt at a gazebo construction in the middle of a camping area that held a basin, running water and a small gas barbeque. Fruit and cold drinks were laid out on the table. The bus would just get bogged on the sandy track to the fishing spot, so Gerald would ferry everyone the ten minutes there. It would take two, maybe three trips. The cab seated five, though more could fit, and there was room on the tray. Those left behind as the crowded vehicle rumbled away waited around the rough, wooden table. Some took out cigarettes, some their phones.

'That was lovely of Dan, giving us those stones,' said Angela.

A man astride a lawn mower rushed around the park and campsites. The mower spat dry grass and weeds, snarled closer and closer in its loops. It circled the gazebo. The driver stared at them, but looked away each time his gaze was held.

'How long before Gerry gets back?'

'Hello, just passing through are we?' The woman was lean, middle-aged and sun-lined. She wore jeans, boots, a denim shirt, a wide-brimmed hat. Her blonde hair was tied back in a ponytail. No one had seen her approach.

Wally and Ruby got to their feet. 'Yes,' said Wally.

'I'm Ruby.' Ruby had her hand out. The woman shook hands grudgingly. 'We're just waiting for the motor to come back, take us fishing at Lake Parndi.' Ruby tilted her head in the direction of the lake.

'How long will that be?'

'Not long.'

'Because, you know, really, this place is only for people staying here.'

No one spoke for long seconds.

'Is that right?'

'Yes, well . . . I'm sorry, but we do have a business to run, you know.'

'We've been coming here for years,' said Beryl, 'since Mr Wellstead was just a boy.'

'Well that may be – though you look a lot younger than him – but anyway we bought the business from Mr Wellstead nine months ago.'

There was another silence.

'We're the Traditional Owners, you know. This is my country,' said Gerrard.

They heard the ute returning, and all except Gerrard turned to it. He kept his eyes on the business owner, and she walked away as the car doors opened.

*

A sandy, two-wheeled track wound its way through spiky scrub: stiff grey twigs, small bunches of bristling spears, flat leaves with spikes reaching beyond their perimeters. Muted explosions of colours erupted here and there. A kangaroo's head and shoulders looped in and out of sight before the animal finally emerged fully formed, bounding along the firebreak the other side of a wire fence. It jumped to their side of the fence, then bounced back again just as quickly. The track turned back on itself, led them between thickly shaded trees and out onto a sheet of rock beside a wide lake.

'Really a lake?' asked Tilly.

'Well, not when there's plenty of rain, might be a river then. Most of the time it's a lake. Call it a lake,' Milton told her.

Small isolated groups of trees stood in the water, a short distance from the rock. Dead, white, their scarred bare arms silently beseeched the heavens, their neighbours, anyone who might save them. A strong wind swept across the water, making a pattern of small slopes and ridges.

The ute went to and fro. Kathy and Wilfred sat out of the wind near a low rock face and a few trees and watched fish leap from the water, throw themselves at the feet of the fishers and flap bright white and silver.

'Better catch yourself some before we end up with too many – gotta clean 'em too, you know.'

Tilly had never caught a fish before. Wilfred was beside her, selecting the line, showing her how to bait the hook though, in fact, he moved too fast for her to follow.

She threw the line. It didn't get far, the line billowing in the breeze, but almost immediately it pulled hard in her hand, and something unseen tried to escape, to lead her away.

'Oh!'

'Pull him in, pull him in.'

She did, throwing the reclaimed line onto the rock, and soon the bream was flapping on the rock, its mouth pursed in dismay and its strong tail agitating ineffectively.

'Get the hook out, then put it in the bag. Hold him.'

The spikes along its spine stabbed her. She felt the muscle of its curve, the gristle of its mouth as she wiggled the barbed metal. The hook came out easily.

'Remember, we have to clean them too,' Wilfred said again.

They heard another vehicle arrive. Doug again. He took out a rod and line and started to fish about fifty metres from one end of their group.

'No police here,' Gerald called out, mockingly.

'Ah, just ignore him, Ger,' said his twin.

Doug was concentrating on his line. Waiting for a bite.

Although Wilfred had warned each of them that they would have to clean whatever fish they caught, Gerrard kept hauling fish onto the rock, every now and then scooping the silver bodies around him into a bag. Then, when they were all packing up ready to leave again Wilfred made sure the bags of fish were all in the ute's tray.

'Men'll clean 'em,' he said.

But in fact when the twins, along with Milton and Wilfred, got back to Hopetown there was a sign at the jetty, its red letters commanding:

Fish Must Not Be Cleaned Here. Fines Apply.

They had so many fish. What to do? Drive back out to one of the beaches?

In a very short time the men were standing at the public bar, admiring the array of colourful labels. This was the place to get some advice.

'Sorry, don't want to buy anything. Not yet anyways; fair bet bunch of alcoholics like us be back soon enough,' they explained.

At first the woman behind the bar had been surprised, nervous. Then suddenly, almost with relief it seemed, she said, 'Yes, of course, yes, Frankie Jones, just around the corner . . . He's got a great set-up for cleaning fish. Ask him.'

'Great.'

She explained where the house was.

'He might want a few beers though. Hire fee, like.'

'We'll have a yarn with him first.'

'This time of day he's probably around the back. If he doesn't answer the front door just go around the side of the house. No dog.'

They pulled into the driveway: two wheel ruts in overgrown green grass. A dilapidated, timber-framed house; paint and boards peeling, it appeared to lean to one side. *Bloody Paradise*, it said in faded lettering on the wall beside the front door.

'You go, Milton,' said Wilfred. 'They'll feel safe with you: old and not so dark.'

Milton looked at Wilfred.

'Go on. Don't wanna frighten them, do we?'

Milton knocked at the front door. Waited, looking back at those in the car. Came down the steps, and disappeared around the side of the house.

The car passengers fell under the enchantment of the car radio's preview of the coming weekend's football fixtures.

'Oy.'

Milton again, at the corner of the house. He gesticulated for them to join him, and disappeared.

*

It was a large backyard, fenced, and as overgrown with lush green weeds as the front, except for a well-maintained vegetable garden and, between it and the house, a long steel table with

233

a trough and tap at each end. Milton and a companion were standing on its other side, doing something with a hose.

Milton called out, 'This is FJ!'

The man held out a meaty hand as they approached. 'FJ,' he repeated. FJ was middle-aged, balding and bearded, with a large earring, an eye-patch and a belly that held his shirt out like a tent.

'Hey,' said Wilfred. 'I've got a parrot you'd like. Sit on your shoulder.'

FJ laughed. 'Shit on my shoulder, you mean.' Then went on: 'Caught yourself some fish I hear.'

'Few,' said Gerrard, holding up a bag with some difficulty.

'No worries. Cost you a few beers with me while you clean 'em is all.'

The men looked at one another. Gerrard was jogging back to the pub before Wilfred had finished his words of assent.

The fish-cleaning table was large enough for them to work side by side, and before long the men were doing just that. The water in each of the troughs was regularly drained into the veggie garden, and the fish heads and guts went into a bin. 'Bury that here,' said FJ, 'or mates've got pigs, chooks – they love it too.'

They raised a storm of silver scales with their blades; sliced, broke backbones, clawed at entrails with their fingers.

'You said your name was Coolman? I knew a Fred Coolman when I was rousabouting, years back.'

'That was my father,' said Wilfred.

'I think his name was Fred. Best shearer I ever worked with,' said FJ.

Gerrard rinsed and put down his knife, went to move away from the table.

'Oy.'

'What?'

'You giving up?'

He'd cleaned the number of fish he'd caught.

'We're doing it for everyone, Gerry,' said Milton.

The other men kept working. The twins looked at one another. Gerrard picked up his knife once more.

'And you need another beer,' said FJ, offering him a bottle.

They worked furiously side by side, no man wanting to fall behind the other; cut backbones, tore heads off, flung intestines into the bin. Rinsed and packed the fish in ice.

'Beers, love,' FJ said to a woman who emerged from the back door. She put down her glass of wine. 'My wife, Penny,' he said by way of introduction, and presented each of his new companions by name.

*

They were in the pub: the largest building in the street. It had an L-shaped bar at its centre, and windows along two walls looked over a huddle of fuel bowsers and a small park – a picnic shelter, a tap – on one side and, on the other, the jetty and ocean could be glimpsed between the scrap of peppermint trees at the edge of the dunes. The fish lay iced in neat silver rows in a box in the back of the vehicle.

FJ and Penny were regulars at the pub, of course. Thus, they were the hosts. But we're the custodians, thought Gerald. He had already resigned himself to a long drinking session, eagerly. Even enjoyed the barmaid's surprise when she saw he and his brother side by side.

'I need a man like you,' she said to his brother. 'Two for one.' Penny shoved Gerrard's shoulder. Gerald wondered if he should warn her. 'Girl ever know who she's with?'

'Back soon,' Gerald said, and fled. The others laughed, then quickly forgot him.

Lifting the box of fish from the ute at the caravan park he saw Angela and Beryl walking to the pub. He realised their abstinence was about to break and that he would join them. Their visit to the massacre site briefly crossed his mind. He called to Tilly. 'Fish ready to be cooked,' and she walked with him as he carried the heavy weight to the barbeque area. 'You might want to get them started, or . . . I dunno who's cooking. Ruby and Wally might. Old fellas have met up with someone. Me and Gerry keeping an eye on 'em.'

'Ok,' said Tilly. 'Most on their way to the pub anyway.' She didn't say anything else. Gerald tried not to breathe; he didn't want her smelling the beer. And he wanted to get back to the pub before anyone else turned up.

'Kathy or Ruby will know who's cookin'.'

He was quickly back in the car. He would have walked back to the pub, but he wanted to get away, the more so when he saw, in the rear-view mirror, Ruby talking with Tilly. He drove around to the other side of the pub. It was in his mind to get inside as quickly as possible, but the sea, swollen and still blue with the light of the dying day, grabbed him; and the rawness of the flayed and retreating sky held him. The big warm windows of the pub showed its interior like a film screen. Already the crowd had grown. Who'd have thought there were so many people living in Hopetown; of course it was the mine, contractors, service providers and farmers. There was a camp for the mine workers on the outskirts of town, new houses peeping from among the dunes, the population now five or ten times what it was just a few years ago. A lot of young people, in party mood. Through the window Gerry saw FJ; right at home in the Great South. In turns, Gerrard and Penny leaned over the pool table.

Gerry two-stepped into the comforting noise, the light and warmth.

Time shifted. The black windows reflected the bar and the crowd. Beryl and some of the younger ones from the camp here too. What was the time?

'Wanna talk to you.' His brother beside him, grinning, tilting his skull to indicate they go outside. There was a stranger beside him; toothy grin framed by freckles, red beard and dark beanie.

'Right,' said Gerald. His voice seemed to emerge from beside him, not from within. They stepped into the cold darkness, then were suddenly a hundred metres away at the jetty car park. There was no light, no moon. The sea was a dark and shifting presence, just over there. They stood by the toilet block.

'Good stuff,' said their new companion, Tommy, packing his little pipe. The stars glittered, seemed to have lowered. They could smell the sea, the old smell of it, and the funk of what Tommy was smoking.

'Got it from another tourist,' the man said.

'We're not tourists,' said Gerald, exhaling.

'But you don't live here.'

'Not yet. We did, once.'

'Huh?'

'I mean, our old people. This is our country. But the massacre . . .'

'Yeah, I heard about that. Taboo.'

'But we're coming back.'

'Oh yeah.'

Gerald saw Gerrard's face, up close, smiling. Might have been laughing. 'Loosen up, brother,' he said, eyes shining. 'Shottie?'

'Nah.'

'Yeah.'

It was easiest to not resist, not struggle. The red-headed

stranger held him, but not forcefully or with real intent. Gerald could've easily broken away, but wanted to submit, to have his will taken away to be obliterated. His brother inhaled deeply, then – palms on Gerald's cheeks – put his mouth to that of his twin and, as many times before, Gerald breathed in as his brother exhaled.

*

Tilly's vision had long adjusted to the dark. Don't go walking alone, she had been told, but a woman has a right, and she felt quite safe at night, especially in relatively open space like this where she was sober and everyone else drunk; she knew how to choose her vantage points in the dark. She watched the twins embracing, how they and the stranger stumbled. The men released one another, staggered apart, one of the twins laughing, it seemed triumphantly. She tried to remember how the one who had dropped off the fish – for she reckoned that had been Gerald – was dressed (not, she knew, that their dress could be trusted). It was dark. She was alone. The twins and their friend could've been devils dancing.

But who could tell devils by the look of them, or how evil?

'Good stuff, Tommy.'

A twin was embracing the stranger, kissing him with the same passion he had kissed his brother, and they fell apart, their breath smoking in the thin light. The other twin leaned back against the brick wall of the toilet block.

Tilly moved away, back along the path through the trees, alert for any sound or sign of movement. The men's voices were very thin, and it was very dark, and the white, sandy path hardly visible. Tilly came to the street parallel to the beach. Staying close to the trees, she saw the three men walking from where she had left them. They were unsteady on their feet and, as a car went past, their shadows leapt and grew and suddenly they were twice the number, distorted and unstable. The car slowed and did a U-turn. Exposed in its headlight beam, Tilly froze. Then, blinded and in the dark again, the car gone, she heard, 'Tilly. Tilly.' There was no running away. The three men walked toward her, and she waited. One Gerry hugged her briefly, surprised her with the friendliness of it; out of his tree, she realised. The other twin held her tight in an embrace. His hand cupped her one buttock, then slid down between her legs. Shocked, she started to struggle but by then he had moved away and was singing some nonsense tune, arm around the shoulders of the stranger.

'This is Tommy,' said the other twin.

'Coming to the pub?' asked Tommy.

'Nah, no ID.'

'How old you?'

'Old enough,' said the groping twin.

'I'm heading back to the camp,' Tilly said.

She left them before the entrance to the pub, rushed from the possibility of a goodbye hug. From a safe distance, she watched them at the bar, so clear in the bright windows it might have been a stage, or a brightly coloured film. Snatches of music and voice reached her. The crowd seethed and rippled. A lot of the family there, even the oldies. Milton at the dartboard, Wilfred at the corner of the bar talking to some young women; a cloth puppet jumped up from his hands, and one woman bent from the waist, the other pirouetted. Wilfred had them laughing; they might almost be his puppets too.

And there is Doug, hands full of froth-brimming glasses, joining a group of people – one of the twins, Beryl . . . others Tilly doesn't recognise. Most everyone blooming, one after the other. But they are clumsy; they bump against one another, stagger and stumble, lean close to hear their partner's words, pull them close in their arms, push them away again.

Standing with hunched shoulders among the fuel bowsers and lidded windows, hands deep into her pockets, Tilly could find no emu in the sky, and the stars reminded her only of the tiny holes in the corrugated iron roof of an old, collapsing shed she'd been in earlier today; pinpricks of light. And now, rising, a thin crescent moon.

*

Back at the caravan park Kathy, Nita, Wally and Ruby were in one of the workshop rooms, Kathy working on a large painting.

'Who?' said Nita as Tilly entered the room.

'Tilly, we were worried about you,' said Ruby.

'Sorry. I'm good.'

'Look at this.'

It was a large painting of a landscape. Strange though: something like a map, something of an aerial view, and something else again. A 'naive' view of a land through which a bright bus moved, following a winding road.

'See?' said Kathy. 'All the seasons at once, and history too. All times together.'

Bright geometries of yellow canola, of freshly ploughed earth, then patches of fire, rivers brimming in dunes, in pools among dry, coarse sand. Animals grouped around fresh green grass; kangaroo, emu, sheep. There were many broken fences. People around the pools, clothed and naked and randomly coloured white, red, black, yellow and brown. The single bright bus, that golden road. Tilly wished for a magnifying glass so she could peer into the bus.

'Not traditional painting, I guess; but it might be one day.'

'Someday.'

'We'll have something for the Peace Park tomorrow, anyway. A councillor rang me today,' said Ruby. 'Would still like a speech. Disappointed we got no song or dance to do. I said we might donate some of the stones to the museum. I'm still hoping that Wilfred . . .'

'They're all down the pub,' said Tilly.

'Yes.'

'That'll be the end of the funding then.'

'I just hope we're right tomorrow.'

'You do the Welcome to Country, Nita, unna?'

'Speeches. Afternoon tea.'

'It's a start,' concluded Ruby.

They drank tea. The women were in tracksuits and coats and sheepskin boots. Yawning.

'You sleeping in the bus again, love?'

Tilly nodded. She'd thought that was secret.

'Safe I guess, if you like . . . Need to be on your own.'

The bus seats were sentries as she lay herself down.

ROLL N RHYTHM

Afterwards, Gerald remembered only fragments. Lay in the lonely hours trying to string them together.

The party was at Tommy's place.

Gerry did not know where he had just been, or why he'd left the party only to now return. Him and Tommy, each with a carton of beer on the shoulder. Last-minute supplies maybe? It was a short walk really, pub to Tommy's place. They wanted to be relieved of their burden.

A fire flickered in the driveway, flame floating in a metal bowl held above the ground, and close to the opened double doors of a carport. Flames, flickering.

Walking from cold darkness toward a flickering fire and light that seemed so thin, yet thickened as they grew closer, held so discretely within the big doorframe. People moving to music, others at a pool table in the back corner. Maybe thirty souls in all, held in amber light, they shuffled and bumped into one another. Gerry saw Wilfred, Angela, Beryl, his twin, a couple of others from the camp. Mostly new people.

Then he was inside, beyond the carport, come from the other side of the kitchen counter . . . was one among a few people sitting on the floor with tubes of smoke, was it? Vapour?

Another stage of the evening, two people played guitar in the open building. Someone doing percussion on a board. Singing. The sound resonated from the walls, into the street and the dunes and the ocean.

In the framed amber light: people swaying, lazy dancing. Bent over the pool table. Flicker of flame just one side. So he was outside, looking back.

And Dougie. It was like a scene on stage: Dougie, so popular, two or three people hanging off his every word. Someone giving him a drink. Arms around his shoulder, thanking him.

An animated Angela talking to him, to Dougie. Gerry was tempted to tear in there, drag her away, but did not. Angela was singing – it surprised him. Had he been in prison that long? No longer the addled carer for an old woman, no longer locked into a vitriolic and co-dependant relationship, Angela was a woman commanding attention.

Tommy joined her, but his singing fell away and he became confused. Angela lost focus, missed a note, stumbled.

Dougie was gifting little packages. Gerry, at least, had an eye for such exchanges, though on this night nothing was asked in return.

Gerald remembered Milton, smiling dreamily as he stumbled away down the driveway. Muttering, 'I'm right, I'm right. Just not so young as I used to be.' He held up the palm of his hand, loosely. 'You stay. Keep that dirty old uncle of yours out of trouble.'

Apparently, Wilfred was still abstaining. An unopened can of some sort of bourbon mix rested in his right hand, as it had all night. Occasionally, he licked the outside of the can.

'No, I don't drink,' he said, 'Not any more. My pleasure now is in the not drinking.' He held the can against his cheek. 'Restrained desire.' The young woman laughed at his voice, punched him lightly on the upper arm.

'You an Elder then?' the girl asked.

'Well, I did have a beard,' said Wilfred, running his fingers across his stubbled face. 'Had long hair, too. All tied up. And I'm getting on in years, true.'

'That an Elder? Just means old?'

'But too dumb to be an Elder – and, us mob down here, no culture of course.' Wilfred shook his head dejectedly.

'I seen how your family respect you.'

Wilfred caught Gerald's eye. Winked.

'Never met an Aboriginal before,' the girl said, 'not to talk to, I mean.'

It was a long time since Gerry Two had been like this. Things fell out of sequence, and cause and effect didn't quite line up as they should.

A young woman turned to Gerald. 'He is, isn't he? An Elder, I mean.'

'One of our Elders, yeah.'

'Oh, Doug.' The girl turned away before Gerry had finished speaking. She followed Dougie down the driveway.

Gerry Two playing pool with Tommy. White ball, coloured ball. Cue and pocket.

Beryl slipped her hand down the back of some man's jeans. The man jumped, then pushed back into the hand. Beryl squeezed, and put her other hand around to the front of his jeans.

White ball, coloured ball. Cue and pocket.

Beryl? She and the man had disappeared.

'We never see hardly any Aboriginal people around here,' Tommy was saying. 'Maybe at the mine, now it's started up.'

Gerald saw Angela leaning into one of the guitarists; the woman. Angela?

A young woman was on Uncle Wilfred's lap, another

leaned into him, breasts against the side of his skull. She twisted around to crouch in front of him, one hand on the other woman's thigh, looked over her shoulder and said something Gerry didn't catch.

The billiard balls seemed to be moving of their own accord, doubling.

Dougie was just the other side of the table, looking along the length of the cue right at Gerald. He gave one of those slow smiles he liked to use, the skin crinkling around his green eyes. 'You look a bit sad, Gerald. Bygones be bygones. Want something, just let me know. All good with the world, you've proved you can go without it.'

The balls exploded between them.

White ball, coloured ball . . .

Where was the white ball? The weight of the cue was resting very precisely between the fingers of his right hand now, held quite differently.

Someone bumped against the table. Gerald realised the look on Tommy's face, the way he was gripping the cue stick.

They resumed the game.

'But was it rape?' Tommy took up the conversation again. He was certainly persistent. 'Why kill someone for that, make all that trouble?'

'Wow!' The woman on Wilfred's lap fell back with surprise and delight. 'That's awesome.'

She laughed when the cloth puppet bowed, and flew to kiss her on each cheek. 'Are you an artist?' she asked. 'I'm an artist.'

'We're both artists,' said the other woman.

'I'm an Elder of puppets,' Wilfred said. 'Puppet creatures.'

'Strings and that?'

'And others. I could show you another way, but I'd have to put my hand up the back of your dress.'

'Go on then.'

Dirty old man, just like Milton said. It was disgusting, and no way for an Elder to behave.

*

'More than rape then,' Gerry Two was trying to explain. 'There's women you can be with,' he said to Tommy. 'They shared women, those days. But other women you couldn't even look at, or else: assassination.'

Angela and her guitarist friend were singing so very sweetly, such beautifully shaped breath. Who knew Angela had such a voice?

'But rape? Lotta women been raped, not just your old great-great-great-granny . . .

'Well . . .' Gerald meant to say, 'well, you try it,' but, throwing Tommy onto the pool table, he lost the thread of the discussion. Tommy didn't know how to fight. Already he'd stopped laughing, had his arms wrapped around his head, was curled up yelling stop, stop.

'Fuck off, mad cunt,' is not convincing when someone has you pinned face down on a pool table.

Gerrard was helping lift Tommy's pelvis, helping get him head down bum up.

'How about' – he grabbed an empty beer bottle – 'I ram this up your arse?'

Gerrard was pulling Tommy's jeans down past his hips. Tommy pleading, whimpering.

'Haven't even started yet, mate,' said Gerrard, laughing.

Gerald suddenly let Tommy go, and stepped back. Gerry One had Tommy face down on the table, jeans bunched around his thighs. He looked to Gerald. 'What?'

'Leave him,' said Gerald, and walked away. Silence behind

him. He kept walking and the voices, though not yet the music, began again.

'Mad cunt.'

'My brother, so shut your hole.'

'Steady now, bruz, be calm.' Dougie's voice. Fuck. Fuck them all.

Jogging. The sound of his own breath, a cloud of it around his head, thin moon and stars bouncing, the gleam of sand and sea. He stopped, heard his own breath and the sea hushing him, hushing.

Gerry closed his hand around the grinding stone in the pocket of his jacket that had been moving so awkwardly when he was jogging. Smooth in his palm, it soothed him. Gerry recited the old language, let it move through him. What had he been doing back there? They didn't understand, none of them.

He would take this stone to the rock pool by the ocean, from where those others must've been carried, taken up the river. Gerry would follow in the footsteps of ancestors, follow the river to the Horton property where this stone had been left, and go on to the Peace Park from there. He was not tired. He could sleep later in the day. He needed to do this, make the path back to the old people complete. He turned back to the party; hot-wire a car and get near the river mouth that way.

*

Tilly felt warm hands, more than one pair of hands, devoted to her only. She relaxed, at ease and loved, thawing. Oil and moist ochre were massaged into her skin, an aroma of incense. Sandalwood? Her mouth made the old word for that tree, breath moving from inside out, shaped by throat tongue roof-mouth teeth and lips, words flowed from her.

People, flickering shadows all around her; Tilly felt the low warmth of a fire. She felt love too, like something radiating. There were voices, and it was as if they were in a cave, the song was all around her, not fading. And then she was the cave, was resonating, was an instrument for this old language, its tune and rhythm.

Wispy clouds veiled her, and the wind was on her cheeks. Washed in sunlight she realised she was held in the sky, was riding easily on people's shoulders, high in a gently jostling crowd gathered especially for her. Glistening with oils and ochre, Tilly glowed in the lowering sun. Still adjusting to the roll and rhythm of being carried, she thought she might fall and then she was falling, alone and in darkness, falling . . .

The smell of plastic, the sound of air rushing around her, the grind and rumble of wheels, an engine. Released from dreams, Tilly realised she was on the bus, and it was moving. Her guardians, mute and stiff, kept their backs turned.

Carefully, Tilly slid along the floor and peered out from behind one of the rearmost seats. Two men commanded the vehicle. Lit a sickly green by the dashboard lights, they might have been aliens, but Tilly recognised them all right. Well, sort of. One of the twins.

She stayed where she was, tucked away on the back seat with her head positioned so she could see down the bus aisle.

Dougie's head moved in the eerie illumination from the dashboard as he checked the rear-view mirror, but of course Tilly couldn't see his eyes. He spoke to the twin, pointed ahead. Did he say look ahead, don't turn around?

Where were they going?

She braced herself as the bus turned, and bumped and slew in soft ground, twisting and turning as the driver worked the gears. They came to a halt. The bus idled for a few moments, and then there was just a softly ticking silence. Tilly crawled back out of sight. It sounded like Dougie was already out of the bus.

'Hey,' Tilly heard. Twin's voice. 'Who's that?' He was coming down the bus aisle.

'It's me. Tilly.' She was on her knees, speaking softly because she was hoping Dougie needn't know she was there.

'Tilly? How come . . .?' Then realised the answer to the question he'd not formulated. 'Sleeping on the bus?'

'Yeah.'

'We had no idea. Shit, sorry, Tilly. But Gerrard took off, he's flipped right out of his tree.'

'What?'

'He lost it. Bashed someone, took his car. We saw it back there, so he can't be far.'

Tilly looked around for Dougie.

'Don't worry. Yeah, I know, I know. Dougie won't bother you again. He's sorry, Til. Changed man.'

'Yeah, well . . .'

'Stick with me. He's not a problem. It's Gerrard I'm worried about.' Tilly felt herself relax. This was Gerald, not Gerrard.

'I'll stay here,' said Tilly.

'He might top himself, Til. There was a fight, see – I could do with you helping. Another pair of eyes, ears – stay close with me. I'll make sure Dougie don't do nothing. Anyway, he's gone down the beach, I'm gunna check the inlet . . .'

'Well . . . I dunno.'

'C'mon, Gerrard's a dickhead, but he's my brother. Your . . .' He used the old word for uncle. 'He's a dickhead, but he's our dickhead. I'll look after Dougie, don't worry.'

'What's the time?'

'Late, Tilly. Early. Nearly dawn.'

There was barely a moon, but the two followed a dull and gleaming path, passed among shaggy old paperbark trees, their pale, rough bark mottled clear. Frogs called out, and their song was all around the man and young woman, beneath them, within them. Tilly followed the man's shuffling footsteps.

'You drunk, Ger?'

'Yeah, bit. That's why Dougie's driving. I'm wrecked. Dougie don't touch no stuff.'

The inlet was in front of them, its surface reflecting starlight, and ripples ran from where fish or insect broke the surface. Tilly was unsettled.

'I dunno if I want to find him. He grabbed me, Ger.'

'What you mean, grabbed?'

'Aww . . . never mind. Yell out for him, why don't you?'

'Yeah. GERALD!'

Tilly thought, Gerald?

Someone grabbed her from behind. 'Tilly, I got something for you. Wanna feel it?'

Holding her from behind so she could hardly move, Dougie pushed his pelvis against her.

'Nothing you haven't had before, Tilly. Plenty of times. You must miss it.'

The twin was watching her struggle. Gerry One. Gerrard. His eyes glossy, the water behind him gleaming.

She was a fool.

Doug's hand forced something into her mouth. A pill? It crumbled, Dougie held his palm over her mouth and nose, and she was forced to swallow, something. She spat out the rest when he took his hand away.

Gerrard was holding her arms behind her back.

Dougie held up his hand as if to slap her. When Tilly flinched, he smiled and let the hand fall.

'I'm not gunna do nothing to you I ain't done before, Tilly dear. You thanked me, remember, once upon a time.'

Tilly said nothing, tried to express contempt.

Once upon a time.

'And me too,' Gerrard said softly, his lips by her ear. 'You're not family enough that I can't fuck you. Is this what you were gunna tell me my brother done?' and he rubbed his hand between her legs, roughly.

'There's no rush,' said Dougie. 'We'll share her. We'll share you, Tilly. You gunna cry.'

A STONE IN THE PALM

Gerald crouched beside the glittering ocean that reached to the horizon but, right by his feet, held these small, smooth stones just below the surface. In his hand he had one of the stones from the farm; his finger fitted into a hole worn into its surface, and it rested so easily in his hand that it seemed made just for him. But it wasn't. One of the old people made it, and Gerry wanted to return it, put it back from where, some time eons ago, they'd taken it. He did not know why he needed to do this. He moved other rocks aside, and placed the artefact – for that's what it was – below the many similar rocks. He took another one from the water, put it in his jacket pocket, and began to retrace his steps to the car.

He was light-headed – the weed, the grog, the argument. Lack of sleep. He'd failed himself, but daylight was coming. There was a word in the old language for this lifting of light, for like when you come out of the forest into a clearing. He said the word now, and turned his back on the ocean. The sun would soon rise somewhere on his right. Be driving back into it, once he found the car.

Gerald was disappointed in himself. The grog and that. He went through words in the old language; it didn't seem they could sustain him, not against his own weakness. Weaknesses. Maybe his connection to ancestral country was too long broken. Maybe it was all bullshit.

He stumbled. Stopped. Considered his breathing, concentrated on being aware of himself, named the parts of his body in the old language, tried to remain in the moment.

The trip to Kokanarup had been very special. Not bullshit. That's why things went awry last night; it had been so intense. He remembered: before they went to the Peace Park thing, everyone was going to the other place, the property where the grinding stones had been collected.

Gerry expected to be disappointed with the Peace Park, the ceremony of its opening, but . . . It was government, it was the big end of a very little town. Still, we have let them down, with the Peace Park, he thought. Let ourselves down. We haven't done our part (other than being nearly wiped out in the first place, he reminded himself). They could have prepared something special, something true to how it had felt after that first night at Kokanarup, when they had felt so welcomed and reassured. The later visit with all of the mob was good, but not so special. Not so spiritual. The word made him wince, but it was true. If not spirit, then what was it?

The river was otherworldly in the dawn. The word for river in the old language was nearly the same as the word for navel. He liked that; it told you about connection. Words hold everything together. And how viscous the water looked in this light, like something that flowed in the body, some life-giving fluid. The paperbarks were gnarled and shabby-clothed old fellows come to visit, leaning over, bending at the knees to look into the dark water, to see themselves confirmed. They were here, the old people. Gerald could feel them.

He heard a scream. Silence. No frogs, no birds; only a

fish broke the surface of the water. Another scream. The first scream had made him notice the silence, now he analysed. It was someone at a distance, but there were voices much closer. Voices he recognised.

*

Tilly was ferocious, enraged; her heart racing, blood pumping, pulse throbbing in her ears. She stopped struggling. Let them do what they would; kill them soon enough. Later. When this was all over.

Suddenly the men stopped pulling at her clothes.

'Fuck. How many?'

'Get out of here.'

She felt herself released. Her legs gave way. Gerry and Dougie – the fucks – were running to the bus. No, they ran right past the bus and down the gravel track, leaving small puffs of dust that the rising sun ignited. The light so warm, so clean it felt like something sacred. Tilly – tracksuit pants half pulled from her, t-shirt ripped – sat on the ground in sacred light.

Someone was calling her name. Tilly got to her feet warily, looking around as she adjusted her clothing. Heard it again, but could see no one. Then, down by the river she saw a great many people, quiet and slow-moving. Women, dark women in kangaroo-skin cloaks pulled close around their bodies. Looking this way, looking at her. Not all in cloaks. Leading them, walking up from the river and lit by the first golden light of the day: Kathy and Ruby, Angela, and then, neither leading nor following but as if compelled by the dark women behind him, Gerry . . . This would be Gerald. Then all those other women stopped, they remained behind, were blending back into the trees, their eyes still on Tilly. Smiling, she was sure they were smiling. She blinked, and they were gone, while Gerry and

Kathy and the rest – look at them – continued toward her, so very serious and grim, their faces lined and twisted with worry. She saw Wally was with them too.

Tilly felt both saved and as if she was the saviour. Was she laughing? Crying? She fell into the arms of the women. So grateful, so relieved; so proud of them and of herself.

*

'Well, we heard the bus go, and we knew you slept in there.'

'And when I woke Wally, he said . . .'

'We couldn't see who it was . . .'

'Something made us go that way . . .'

Over and over again as they drove back in the bus, they told the story of how they'd found her. Tilly assured them she was unhurt; her clothes were ripped but nothing really happened; just a fright.

'You sure it was them?'

She was.

'They run all the way home?'

'Two little piggies run all the way home,' said Wally from the driver's seat. They smiled, partly from relief and good manners, but mostly just because of Wally's strange sense of humour.

Gerry had waved them away, said he'd join them later. They'd tried to persuade him otherwise but he'd borrowed a car, he said, and wanted to get it back. Stole it, they agreed; that's why he wants to get it back. Stole it from that fella he was gunna beat up on the pool table last night . . . And then they had to tell that story too.

Ruby would have to hear it later; she was in the car they'd driven here, looking for Tilly.

'Borrowed it from Wilfred's new friends,' Wally said. 'They come home with him. Very taken with our old Elder, unna?

Gunna help him finish off whatever it is he's made for the ceremony today.'

Tilly was surprised she was not more upset. Perhaps it was because of what she'd been through before, and this time Dougie hadn't been able to do anything, not this time, not now. She felt betrayed, yes, by the twin; but his brother had led the rescue. The size of the crowd, all those women behind him . . . She didn't question it.

'No. No police,' said Tilly. And no need for the hospital. Really. She smiled, and conversation bubbled and flowed within the rushing vehicle.

*

When Gerald got to where he'd left the car, there was nothing but its tyre prints. It had accelerated away, that was clear from the way the soil was scattered from the arc it had left in the dirt. He imagined Dougie placating Tommy; wasn't us that took it, was that mad cunt Gerald. We brought it back to you, you should thank us. Here, have this. He'd give him drugs, help smooth it all over in the way only Dougie could, put himself in your line of dependency. They might get the cops on him, Gerry; but they couldn't prove nothing, and his brother . . . His brother wouldn't want that, wouldn't do that to him again.

He was going to walk the river anyway, just like his ancestors had done, carrying stones worn and smoothed and delivered by the ocean. It would have been the young men, probably younger than himself. But it was harder today. He followed in their footsteps, but must travel a little further too.

He reckoned it would take about four to six hours to reach Dan Horton's property, at least that part of the riverbed where his family had collected all of the stones. The Peace Park ceremony was in nine. He had time. He would meet all the others there.

A smooth stone cupped in the palm of each hand, Gerald was one of many moving among the paperbarks, there in the shadows near the water's edge. Gerald was gently compelled: go this way, that way. And then there was a thin path through rushes and he strode out briskly, his muscles long and loose even so long without sleep. He breathed deeply, free of anxiety. The stones reminded him; let gravity ground you, your spirit soar; let the energy of this old path move you; let it set the direction and you just stay by the tiller.

Darkness became more than monochrome, light rising from the ground. Again and again Gerald sensed a figure – figures – at a curve just ahead of him, slipping behind a tree and away into some other world. Back again.

He detoured across coarse river sand to a small, deep rock pool. Dropped to his knees, put the stones either side of it, cupped his hands, drank. On an impulse, reached into the water. His fingers closed around a fist-sized stone. He drew it out, dripping, and laid it on the sheet of rock. A hollow had been manufactured at its centre. Who left it, how long had it waited? Gerald placed one of the stones he'd been carrying into the pool, and carried this new one away with him. He saw no skull, jammed among rocks, nor how his own face remained, for a moment reflected in the water there, the wan sky behind. The moon was almost gone. Light rose from the pale sand of the creek bed, flowed in the tumbling gully he entered.

Later that same morning, still walking strongly, Gerald heard thunder. He looked up, a clear, bright sky; if thunderclouds, he cannot see them. The treetops writhe, but he is sheltered in the creek bed and the canopy closes again.

He hears crickets. Frogs. Rumbling thunder.

And, surprised, himself singing, one of those songs in the

tongue of this place. Thunder and his own voice rolled along this creek bed, these gullies.

His feet crossed sheets of rock, wide banks of coarse river sand. Trees leaned over him, made a canopy above him, opened again.

Another waterhole. Gerry drinks, reaches into it. Leaves the stone he's carried from the last, takes another one with him. Smooth stone in the palm of each hand.

*

Dan had gone to bed thinking about the opening of the Peace Park, and when he awoke was thinking about it still. He worried about the weather – not unusual for a farmer in this or any part of the world. The forecast referred to the possibility of a storm, and isolated gale force winds. It wasn't because of the Peace Park opening that he worried – that could go ahead with a bit of rain and wind – but because of business. A bit of rain was nearly always valuable, especially now that the crop – such as it was this miserable year – was harvested. No, he wasn't so worried about rain, but everywhere was so dry and the soil so loose that a strong wind would blow the best soil away.

Rain this year in particular had been isolated and patchy, and the yield had been extremely poor – some areas had no harvest to speak of – except there was that one paddock adjoining the sites he wanted to show Tilly and the others later today. It must be something to do with the topography there, the river valley, or that ridge to the west, but something seemed to ensure that small paddock always had a good yield. Every year when they ploughed, countless yams came up with the turned earth. Perhaps there was something in the soil there.

The early sun was large and red; dust in the air already, then.

He expected to figure in the Peace Park ceremony, to at least be mentioned, especially since the Wirlomin group apparently intended donating some of the grinding stones to the Historical Society. Janet would've been thrilled by that, and it would make the rest think of how they should have included him more. He expected some of the Aborigines this morning, so he could show them the area where most of the stones had been collected. He was looking forward to it.

He'd asked that Tilly be among those who came. He had a plan; perhaps it was a wish. He'd talked to his brother, Malcolm, about it already.

'Malcolm, I want to give them the property.'

'What? Who? Them Aborigines?'

'Yes, in a way.'

'Tell me what way.'

'Well, I'll show them around first, show them the "sites"; the riverbed, the springs, the rock hole and that.'

'Yes, where their ancestors were.'

'Yes, they're all very interested in their old culture. It means a lot to them, and some of what they say, it's like God. Janet used to talk about it all the time.'

'Yes, pagan . . .'

'And Doug, see. I told you he's with them?'

'Yes. I'm happy for you that he's back, Dan, really I am.'

'I talked to him a little bit the other day, with them at the camp. It'll take us time, I know. I think he might move back. And I could donate this farm, with its special places and that, to Tilly and to Doug both. Just this property. Tilly representing them, the family, and Doug . . . They could run it together, like these camps they do, and wouldn't need to stay in the caravan park, and the waterholes . . .'

'I see, but . . .'

'I'm thinking about it, that's all. I'll sow the idea . . .'

'You'll need a lawyer.'

'Of course, but . . . I want to put the idea to them today . . .'

'Well, of course it's your decision, Dan. It's a very Christian thing to do, really. But with a lawyer, Dan; a lawyer. But I guess you can broach the idea with them first, if you feel you must.'

Dan had already decided he must. It was a Reconciliation thing, real reconciliation. And to have Doug back . . . Doug seemed so interested in these people and what they were doing. It would be family – Tilly and Malcom and Doug – together with these Aboriginal people. One family, descended from Adam and Eve. Janet had dreamed of something like this.

He checked the clock. Hours yet before they arrived.

The dogs reminded him it was time to get out of the house. Yes. He'd wait in the shed, do some repairs and tidy up a bit while he waited.

He stepped outside and into a dry, stinging hail of soil.

The shed door slid easily, the concrete floor was neatly swept. The truck and its trailer were loaded with wheat. He touched the tarpaulin, checked (unnecessarily) that the cords were tight. The last decent load; he'd take it to the depot today, weigh-in after the ceremony.

It had been a terrible year, generally. Most of the crop had failed – lack of rain – except that one paddock where the yams were.

The wind howled around the shed, threw sand and leaves against the corrugated iron walls. Just as suddenly dropped again.

Dan gazed upon the tools hanging on the wall. There was the house to keep tidy as well, now that Janet was gone. He couldn't keep up, not by himself.

The sound of a car pulling up startled him from his thoughts of Janet, the past, Janet, a diffused anxiety about the future. Janet. He ventured to the doorway; saw a strange car, and his estranged son. Returning. Doug walked toward him beaming. 'Not trespassing am I, Dad?' He'd made the same joke yesterday. Behind him, one of those twins laughed.

'I feel better here than at Kokanarup,' his son said, shaking his father's hand warmly. Dan felt absurdly grateful that the boy – the man – had returned and was not ashamed to face what it meant to live on this river, its history. They had so much to talk about, he and his son.

'You know Gerry, I think?' Of course Dan knew Gerry, and Tommy, the driver. They shook hands.

'I wanted to show them our sites,' Doug said. 'You know, around where we found the rocks: the springs, the clearing. Heard you showed them the other places already.'

Dan nodded. 'The others will be here later this morning.'

'That's bad luck. Me and Tom and Gerry gotta be back in King George Town today. Can't even stay for the Peace Park opening.'

'Oh, that's a shame. But you'll be back?'

'Yeah. I know, I'm sorry, but like I said, Dad, I want to come home.'

'Wonderful. We need to have a chat sometime, soon?'

'Yep, but not just yet, hey? I wanna show 'em our sites, what you're gunna show the rest of them, but then we have to go. Rush.'

'Doug, I want to give this property to you and to Tilly, together, so they can do their camps, their language and that, here, and it will still be a farm and you and Tilly, representing her people. Your mother . . .'

Dan wanted to tell him all this, but Doug drove off before he'd hardly begun.

Dan watched them drive toward the river, the dust rising behind their vehicle. He returned to the shed. Increasingly, he found himself at the workbench, daydreaming. As if lost. Stranded. He stood in the wide doorway, looked to the sky. A fire somewhere? Sandstorm? Some menace in the air? He smiled; it could be nothing he'd not dealt with before.

STICKS AND STONES

The light was strange, as if there was a distant bushfire, but the smoke was very high and must've been well above the wind that was gusting so irregularly around them. Wally, Ruby, Nita and Kathy were by the campfire, having separately scouted around to see who'd not returned from the pub and the party.

'Most of 'em here, but . . . They'll have to start their rehab all over again.'

'Yeah, well, not the first time,' said Ruby. 'I've got the artwork to get ready for later today, such as it is. Not much or much good actually. Might be a bit embarrassing.'

'Well, not the first time for that either.'

'Seen old boy's harem?' Wally tilted his head toward where two bodies rose, fully clothed, and stood in their rumpled bedding on the veranda of the hut where Wilfred slept. They lifted their arms, stretched, rubbed tousled heads. Two women, Wilfred's artist friends from last night.

Wally waved to them from the fireside. They waved back, and made their way over to join them.

'Cuppa?' asked Ruby, before they'd arrived. 'Cups and tea and that in the breakfast hut.' She pointed.

They returned a little later, each with a steaming mug in their hands.

'Sylvie,' one of them introduced herself. She was a small woman who, having uttered her name, immediately retreated behind her cup, eyes twinkling in the gap between its rim and the large, blue beanie pulled low over her skull.

'Susan,' said the other, holding out a hand that proved to be surprisingly callused. She wore heavy boots, jeans and a large jumper. Her salt-and-pepper hair sprang out around her head in a way that made her seem a startled cartoon.

'Met Uncle Wilfred last night,' Susan said. 'Drank too much and ended up here.'

'He reckoned he needed a hand, anyway,' said the smaller woman, Sylvie, 'to finish up something for the opening of a Peace Park today?'

'Oh yeah, that's good then,' said Wally.

'We're artists,' one of the women said, and the other nodded agreement. 'It's a privilege to meet someone like Uncle Wilfred, to work with Traditional Owners on such an occasion.'

'Oh yeah.'

'Glad you can help.'

'Uncle Wilfred said he was going onto a property, before the ceremony. To get some materials, consult the spirits?'

'Oh yeah,' said Ruby. 'He hungover today or what?'

'Oh no, he wasn't drinking,' said Sylvia, earnestly.

'Thinking about it all the time though,' said her companion. 'He an alcoholic?'

Wilfred was walking toward them. 'Sorry camp this morning, unna?' he said as he arrived.

'You! Old man, what time you get in last night?'

Wilfred looked to Susan and Sylvie. 'What time was it?'

'About 3 am I think. I was pretty drunk myself.'

'Me too,' said the other one.

'Special day,' said Wilfred, looking to the sky. The light had a red tinge, the sun was a coppery disk. At intervals the trees writhed and tried to tear themselves from the ground.

'Tilly alright?' the old man asked.

'Yeah. You hear?'

'I heard you all talking when you pulled in, musta been around sunrise,' said Wilfred.

Wally put his back to the smoking campfire. 'This lot came in all hours, dribs and drabs.' The smoke rose in a thin, frail stem; was suddenly shredded by a gust of wind. The trees shuddered and throats of dry grass and leaves called to them.

Ruby said, 'We'll be all morning getting them moving.'

'Well, I promise you they'll all be there. Kick up the bum. Failed rehab, not gunna be missing the Peace Park opening . . . They need to have a good look at themselves . . .'

'Staggering around like the walking dead.'

'Well, it is a massacre town.'

'But, we're coming back to life, we are,' said Wilfred.

'Yeah, slowly. Maybe tomorrow.'

'How's Tilly? Seriously.'

'I told you, she's right.'

'Maybe me and the girls here,' Wilfred indicated the two newcomers with a sweep of his hand, 'and Tilly . . . We'll go see Dan and have a look at this property of his. Musta been a place . . . I've got something that we can use, like an exhibition, a display. Just need to finish it off at Dan's farm, he'll have what I need. Have a look around. Nita can speak at the Peace Park, Welcome them in language. It always works out, don't worry.'

'Well, get there at least half an hour before it starts, I promise you – hangovers, DTs, withdrawals or whatever . . .'

'Bus ok?'

'Oh yeah.'

'Here she is now.'

Tilly was walking toward them, hand in hand with Nita. It could not be said who was leading whom. Again the wind gusted, and lifted ash from the fire. The old woman paused in her approach, steadying herself in the wind. Tilly looked to her companion, waited, and they continued, their shadows tremulous in the strange light.

'Fire somewhere,' offered Susan as they waited for the two to reach them.

'Sandstorm,' said Wilfred. 'Overcleared all down this way; bit of wind the soil lifts. Might be a proper storm inland, rain even, but it's the sand makes the light like this. Fire too.'

'Might get a bit of water running down the riverbeds,' said Wally. 'Most weather from the south-west round here, but sometimes storms inland.'

'Quiet camp this morning, unna?' said Nita as she joined them. ''Cept this wind.'

'Morning, Nan.'

'Angela's crook,' the old woman continued. 'Grog sick. Got home just now.' They listened to the wind and the trees and saw their shadows rippling on the ground. 'Tilly's the one had a hard time, I hear,' the old woman went on. 'She's steel, this one. Gold too,' she added, confusing the image and Tilly saw herself as some sort of Tin Man from Dorothy's Kansas, walking a sandy version of a yellow brick road, shining with stainless steel and cheap strips of gold alloy.

'Tough and precious,' said Wilfred, 'like . . .' and then he named sandalwood and jam tree in the old language. 'You like our backbone, Tilly. Our skeleton,' he continued, seeming to make it up as he went. 'Precious that way. Hold us together, you and the younger ones. Better than bones; voice and spirit.'

The two newcomers hung off his words, doe-eyed and reverential. They stared at Tilly, looked away. Glanced again.

'Meat and bones, you mean,' said Wally. 'Want some breakfast?'

'Cup of tea – proper sized, mind,' said Wilfred. 'And then we'll get going, eh, Nita? Check out this other property of his, and get ourselves ready for the Peace Park thing, all going well.'

Wally hitched up his trousers. 'We'll get these drunks and party animals sorted and be right there with you. They can sleep later – keep 'em out of trouble tonight.'

'And Gerry – Gerald?'

'He'll get there alright. He's got some help,' said Tilly.

*

Dan had not expected a whole busload to turn up, and was not sure if the bus could get down the track. But otherwise they would have had to ferry people . . .

'I'll follow you, give you a toot if I get nervous,' said Wally.

Then another vehicle arrived, Wilfred and two women. Wilfred was quickly out of the car. 'Susan and Sylvia,' he said, gesturing over his shoulder. The women waved, but remained where they were. 'You gotta bench drill I can use, Dan?'

'Yeah.'

Wilfred surged ahead of Dan as they entered the shed. He seemed very excited. 'Just gotta finish my artwork for the ceremony today, for our presentation. They wanna help,' he tilted his head back to the women in the car, 'but I don't want them, not this last, tricky little bit.'

The bus idled, passengers still in it. They leaned their heads against the window glass.

'Bit cramped, but,' said Wilfred, entering the shed.

''Cause of the truck,' said Dan, stating the obvious. It did

269

take up a lot of the space in the shed. 'I got a load of wheat on, gunna drive it to town, drop the load at the depot afterwards.'

'Me, I got some timberwork I want to string together. All articulated, you'll see what I mean. Very delicate operation, getting it right.' Wilfred produced a thin, carved piece of timber the size of a bony forearm from a bag. 'Once I put it together I might just drop it on top of the wheat until we get there. It's clean, no dirt or nothing on it to taint . . . but it's delicate, and will be too awkward to fit in the car or bus, especially with that mob.'

'Yes, alright.' Dan turned to the bus, concerned not to keep them waiting too long.

'Go on, I'll catch youse up,' said Wilfred. 'I think I know the place; springs in the riverbed, bit of a clearing?'

Dan concealed his surprise, nodded.

They followed the fence line down a gentle slope. Small trees the other side of the fence on the left, and trees on the right too. The trees moved closer, pressed up against the fence, limbs reaching over the wire. They went through a narrow corridor of whispering sheoak and jam tree, and then it opened and they rolled onto a wide sheet of rock. An old campfire; charcoal and ash in a small heap, a metal grill.

The sound of tyres gripping the rock.

Then silence; but a bird called, the trees whispered. Was that the sound of running water?

Someone on the bus pointed out the horizontal slab of a lizard trap. Another. Many.

Granite sheet under their feet, the sky widening above them, they left the vehicles behind. The riverbed – red and brown and grey granite too, scattered ledges and fissures and crevices, boulders strewn here and there, water making its way patiently, a thin trickle sometimes hard to find, but pools everywhere. Flat areas or rock-like terraces stepping down from bony crowns, trees in small groups, their trunks lifting and bringing their heads together in shady canopies. Three long pools, one after the other, stretched across one wide, level floor of rock little higher than the clean sand surrounding it. Spring water in a land of salty pools. Small, green leaves floated in the first pool. They tasted sweet, fresh water.

'Never dries,' Dan told them. Rejuvenated, people scattered along the lengths of the river, up its slopes. 'We used to hang around here all the time, when we were children.'

He led a few of them along a path into wispy, whispering, thin grey-green leaves. There, a mark in dark sand where two kangaroos slept, time after time. Elsewhere, furious scattered diggings of an echidna and small, decorous arrangements of droppings. They picked their way along ribs of stone, under the trees, around tufts of vegetation. Spider webs made airy skins stretched between the thin tree trunks, leaves and dry insect bodies clinging to each ethereal surface.

Then, a clearing.

Dan had said, 'There was a bit of an old fence around it and I thought it must've been the sheep kept it bare, but . . . Still cleared, nothing ever grows there.'

It is an old dancing ground, the earth compressed by count-less generations of pounding feet, of saplings plucked and put away. Very old sandalwood trees, most of them dying and with lichen clinging, stood in a vast circle around the space, a vast crowd of trees behind. On the lower side, closest to the river, a small collection of stones on the soft ground. A grave?

A glossy black snake raised its head, opened its mouth to show fangs and flickering tongue at the end of its arcing body. They backed away, from the grave and its guardian.

Going gently downward they paused on a flat ledge of stone. Beside it a towering tree, grey and shining, and it seemed dead, except for green shoots near its base, and there, above their heads, a heavy tangle of twigs. More than a nest it seemed, and large enough to hold a group of children. Wilfred said the old word for eagle. Before then a steep two-metre drop to a rock pool, a couple of metres across. Similar walls of stone at rough, right angles on three sides around the pools almost made a courtyard. They followed another sandy path between the huge boulders to the water, their voices multiplied by rock and sunlight falling from the open roof above them.

Some were rubbing and scratching themselves. 'Mozzies,' said Dan.

It was a place that would once have been approached with smoke, with scents of jam tree and sandalwood and oils and unguents in your skin. For ceremony and respect, but function too.

After, they walked back along the riverbed, following a wet and thin black line that flowed along and among all this stone, marking the river's persistence and, now and then at some steep change in the level at these, its dry depths, they heard the melody of water.

Tilly began one of the songs from the workshops. Stopped.

Dan said, 'When the river is in flood you can hear it from the farmhouse. Oh, but that's quite something, it's lovely, what you were singing.'

Tilly sang again, her voice bouncing among rocks, escaping from gullies, sinking in sand.

A crack of thunder, rumbling among the rocks. A hungry silence followed and then another voice, not Tilly or that of thunder, but some other, as if replying.

A figure, tottering a little but nevertheless nimble, was making its way toward them.

*

Downriver, some hours earlier and at a breakaway in the riverbed, Gerry had heard someone crying, and ventured a little way into a gully. Suddenly, unimaginably, he saw the old stone house in the distance, further up a bleached slope. A Noongar woman dressed only in a petticoat was running from the house. She paused to tear off the petticoat, looked back up the slope but there was no house there now, and resumed her flight. Tears streaked her cheeks. Tilly? No, she was too dark-skinned. Gone.

Gerry turned around and around. The gully, the twisted earth opening to bird song and sky. More figures, women, moving back among the trees, except for one, the same very young woman again, and now this Tilly moved away from him. She glanced over her shoulder from further along the gully, making her way up out of this tangle of earth and trees, up a yellowing, dry slope toward some house of bone? Wanted him to follow her? Light pulsed and dazzled in the tree leaves, and the treetops were alive with birds, rustling, calling . . .

Or perhaps he fainted. He was sitting on river sand; there was a small pool nearby. After all, he had been up all night, had been drinking, hitting the gear. Expect to become disorientated.

He heard a human voice singing, and moved toward it. Yes, a song in language. Then a crack of thunder, and his whole body seemed a chamber for that great voice, and he was shaping his renewed breath, had become an instrument for this old sound.

His people, his old people, in his blurred vision ahead. Clustered on a wide flat sheet of stone, a stone courtyard behind them, tilted shafts of sunlight in its shade. The song had reached him first, and now they came, now they welcomed him.

*

The little crowd who'd been camped for days at the caravan park in Hopetown had scattered across the dry riverbed, and now they reformed and took Gerald into their centre. He was fine, he told them. Fine. They began to slowly pick their way back in the opposite direction to the thin stream wending its way among the rocks and pools, barely more than a trickle.

Wilfred, late to join them and the only one apart, called from further upstream. When he realised that Gerry was among them, the two men hugged. The others stood around them, patting the shoulders of the two men. Gerry seemed completely recovered from his long walk and hours without sleep. Wilfred led them to a declivity in the riverbed a little upstream from where they'd parked. It was filled with river sand that had absorbed the blood-red stream trickling into it, and was now beginning to seep, to let the red stream continue.

'Raining inland, this is the first of it.'

'Red from the ochre, like you know that place we been? It'll dilute with more rain.'

Walking back to the vehicles, Wilfred and Dan were side by side. Wilfred called for Tilly to join them. Dan did not hesitate. 'I have a plan,' he began. 'I'd like to, what I'd like, if . . .' Tilly and Wilfred waited, the three of them kept walking. It was hard to say.

'One day, I'd like to leave the farm, just this property, I mean, not the others, just this one, to you, Tilly. You and your people, and my son. Representing us. Partners. Business partners. Real reconciliation, I mean. Not just a park. You can have those workshops here, no need to stay at the caravan park.'

Tilly blanched as if she'd tasted something vile.

'Doug is on the property somewhere today, I saw him earlier. I tried to tell him, but I don't think he heard . . .'

274

'But your son, Dan, what he's done,' said Wilfred, placing his hand gently on Dan's shoulder. 'We need to talk, I will tell you.' Tilly had already walked away.

*

Wilfred had known it would of course be a shock, but had not expected such a reaction. Dan thought it was a joke; then shook his head, looked incredulous. For a time. Did not want to believe. Then confronted the truth of Wilfred's account, and next moment was in his car and leading a cloud of billowing dust toward the farmhouse.

The rest got on the bus, and Wilfred and Tilly piled into the car with Susan and Sylvie.

*

They drove in Dan's dust, and only as they reached the homestead did they see the vehicle itself. Dan was walking from it toward the shed, his hand held up to halt the car emerging from there.

The old man pulled open the passenger door of his deceased wife's car. The vehicle sat quietly for a moment, and then Dan fell into it and the car accelerated away.

'Peace Park, unna?'

Wilfred walked over to the bus. He leaned against Wally's door and spoke to him through the window.

'I left my art-thing in the trailer, back of the truck. Can't take it in the car. Got it in the wheat bin, otherwise it'll fall apart. Dan was gunna drive it in for me and dump his wheat at the silo, but I'll take it – and the wheat.'

'I'll come with you,' Tilly said, softly.

*

Wilfred and Tilly hauled themselves up into the cab. The shed resonated with the motor.

Tilly looked down on the gate posts, and felt the wind whip and pluck at the cab. Black and blue thunderclouds bulged in the distance, and ahead of them a vast, dark cloud raced across the paddocks. Sand hissed against the windscreen and Tilly, protected by glass and metal, cringed with the imagining of it. The truck slowed: hard to drive in this red and gloomy light, surrounded by this hissing.

Then they were out of the sandstorm, and there was the roaring motor, the eerie light. The sun was a coppery disk. Lightning flashed from the ranges inland.

They reached the speed signs at the crest of the hill, the edge of town already. Tilly looked to Wilfred, thinking why not slow? and realised his agitation.

'No brakes.'

He changed gear. The truck convulsed, the motor roared, but they slowed only a little. Wilfred tried to change gear again; the gears grated, crunched, something screeched. The motor screamed, but they sped on. Wilfred glanced at Tilly. Frightened? He gripped the steering wheel, glared ahead.

They were rolling down the main street.

'Trust your ancestors, I always say.' Tilly could hardly hear him.

She leaned back, gripped the seat. Nothing she could do.

'Fuck.' Wilfred again.

Tilly agreed, with his sentiments at least; ancestors could not help them now. The street seemed mostly empty but, ahead, Doug stepped onto the road's edge, expelled from a little group of people gathered there. Wilfred sounded the horn, and Tilly could've laughed at Doug's fear as he ran, arms flailing. Wilfred swerved to avoid him. Tilly was disappointed.

Faces turned to them as they rushed past. Dan was at the front of a group, the Peace Park crowd. One of the twins stood with Dan. Tilly saw the open faces, all heads turning . . .

Wilfred scanned not just the road, but to either side and further ahead.

'Brace yourself.'

Tilly put her feet up on the dashboard. They left the road, were bouncing, helpless, riding their momentum, slapping trees aside, bellying boulders, and they rose and Tilly saw the sky, and they slowed, the truck rose again, and then went sprawling onto its side.

Tilly heard birds, a creaking and ticking, the rumble of wheels spinning. She hung in her seatbelt, braced herself again with her legs and looked down at Wilfred. Blood flowed from his forehead, but he was still in his seat, his hands still on the steering wheel.

'Unna?'

The window still worked. Tilly wound it down, grabbed hold of the door, unclasped her seatbelt and began to climb from the vehicle. It was surprisingly easy, as if she was being lifted, gently pushed from behind. Adrenaline, perhaps. She stood for a moment on the side of the upturned cab, saw a car approaching, people in the distance rushing down the street toward her. Then she reached in to help Wilfred, but he was making his way, and he gestured for her to give him room. He hauled himself out as she made her way to the ground, and sat for a moment on the cab. 'Do that again?' Began climbing to the ground. Tilly saw there were eagles in the sky, far above, circling.

The wheels, still spinning, rumbled, and wheat spilled slowly from the truck and its trailer, small runnels pouring to growing, golden heaps, warm and golden like great wealth. A luxurious sound, soft and comforting, that whispered it might go on forever.

Come close. Closer.

The sound of the grain running, a rumble of thunder. Grain, smooth and reassuring; thunder, to demand attention.

Transfixed, Tilly and Wilfred watched a pile of golden wheat grow beside the trailer. The tarp had split, thus the runnels of grain, and they saw the outline of Wilfred's puppet creature beneath its skin. The tarp shifted, the figure slid down, and as the grain continued to flow they could see, behind the edge of tarpaulin, a small dark dome beginning to appear. A skull? It was too dark to be bone. The tarpaulin shifted again and, like a body in a draining bath, shoulders were revealed, then upper torso, knees . . .

Tilly glanced up the street. People from the Peace Park were at the bridge, were picking their way along the wheel ruts through the sand and broken scrub toward the overturned truck.

A golden dust hung in the late sunlight, the grain continued to run, revealing more of the figure. Skeleton? Mannequin? The tarpaulin shifted and suddenly – it must have been the grain sliding and spilling that pushed the figure, because its legs and pelvis shifted and, leading with the head – it rose from the spilling grain and stood, swaying on still invisible feet, in a shimmering shroud of golden wheat dust.

The wheat dust, the light, perhaps the after-effects of the accident; it was impossible to comprehend the whole figure. Something like a skeleton, but not of bone, or not bone only. Some parts – the dark and burnished skull – were timber, and the teeth shone in pink gums. Kneecaps were smooth river stone, the fine and intricate hands and feet made of bone and seed and woven grasses. The timber of limbs and ribs glowed the colour of honey, coffee and caramel as if liniments and oils had been lovingly rubbed into their depths. Bright feathers decorated an upper arm, and jutted jauntily at the side of the skull. Neat cords of ligament and sinew, of neatly knotted fishing line and human hair wove together each mobile joint.

It must've been the still-spilling golden seeds that pushed, compelled the figure to make one step, two steps toward the girl and old man, and to reach out a hard and delicate hand. Its whole being seemed to smile.

Tilly clasped its hand firmly.

And now the wind of the storm came up again, and began to move musically through the figure, through the hollows and whorls of its meticulously carved sinuses and along and between its curved ribs. Timber limbs clattered rhythmically, and again a voice of thunder came rolling along the old river valley . . .

The figure teetered, began to tumble.

A voice called out Triumph. Victory. Called it out in the old language. Then: 'Did it, Tilly.'

*

Dan had hardly moved. He wished he had followed the others toward the crash, instead of being so fixated on his son that he had remained at the edge of the Peace Park, glaring.

'That is not your car to take as you please,' he said again, rather feebly; Doug was out of earshot anyway. His son looked back across the distance between them – a vast distance, it seemed to Dan – opened the car door and slid into the driver's seat. The windscreen reflected clouds, and Dan could not see his son as it drove away.

He turned to walk down the street, and glanced at the Peace Park: some dignitaries beside a microphone at the far side of the grassed area, looking around at the no-crowd. The dignitaries must have just stepped out of the building.

The sound smacked him; singing, a rhythmic tapping. Moving almost as one, a tightly packed crowd – those who had raced down from the Peace Park, those in the truck, the bystanders – was moving up the street from the river crossing. They carried someone – Tilly – held her in the air, on their shoulders, and her arms were full . . . of polished sticks? Gleaming bones? Bright feathers? Her arms were full of all these things. Tilly shone, she glistened in red light as if it was sunset, or sunrise. Wilfred walked alone in front of this solid little crowd, lightly clapping his hands and leading the singing.

Dan wiped his leaky eyes.

They walked . . . no, understated but undeniably rhythmic, they danced up the slope in a haze of golden dust, shafts of sunlight like spotlights against a backdrop of red and purple thunderclouds that glittered with lightning. The red river sent a leading edge, an investigatory cusp pushing at rocks and boulders, detouring, snaking between banks of sand.

There were so many coming up the street, not a small crowd at all. Dan saw many others joining the rear of the procession . . .

Later, those who had been in the street finishing their beers, having been pulled from the bar by the runaway truck, reported that a great many dark and thin-limbed figures continued to come up the hill as the river rose.

And so began the Peace Park performance.

*

Many years later, as an old woman collecting wood to make a secret campfire as she rested on her drive back to the little property on the river, or anytime just staring at dappled light laid across a forest floor of branches and sticks, Tilly would see the timber limbs as our own, fallen and broken; would see peeling bark as an unrolled sleeve, a fringe of leaves like decoration.

Would see not timber limbs but the bones of something both new and ancient, something recreated and invigorated, and would think of when she first heard a voice rumbling from a riverbed, and how something reached out to her.

AFTERWORD

Although this is a work of fiction, it touches on real events, people and landscape. At one stage of the novel readers who know me well may recognise the old hairstyle of our Uncle Russell. And it is true our community has twins, though more than one set. A few of us drink too much, and some know about the inside of prison. We have a number of generous souls and courageous women. We are acquainted with brothers who own farms. I could continue like this, but it is the issue of beginning with real landscape that caused me to hesitate in writing this novel. Writing fiction, how does one do justice to stories and language 'abiding' in place; how does one do justice to such stories and language even as they are being 'revived' and consolidated in a home community and place of origin? Perhaps it is impossible.

Taboo is a novel. It exists in a tradition of stories-in-print and this author chose to proceed in what might be called a trippy, stumbling sort of genre-hop that I think features a trace of Fairy Tale, a touch of Gothic, a sufficiency of the ubiquitous Social Realism and perhaps a tease of Creation Story.

In narratives of identity, particularly, I like to emphasise land and language. However, as writer, artist and cartographer Tim

Robinson (1996) says of Ireland and its indigenous language: 'In talk about land and language, there is always a whiff of a third element, blood. The three have historically made up a deathly stew.'

Taboo is written in modern Australian English; the 'default country' for which, Jay Arthur (2003) has explained, is England. England is narrow, green and wet; inevitably therefore, Australia becomes wide, brown and dry. The word 'drought' unfairly labels our naturally irregular rainfall. The Todd 'River' cannot account for its waters going underground near the continent's heart, and does 'river' adequately explain those series of pools with more distributaries than tributaries and which rarely reach the sea? Australian English place-names tell their own story: Lake Disappointment, Mount Misery, Useless Loop. Starvation Harbour. The Barren Ranges, Cape Arid, the Doubtful Islands . . .

And then there is Kokanarup.

Cocanarup is a word derived from the ancient Noongar language of south-west Western Australia, and a place name on official maps. A report concerning aspects of the region's history by Noongar author Roni Forrest (2004) uses the name Kukenarup. In this novel I write Kokanarup. Cocanarup is a real place. Kokanarup is not, although I am perhaps trying to make it so. Cocanarup sits on the Phillips River, and near the town of Ravensthorpe. This Cocanarup is the origin site of – some people say 'massacre', others resist the term – a series of incidents involving killings of Noongar people in the late nineteenth century. Reports of the time vary, but most agree that the catalyst was the killing of a European, John Dunn, at Cocanarup Station in 1880. A Noongar man Yandawalla (a.k.a. Yungala) was arrested and charged with the crime. Reprisal killings of Noongar people seemingly occurred both prior to and following the trial even though, or perhaps because, the accused was acquitted of the murder.

Half a century later, a newspaper describes a visit to the Phillips River:

'. . . *one of nature's beauty spots. It is situated in a rough boulder strewn gorge, the steep sides of which are carpeted with luscious grasses, daisy everlastings, and rock fern, over which tower the tall Yate and smaller Jam trees, the blossoms of which feed hundreds of screeching parrots and parakeets. By following the watercourse up into the gorge one comes to a small waterfall forming a cul de sac, and there . . . jambed down a deep crevice between two huge rocks, lay a whitened human skull.'*

The article continues to explain how the human skull came to be there, and after referring to the aforementioned trial, continues:

'. . . *members on the station were then granted license to shoot the natives for a period of one month, during which time the fullest advantage was taken of the privilege. Natives were shot from the station through Lime Kiln Flat, Manjitup and down to where Ravensthorpe is now situated. In the course of their guerrilla warfare the whites arrived one day at the Carracarup Rock Hole, and, knowing it was a watering-place for the blacks, they crept quietly over the hill until they could peer down to the hole. There they saw two natives who had just risen from drinking. Two shots broke the stillness of the gorge and two dusky souls were sent home to their Maker. The bodies were left lying at the rock hole where they dropped as a grim reminder to the rest of the tribe of the white man's retribution.' (Western Mail, 1935: 8)*

I used these historical reports in *Taboo*, along with snippets of other true events and places. This novel is artifice and – though perhaps not so cleverly as the strange being that prowls its entrance and exit – is made-up of bits and pieces.

Along with the 'language of the default country', Australia has its own unique languages, and they have been crushed and discouraged. Obviously, the author agrees that more recently attached languages are also of great value.

Noongar language is endangered. But, listed as 'extinct' in the Summer Institute of Linguistics (SIL) catalogue until 2009, it was updated to 'living' in 2015. Elsewhere, it has been classified as 'threatened' (Lewis et al., 2013), and statistical data says it was spoken at home by 163 people in 1996, 213 people in 2006 and 369 people in 2011 (Australian Bureau of Statistics, 2015). It is stronger than that. The written language seems frail; even its name spelled in various ways: Noongar, Nyoongar, Nyungar, Nyoongah . . .

But, despite a harsh colonial history, Western Australia's vernacular is imbued with this language. There are all the place names, for one thing – many names of towns and localities derive from Noongar language and a glance at a map demonstrates their uniqueness. Noongar words provide the common names for Western Australian plants (jarrah, karri, tuart . . .) and animals (chuditch, quokka, numbat . . .). A peculiarly Western Australian word for spear – gidgee – is derived from Noongar. Such usage shows the pervasive connection of land and language, and hints at what such a heritage – an ancient tongue, its narratives of a unique environment and community – might contribute to a sense of regional 'belonging' and identity.

There is little literal Noongar language in *Taboo*. I would have it speak to a wider audience and do more than posture difference.

Tim Robinson again:

'We, personally, cumulatively, communally, create and recreate landscapes – a landscape being not just the terrain but also the human perspectives on it, the land plus its over-burden of meanings.' (1996: 162)

Robinson is talking about Ireland. Although my ancestry includes Irish people along with Noongar, that land is a world's distance from home and it is Cocanarup, much closer, that inspired me and has a rhythm with which I would resonate. *Taboo* offers a little band of survivors following a retreating tide of history, and returning with language and story; a small community, descended from those who first created human society in their part of the most ancient continent on the planet, provides the catalyst for connection with a story of place deeper than colonization, and for transformation and healing. But of course *Taboo* is only a book, only a novel. Cocanarup is Kokenarup is Kokanarup is Cocanarup...

ACKNOWLEDGEMENTS

I would like to acknowledge the inspiration gained from the Wirlomin Noongar Language and Stories Project and, in particular: Hazel Brown, Roma Winmar, Iris Woods, Olivia Roberts; Jason, Justin and Graeme Miniter; Albert Knapp, Bobby Woods; Darryl and Errol Williams; Ezzard Flowers, Russell Nelly, Helen Hall, Henry Dabb, Connie Moses, Gaye and Aubry Roberts; Clint Bracknell and Ryan Brown. I would also like to thank my sons – Sebastian and Declan – for their great strength and support. And finally I would like to express my gratitude for the tact, patience and encouragement of Geordie Williamson and Mathilda Imlah at Picador.

Extracts from earlier drafts of this novel appeared in *Review of Australian Fiction* ('Departure') and *Kenyon Review* ('Collision').

ABOUT THE AUTHOR

KIM SCOTT grew up on the south coast of Western Australia. As a descendant of those who first created human society along that edge of ocean, he is proud to be one among those who call themselves Noongar. His second novel, *Benang: From the Heart*, won the 1999 Western Australian Premier's Book Award, the 2000 Miles Franklin Literary Award and the 2001 Kate Challis RAKA Award. His third novel, *That Deadman Dance*, also won the Miles Franklin Literary Award in 2011, the Commonwealth Writers' Prize and the Western Australian Premier's Book Award. Kim lives in Fremantle, Western Australia, and is currently Professor of Writing at the School of Media, Culture and Creative Arts, Curtin University.

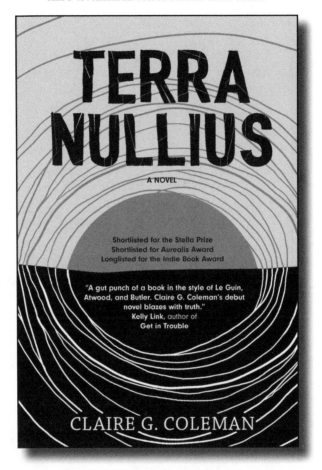

Shortlisted for the Stella Prize

"Deftly twists expectations. . . . a debut that leaves you
excited for what's next." — NPR Best Books of the Year

★ "Coleman stuns with this imaginative, astounding debut about
colonization. . . . Coleman universalizes the experiences of invaded
indigenous populations in a way that has seldom been achieved.
Artfully combining elements of literary, historical, and speculative
fiction, this allegorical novel is surprising and unforgettable."
— *Publishers Weekly* (Starred Review)

paper · $17 · 9781618731517 | ebook · 9781618731524

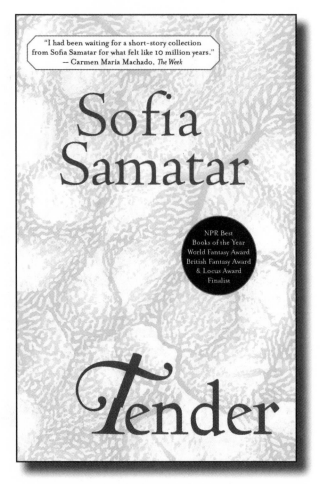

"I had been waiting for a short-story collection from Sofia Samatar for what felt like 10 million years." — Carmen Maria Machado, *The Week*

Sofia Samatar

NPR Best
Books of the Year
World Fantasy Award
British Fantasy Award
& Locus Award
Finalist

Tender

"Daringly explore the overlap of familiarity and otherness."
— NPR Best Books of the Year

"Equal parts brutal and beautiful, flinty, and acrobatic, Samatar's stories explore lesser known territories of the imagination. The results chime with all the strangeness of dream and the dark-hearted truth of fairytale. I loved it." — Lauren Beukes, author of *The Shining Girls*

★ "These stories are windows into an impressively deep imagination guided by sensitivity, joyful intellect, and a graceful mastery of language." — *Kirkus Reviews* (starred review)

paper · $17 · 9781618731654 | ebook · 9781618731272